# MAGGIE'S WARS

ALL CLASSIC NOVELS

ISBN-10: 1-938759-13-3
ISBN-13: 978-1-938759-13-0

**Publisher's Note:** *This is a work of fiction. Names, characters, places, and incidents either are the product of the author's imagination, or are used fictitiously, and any resemblance to actual persons, living or dead, events, or locales is entirely coincidental.*

American Book, Inc./All Classic Novels
Manufactured in the United States of America

# MAGGIE'S WARS

## Phil Pisani

"Know'st thou not there is but one theme for ever-enduring bards?
And that is the theme of War, the fortune of battles,
The making of perfect soldiers."

Walt Whitman

# DEDICATION

To my wife Joanne, a wonderfully beautiful lady.

# PREFACE

The plane banked towards the sun; it hit some turbulence then leveled, heading northwest. The ink blue of the Pacific below reminded me of my first transatlantic crossing. How amazing—that one chance incident changed the course of my life. Or maybe it wasn't chance, but instead a grand design by some cosmic source, playing us at its whim. Or maybe it was a bit of both, chance and design coexisting in some fundamental game of destiny, where one's drive and ambition collide head on with a divine plan, becoming part of it and reshaping its course—Hegelian in a sense.

The plane banked again, giving another wondrous look at the ocean; this time the blue dabbed with white like an impressionist painting. What a difference a few years makes in one's life; years when one thing leads to another, and then everything runs together.

# PART I
## New York City, 1944

**MAGGIE**

I knew I would love New York City. From my very first days there, its thrills, its hurried people, and its splendid, stately buildings soaked me with eagerness and fervor for adventure. With war raging across both oceans the city's people displayed a measure of recklessness while preserving their determination to win. Their liveliness and vigor breathed through the streets they walked, and the small shops, restaurants and department stores they frequented.

I tried harnessing this energy in my job search for a news reporter, but it didn't work. A blockade of foolish obstacles prevented me from even getting an interview. So I decided to spend the first several months in graduate school at Columbia. It helped at least initiate a response from The Herald Tribune, but it was much more than my schooling placing me at one of the reporter's desks.

It happened on one of those days that everything went right, from the perfect fit of my Gabardine suit, to the editor who liked me immediately. But the most memorable part of the day was when I met Johnny Pero. The crystal clarity of the moment lived with me everywhere I went, in every corner of the world no matter how remote, the moment was always with me. Little did I know at the time what an ongoing impact he would have on my life.

He helped me right from the beginning, showing me to the sports room and introducing me to the sports editor, a burly man who smoked large, smelly cigars. The editor's gruff voice scared me until I realized it was natural and misplaced on such a gentle man. After talking with Johnny for a few moments, Mr. Hurd escorted me to the city room. I waved to Johnny as we left and mouthed a "thank you," hoping to see him again.

The city room was a long, rectangular, high-ceilinged room filled with four rows of desks occupied mostly by men pounding away on typewriters, oblivious to their surroundings, the smell of ink mixing with the reporters' sweat. There were several ceiling fans that turned leisurely, seemingly displaced and out of rhythm in such clamor and busyness. Mr. Hurd's voice barely reached me over the clatter of the typewriters when he stopped and pointed to the middle of the room.

"His name is Englewood. Over there. Go to him yourself, he'll like that better," he continued as he watched me hesitate, and then nudged me a bit with his fat hand. "Everyone calls him Engle."

I saw a big man at the largest desk in the middle of the room. He looked like the queen bee of the hive, with the reporters clacking and working away as his drones. The scene intimidated me, but not enough to keep me from following through with my plan. After Mr. Hurd's nudge, I walked to his station and stood patiently in front of his desk. He continued to work, reading and typing without a glance up at me.

I coughed to try to get his attention, but it didn't work. I was close to turning away, but held firm and plopped myself into the chair at the side of his desk. As I leaned forward, properly but close enough for him to get a scent of my perfume, Mr. Englewood stopped his typing and looked at me. "Who are you?" he asked with a slight Texan accent.

"Marguerite Hogan."

"And what does Marguerite Hogan want?"

"I want a job...as a reporter," I said.

Englewood smirked. "So do eight hundred good male reporters." He hesitated, and I knew this was a good thing. "If there wasn't a war on. Whattaya got?"

I was quick to lay out my scrapbook. "I'm a Berkeley grad and worked the paper there. Columbia, too. I'm good, Mr. Englewood, you won't be sorry." I spoke fast but distinctly and smiled. My eagerness got through. I saw him soften and then he smiled.

"We need reporters. The war has taken all the guys." Then he resumed his typing. "I'll keep you in mind, Marguerite."

I knew the conversation was finished and didn't think it wise to linger, so I nodded and stood, looking directly at him and said, "I'll be waiting, Engle."

Engle paused and looked up. I saw that he was surprised that I had already caught on to his nickname. He gave another small smile and then went back to his work. I smiled, too, assured of my small victory.

It was only a few days later when Engle phoned the messy, cramped Greenwich Village apartment I shared with my good friend, Flora Lewett. Flora was an attractive blonde, recently graduated from Columbia University and hoping for a newspaper career, too. It must have been my day for phone calls because just before Engle, my fiancé, Stanley Hampton, had phoned. Flora sat on the small couch spilling over with papers and books, and watched me as I listened to Stanley.

Stanley and I had met at Berkeley. His aristocratic nose and pointed chin might have been considered plain looking, but his light blue eyes glinting with intelligence fit well on his tall slender frame turned the whole appearance into a handsome looking man and coupled with his idealism. He felt perfect to me and so easy to love. He was from a money family, and I probably should have known from the beginning that he and I would never become a team. He asked me to marry him rather quickly and I said yes, but

13

because of the great distance between us, me in New York and him in California, I thought a wedding in the later future, rather than the present, was the most reasonable. I was wrong.

I answered him in short, soft tones so Flora couldn't hear, and I tried to be excited, yet I didn't want to commit to a wedding. The distance was the main problem, I kept telling myself. But I found this was not the case. After falling in true, real love, I learned the real impact of distance on relationships. The yearning for intimacy makes one's reason erode, and when you search for answers about your love, the questions dangle in purposeless despair. Petty fears and jealousies mushroom into mistrust and loss.

Stanley and I were not like that. We were young and idealistic. I think the love blossomed from this romanticism, fueled by our ambitions, and when I came to New York to find a career and he stayed in California to begin his, the distance between us did not cause me any grave discomfort like it should have. Once I realized this, I wondered if our relationship would last.

I put the phone down gently and pondered what I had just heard. Flora pretended to be reading from her book but peered suspiciously over the top, knowing full well that when I ponder, something big is reeling through my brain. Impassively she waited for me to speak. "That was Stanley," I said, trying to be as emotionless as Flora looked.

I knew she had an inkling it was Stanley by the way I talked, almost cooing. Generally, I'm very aggressive and direct. She shrugged and pretended to continue to read, but I knew she was listening. "He wants to marry me as soon as possible."

That got her attention, and she lowered her book. "That's your liberal professor lover, right?"

I threw her a snide look. "He's my only love."

"I said lover, not love, dear."

"Ahh Flor, com'on. You know I like guys, but truthfully, what do you think?"

She closed her book and sat up a bit. "Big commitment. It's one guy for life, and it'll make you a housewife quicker than a reporter." Her lovely, hazel eyes looked sincerely into mine. "Most importantly, you must truly love someone to marry. Do you truly love him?"

She was right, and it made me think for a few seconds, turning toward the small window that overlooked the street. I turned back. "I don't know. I think I love him, but truly? I don't know. Since I came to New York, my only thoughts have been to make something of myself. To excel, to do something no other woman ever did before. That's my true love, Flor. I know it's selfish and not very flattering for a woman to choose a career over a marriage, but with the war and everything, the world's just crazy. I want to tell people exactly that and why it's so." I surprised myself. I always felt what I just said but never said it to anyone.

Flora smiled slightly and slowly nodded. "I thought so." She placed her hands on her knees and looked at me again her wisdom sparkling in her eyes. "Then you must tell him."

She was right again, but it scared me. If I cut the tie, would I feel vulnerable? Did the bond of engagement, no matter how fragile, give me enough security to take risks for what I really wanted? "I will. I'll tell."

"Sooner than later, Maggie."

I waited a few weeks before telling Stanley I didn't want to get married. He took it well, almost like he was still hopeful it would happen in the future. I felt good at first, relief I guess, but then I began to wonder if I did the right thing. In order to forget, I concentrated on my career. I went to the Tribune office dressed in my light green cotton dress that flowed in the light breeze. I wanted to charge into that building with all my enthusiasm and energy and show Engle I was the woman for the job.

When I reached the city room door, my confidence and direction were at an all-time high, and I walked right to Engle's desk. He didn't look up, although I knew he saw me out of the corner of his eye. I waited for some acknowledgement, moving from side to side, but Engle continued with his work. Finally my eagerness overtook me, and I knocked on his desk with short quick raps. "Hello, anyone home?"

Only then did Engle pretend to notice. "Oh… yes uhm… Marguerite… a…"

"Hogan. You phoned me yesterday and told me to come today."

"Yes, yes, the Berkeley and Columbia girl right?"

"Yes sir, and I–"

"Listen Hogan, most of the men in this city are fighting a war, and I need someone to fill in while they're gone." I didn't understand his indifferent tone.

"Yes sir, I'm your man or woman or…"

"When can you start?"

The words floored me—I had a job as a reporter. My whole body seemed to fill with air, beginning in my stomach, moving upward, and spreading into a grin. It was as if I had received the leading role of a Broadway play. I told myself to relax and caught myself before I said something too eager. I bridled my excitement and responded with just the right amount of dignity. "Show me my desk and give me an assignment," I said evenly.

My first assignments were boring and uneventful, picking up facts and figures—the where's, when's, how's, and whys for pages fours and fives. I kept trying to land a bigger, more important assignment but the newspaper business was very chauvinistic. I learned that to become respected, to gain the notoriety that presented opportunities, a woman had to use every talent, every God-bestowed attribute. Every day was a battle, and I needed a better weapon. I looked at myself in the mirror one morning and saw I had plenty to work with, so I decided I was going to break this male dogma, with my newly founded offensive.

The first coup came as I was researching the mayoral race with Fiorello La Guardia. I was following the trail of money left by campaign contributions—real boring stuff—when I stumbled on an interesting piece of information: Madame Kai-shek.

I asked Engle if he would assign me the story, and he humphed about it. "She doesn't do interviews. But if you want to give it a try, go ahead."

I asked several of the reporters why no one had the story assignment and the answer from everyone was the same: "She won't interview." Now, the words "won't" or "can't" only add to my determination to get the interview, so like a flash I grabbed my purse, pad, and coat.

I arrived at the Waldorf Astoria and asked the clerk for Madame's room number. His thin frame worked busily, and his eyes worked just as fast as he shot me sideways glances, then murmured the room number, jumbling the information with the proviso there were to be no visitors. Luckily, I knew Henry R. Luce from *Time* had planned a dinner that evening for the Madame and twelve well-known Republican governors. Madame Chiang Kai-shek had come to the States to bolster support against the threats from the Japanese and the Communist Chinese, and she had hoped to speak to the dignitaries on her country's behalf.

After the dinner, she was afforded her chance to convey her country's need for help. Unfortunately, not all the reporters received an invitation, but instead received a visitors' list with some information on the topics of discussion. That was it. Most of the reporters left; actually everyone did except me. So I dug in and cornered Mr. Luce, smiled and looked directly in his eyes. "Mr. Luce, any possibility I could have access to the meeting?"

Luce smiled back. "You're Hogan, aren't you?

"Yes sir, Marguerite Hogan."

"I'd like to, but if I allow you in, I have to allow everyone else."

"Everyone is gone. I stuck around."

Luce looked at me, smiled again, and shrugged his shoulders. "If you can convince the Secret Service guys upstairs, I'll have no problems with you sitting in."

Perfect. The Secret Service men and I got along quickly, after a few smiles and the promise of a few future dates. Soon I was sitting in the room with the Madame, John D. Rockefeller, General Hap Arnold of the Air Corps and twelve governors. I think everyone thought I was some kind of secretary, but I listened, took notes, feeling almost giddy on my triumph, but even more importantly a newly resilient confidence.

When I returned to the city room with the interview, Engle was so impressed he hired me full time—the second woman in the paper's history to be a full-time reporter. For the first time since I started at the Trib, I felt like an equal, and it was exhilarating.

But I was still considered less capable than the men. I pleaded for assignments, cranking out mundane stories none of the men would take, but figured eventually I'd get a break on a big one. And that is exactly what happened on July 6, 1944 in Hartford, Connecticut.

I was the only reporter around when the news of a massive circus fire in Hartford came across the ticker, so I landed the assignment and was out the door before Engle finished his statement. I paid the cab driver extra to break the speed limit on the way to the train station, where I bought a ticket and tore through the gate like a mob was chasing me. When I was safely on the train and rolling down the track, I looked down and saw my wrinkled blouse and twisted hose, and with my compact the ink splattered on my face. Then I thought of the fire sweeping through a circus, and it dawned on me that what I looked like really didn't matter. I learned quickly that disaster was as indifferent to looks as it was to cries for mercy.

I wasn't ready for what I saw when I arrived at the scene. My insides felt all jumbled and twisted. I froze at the devastation. I almost vomited as I took in the smoldering tent and the performers helping the rescue workers uncover some of the bodies trapped inside. People screamed and cried. The mangled bodies, many of them children, were loaded into various kinds of vehicles for transport to the hospital or morgue. It was one of the nation's worst disasters at the time.

As I took in the carnage, my heart urged me to help, but I knew I had a job to do. The battle between my heart and mind tore at my soul, as the event became my first lesson in the world's cruelty. Watching more of the gruesomeness unfold, I jotted down notes and walked slowly around the scene. I saw a man standing with the fire chief, so I approached them.

"Excuse me; I'm Marguerite Hogan from the *New York Herald*. Can I get your names, please?"

The fire chief answered right away, but the other man fidgeted. I noted his discomfort, but it would be years before I knew enough about people and their body language to understand him. Nevertheless, I've always remembered his attitude and how it alerted me that something was being omitted, which is the same as a lie to me. This intuition became my greatest tool to unravel a story.

"I'm Fire Chief Williams," he said professionally, although his eyes screamed the anguish of death.

I looked at the other man, recording the chief's name on the pad without watching the paper. He fidgeted again and then spoke sheepishly. "I'm with the town council."

"Do you have a name?"

The councilman shifted, looking more uncomfortable.

"How could you let something like this happen?" I looked directly at the councilman who swallowed hard.

The fire chief came to the councilman's aid. "Now wait a minute. Nobo –"

"I didn't ask you. I asked him. How could something like this happen?" I sensed I was being too accusatory, so I backed off a little.

The official just shook his head in shock.

"Who's responsible in a case like this?" My disgust was mounting, and I wanted to focus on accountability.

"We're looking into that," the chief said.

"How many are dead, and how many are children?"

"We're looking into it that, too. No final count yet."

"There are many injured that are borderline."

"Who brought the circus into town? Was it the city? Isn't there some kind of code for fire safety?"

The councilman gave cursory answers, not taking any responsibility and giving up as little as possible. It was the grand tradition of politicians, and I would soon understand that it was their self-preserving, self-absorbed way of life. I tried badgering the guy, but afterwards he clammed up like a child with a secret.

It was a long day and a long night. I got back to the city room in the early morning hours and began pounding away at my typewriter, my face and hair dirtied from fire soot, and my body wracked from a tiresome and stressful day. When I finished the story, I read through for errors and, though the facts were right, the story still sickened me. As I relived the ghastliness, I felt my eyes widen in amazement and fill with tears. I dropped the story on the desk dozed for a few seconds, but the thought of the victims flashed through my head like signal lights in a rail yard.

I slowly raised my head and looked to the ceiling, wanting to disbelieve what happened that day. Then a new reality smacked me between the eyes—I had become part of the story itself. What people would read in the morning would be what I saw, what I heard, what I smelled, and what I felt. It was then, sitting alone in the city room, solitary with my thoughts of horror, carnage, and sorrow that I understood the responsibility of being a reporter. I had to transform what I learned into sentences and sent directly to the people, to give them the truth of what happened, and why and how. What I didn't know at this time in my career was how difficult the truth was to deliver.

***

A few nights after the fire Johnny Pero didn't see me as I sat at a corner table at a bar. I was there with another man, John Webster, an Irishman and damn fine reporter. We were having drinks after work—a lot of drinks. I thought him good looking and we had fun together, but John was already half in the bag and it was really turning me off. I felt alone, and I missed Stanley and intimacy. John wasn't about to give me that, nor did I want him to.

But none of that mattered because when Johnny came into the bar, a spark lit in me. He had dark, smooth skin and broad shoulders tapered to a thin waist. He was medium height and carried himself with a sureness that bordered on cockiness. I could see in his eyes an enervating mystery mingled with a kindness that softened the chill. I knew something was amiss when he weighed the pool cue in his hand. My instincts told me that he wouldn't take the verbal lashing the drunk across the table was throwing at him, but what he did tore through me like two converging rivers, one a torrent of awe and the other a surge of apprehensive respect.

Johnny calmly picked up the cue ball and flung it, exploding the drunk's face in a shower of blood. First, I felt repulsed, but then I found an off-hand justification rush through me, as if by instinct not reason. I learned quickly that a different law applied in this room, in this neighborhood. No one moved to help the drunk, but watched impassively while Johnny tore the guy apart. When he was done, Johnny straightened his clothes and bought everyone a drink.

It was as though the fight had taken place elsewhere, and it stirred me. I felt something burn within, a yearning fueled by his toughness, his measured violence, and his detachment from it all.

The feeling made me calculate a way to have him see me, so I asked John to take me home. On the way out, I stopped in a surprised fashion, said hello, and slipped him my phone number. He didn't know how desirous he made me when he looked into my eyes and smiled, but he did. He charmed me, standing there and smiling as though the brutal beating had never happened. I was about to say his name, but something in his eyes was pleading with me to stop. It was so different from anything I knew.

The next several days, my enthusiasm for my work waned against my anxiousness for Johnny to phone. When he did, something unique swelled within me. His voice melted its way through the confidence I built over the last several months, yet the anticipation of seeing him again gripped me with a thrill as if I landed a scoop story. It frightened me, and I loved it as I answered a stammered "yes" to his question for a date.

We met in his neighborhood bar off Mulberry Street, a dark place with some tough looking men surrounded by cigarette and cigar smoke. Johnny took me to a table in the back away from his buddies. Their eyebrows rose when I pecked him on the cheek, and they watched as we walked through the place and sat.

He was honest with a boyish charm that barely concealed his steel side which came out under my scrutiny.

"So the job goes okay?" he asked, and I knew he really meant it.

"Yes. Yes, it does, and how did you do it? I wanted to ask you. How'd you get me in there so easily?"

He shrugged. "Like I said on the phone, I know guys. They did me a favor. You know, neighborhood stuff."

"Sam, right?"

He leaned towards me, "But in the end it was you who got yourself the job."

"You know I asked him to contact you to tell you about our celebration on getting hired."

"Yeah, I know. I got busy. I really wanted to make it. I tried. Really."

Now throw modesty into mix, and I didn't know which quality I liked more in him, but taken together and blending with his looks he was a really sexy man. We talked more. I asked him about being a gangster but he shuffled that question aside quite adeptly. We laughed and everything felt comfortable and natural in our conversation. As we walked to my apartment, I resisted the urge to kiss him, only weakening when I knew the evening was coming to an end. We kissed under a streetlamp, softly at first, then harder as the kiss drew on. It took all of my reserves to keep from taking him up to bed, but he was a gentleman. We parted with the assurance of another date, this time for dinner at my place, and I knew before he did that we would make love. What I didn't know was that I would use him without really wanting to.

It was a lovely evening, beginning with my own version of beef braised in cognac. Johnny brought the wine, which he told me he had purchased from the private reserve stock of some older Italians. It had a romantic ring to it, so I believed him. I could feel his eyes burning into my back as he watched me pour the cognac onto the beef, whooshing into a cloud of an aged oak and grape aroma. Johnny circled his arm around my waist and his leathery scented cologne mixed with the cooking smells. He squeezed me to him and everything made me feel safe and warm and sexy. The wine was strong and had us giddy before the bottom of the bottle.

After dinner, we shared the rest of the wine, and the kisses became longer and more intense. Once in bed, I learned that Johnny was a wonderful lover, with a knowledge of where to touch and kiss, and when to bring the passion to its climax. He was beautiful, and he was gentle afterwards. I lay in his arms and we continued kissing, fulfilled with the lovemaking, but the reporter in me kept nagging until I started my questions.

"Does your job, your work, deal with union people?"

"Sometimes," he said staring at the ceiling.

"Like how?"

"Like business matters." He turned on his side and stared at me. "Why?"

I really didn't want him questioning my motives for the night, but I wasn't getting anything from his answers so I danced around with my questions until I finally centered on the music union president.

"Petrillo, Dominic Petrillo," he interrupted. "I know him. Now tell me why."

"Well, it would really help me in my work if I could interview him. He's making some movements in the business that my people at the paper want to know more about. If I could get an interview..." I stopped quickly hoping my eagerness was catching him.

He nodded his head and squinted his eyes. "I think I can do something for you there." I grabbed him so fast and then smothered him with kisses.

Johnny left early in the morning, saying he had to see some people and that maybe with luck we would meet in Europe. I wanted to dig into his meaning further, but thought it more important to get to Petrillo. I felt a pang of guilt having used Johnny for the Petrillo contact, but I also knew I really felt something deep, different about him and truly made love to Johnny Pero because of how I felt and not to get the Petrillo contact. I told myself that until I almost believed it, and it masked my anxiety over my clandestine intention.

Johnny fixed up an interview with the music czar at the Waldorf, endearing himself to me even more. Within a week, I found myself in the lobby of the beautiful hotel again, speaking to the desk clerk who checked my clearance to Petrillo's room. He found that indeed I had an interview and directed me to a room on the top floor.

When I arrived, the door was ajar so I nudged it a bit and looked in. Petrillo was standing in front of the window of the sitting room, talking rapidly into the phone. A pot of espresso and demitasse china sat on a small coffee table near him. Petrillo was a large, broad shouldered man and had a head of curly black hair. He was dressed in a silk robe and smoked a black, thin, crumpled stogie that ranked of burned bark. His arms moved Italian style as he argued his points in a gruff manner. His teeth were yellow, most likely from cigar stain.

"I don't care what the radio says or what the juke box people say. If my musicians' tunes go over the air or entertain some Goddamn roomful of diner people, my guys are gonna get a percentage!" Petrillo slammed the phone down and knocked one of the glasses onto the floor. He was fuming, puffing away on his stogie, the end a long glowing ash adding to his mean and angry face. I knocked on the inside of the door and a quizzical look crossed his face when he saw me.

"Get outta here!" he yelled with the cigar clamped in his teeth, the ash spilling to the floor. Who the hell are you? Get out, now." He pushed up on his chair like he was going to jump up and physically grab me and throw me through the door.

No one ever spoke to me like that. Intimidated, I answered with a small, far-off voice.

Petrillo glared at me with one eye and cocked his head like a rooster. He shrugged and seemed to soften, turned his head so both eyes stared at me as he sat back down beside the phone, took his eyes from me and then directed them to the phone as if waiting for it to ring. I entered the room and approached him with a mixture of fear and curiosity. Even seated in the floral armchair, his size and the steady stream of smoke was overwhelming. He still wasn't paying any attention to me, so I continued to move forward until he caught sight of me out of the corner of his eye. It made me feel like something explosive was about to happen, and it did. His reaction was immediate.

He suddenly leapt to his feet, defending his domain. "What, who, tell me now dammit!"

As I tried to regain some composure and exude a professional air, I repeated my name to him.

It was clear from his face that Petrillo didn't know if he was angry or amused. Someone had intruded on him, yet I think he saw me as a pretty, feisty, and somewhat unnerved young blonde that reminded him of someone. He softened. "And who the hell is Marguerite Hogan?"

The tension eased. We smiled at one another and my cheeks reddened with excitement. "I'm the reporter for the Herald Tribune. Johnny Pero called you?" I began to wonder if Johnny had messed up or forgotten.

Petrillo pointed to the chair and we both sat. "Johnny, yes, he phoned. He's a good man. You know him, huh?"

"Yes, he's a fine young man."

Petrillo eyed me again, no doubt digging past my facade to see how well I knew Johnny. Some men just have that look that pushes right through you.

"You've heard I don't give interviews?"

"Yes, but Johnny said he would ask," I said, pushing forward from my chair, trying to show confidence as well as courage. Petrillo smiled again, and I think he liked my spunk.

"I thought –"

"What's a pretty thing like you doing in a man's job?"

I hated that and my Irish poured forth. "Mr. Petrillo, I'm as good as any man, and if you would please let me begin, you will see why."

Petrillo seemed amused by my outburst, giving me a patronizing smile and shaking his head like a long-suffering father. "Johnny told me you were a fireball. He wasn't shi – excuse me. Okay kid, ask your questions."

Silently thanking Johnny, I did it. I began the first interview ever given by one the most powerful union leaders in the city.

I was the talk of the city room for several days. Nailing down that interview would have been a challenging scoop, but for a woman it was a dauntingly impressive coup. I tried to find Johnny and thank him, but he didn't have a phone and the couple times I stopped at the bar, he wasn't there. I left messages, but he didn't call or try reaching me in any way. I began dwelling on the memory of his kisses. The guilt started making me irrational, so I buried myself in work. I couldn't help but think that he was mad at me, maybe thinking I manipulated the whole evening to get information. I did, kind of, but I also wanted to be with him.

After my day of glory, I realized that something more important than any man was nagging me: my career. It scared me to think like this, putting work ahead of people I cared for, but I couldn't help it. I was getting more important story leads, making a name of myself in the papers, but the real stories were about the war, which was drawing to a close. The Normandy invasion had been successful, and it seemed war in Europe would end and Hitler either would surrender or die. I needed to get to Europe, so I decided to pitch Engle one day while still basking in my glory of the Petrillo scoop.

Learning from my experience with Petrillo, I decided on a straight-ahead approach. "I've been good at everything, have done my duty, written good stories, scooped other papers. I deserve a chance at the war, Engle."

Engle wouldn't even look up. "Men fight wars, woman watch. Men report the wars, woman read the reports. It's not negotiable, Maggie."

"I'm better than men at stories. I did the Hartford fire; what could be more brutal than that carnage?"

"I would have sent a guy, but no one was here. I have work to do."

That was it: a real dead end. So I decided to sulk and write some copy. Thanks to the hot stories, I had moved from the obscurity of the far reaches of the room to a more prominent place, and it felt good. I was with some of the old timers, some of the real pros, and they liked me. They always glanced up from their typewriters and watched me feverishly pounding at the keys, my hair disheveled and the trademark carbon on my cheeks and neck from hand rubbing. I tried washing it off but it seemed to always mysteriously reappear.

Engle's rejection of my proposal ate at me until a good friend of mine from California, Jean Creights, appeared in the doorway. She was beautiful, with long dark hair and an air of sophistication that was underscored by her elegant suit, hat, and gloves. My practiced reporter's eye spotted her right away, and I rushed to greet her. Jean was clearly surprised by my appearance—from the carbon smudges to my soiled skirt, the look on her face showed her shock. Then she smiled, and shook her head and we hugged. It was good to see her.

After showing her around and introducing her to the crew, we cut out and went to dinner. We talked about my career until I could find a way to bring the subject around to Johnny. I loved to talk about him because I found if I talked about him to someone, was as if he was there with me. I wished he were.

Later, we returned to my apartment, and Jean was just as surprised by the looks of it as she was with the looks of me. My roommate had moved and she was the one who usually cleaned, so dishes stacked in the sink of my small kitchen spilled onto the counter, and everything was covered in dust. I just didn't have time to clean.

I tried to be nonchalant about the mess and plopped onto the pullout sofa in almost complete collapse, beat from the day and sour towards Engle. Jean inspected the couch, searching for the cleanest spot, before sitting down gingerly.

"Whew! I'm beat," I said. "It was a long day."

Jean didn't respond; instead she seemed to mull something over. She obviously wanted to say something, but wanted to say it with tact. She decided to be blunt instead.

"Do you miss Stanley?"

"At times, yes."

"You don't act it. I mean, telling me about this Johnny guy."

"Why? I broke it off with Stanley."

"I know, but from what I heard you kind of left an opening for him. At least he could think that."

"That's what you heard or know?"

"Oh, come on, Maggie, don't play reporter with me."

She was right. I never really told Stanley it was completely over, so I had left some hope for him. After not hearing from him, I had just figured he'd moved on. "Listen, I'm not attached to Stanley anymore, so I can date other men. I like Johnny, he's helped me more than anyone else in my career. He really started everything going."

"Well, tell Stanley not to hope. Don't let him dangle."

"Listen, times are different. There's a war going on and things are nuts. Guys die and everyone's got this let's-have-fun-before-I-go attitude. I'm the same way. Listen, I like guys, but truthfully, I love my work. That's my true love."

"Don't you think you're a little promiscuous?"

I didn't like the sound of the word. "Why do you say that?"

"By the way you talk and from what I hear."

"Hear or know?" I asked angrily.

Jean winced and apologized.

"Don't hate me, Jean."

She looked into my eyes, which must have shown a longing for some kind of redemption because she hugged me and began stroking my hair. "I don't hate you, dear."

Jean didn't stay long. We had fun, but my work was demanding and my lifestyle put her off.

Several nights after Jean left, I found myself in Bleek's Restaurant. It was a wild night, and everyone in the joint was bombed. I was sitting with a bunch of the city room guys and John

Webster, and I had really been enjoying the booze. I had my hand under the table and just poured kisses onto John, who was loving every minute of it as "Buggy Woogy Bugle Boy Of Company B" came on the jukebox. I wondered if Petrillo got his nickel as I played with John, my hand finding its place. I had to almost shout for John to hear.

"I want to be a war correspondent."

John, plastered and loving the moment said, "We all do."

"How do I do it?"

John looked at my eager face and felt my strokes below, and I think he felt obligated to tell me. He leaned into my ear and said, "Get to the owner's wife, Helen Reid."

I knew when he said it he was right, and my mind raced in its new direction. I looked up, took my hand from underneath the table, and watched a well-known actress climb up on a table and begin a sultry dance to "Moonlight Serenade." As she writhed to everyone's cheers, she slowly lifted her dress to reveal she was wearing no underwear. The place erupted with cheers, and I remember thinking how I was still a novice in this world.

I mulled it over the rest of the night and into the morning. I wasn't sure if I should go over Engle's head and right to the top for my request to go overseas. I didn't want to betray Engle or lose his friendship and respect, and I understood that he was locked in a dying mindset about a woman's role. Having a job was outrageous to men like Engle; having a job as a newspaper reporter was despicable, and having a job as a war correspondent bordered on heresy. I chose heresy and risked Engle's friendship.

Driven by uninhibited ambition, I phoned the top office and asked if it were possible to see Mrs. Reid. I was hoping to play on our common ground as women working in a man's field. I was surprised when the receptionist came back on the line and told me that Mrs. Reid would see me in the afternoon. I was anxious all morning, and even tried to give Engle one more chance to clear my request, but he gave me the same tired line. The war was no place for a woman, he insisted. I decided it was.

The Reids's office had three rooms: one for the receptionist and waiting area; one for Ogden Reid, the paper's patriarch; and one for Helen Reid, who people murmured was the real brains and power of the outfit. When I entered the room, the receptionist, a pretty redhead, was reading the newspaper on a seemingly quiet afternoon. She looked up from her reading and smiled. Cleaned up, no carbon on my face and my clothes neat and pressed, I was ready.

"Mrs. Reid is waiting for you," the redhead said without dropping her smile. "The door to the left; it's open."

I craned my neck at the open door, fear creeping into my stomach. This was my one shot for the big time, and I was risking my entire career. If I failed, Engle would never forgive me for betraying his seniority. I took a deep breath and walked into the office.

It was elegant, with a large mahogany desk and high-backed leather chair where Mrs. Reid sat, looking distinguished with white hair pulled into a tight bun and a prominent nose. She fit nicely into a dark blue suit and was eyeing me with a faint smile as I approached. That little smile was just enough to help me square my shoulders and cast my fears aside—it gave me confidence.

"Sit down please, Miss Hogan." Her voice was soft, with just enough authority to let one know there were no pretensions.

I sat in the leather chair she indicated, feeling stronger with every passing moment.

"Good job on the fire. A horrible, tragic event."

"Thank you, Mrs. Reid. It was very sad."

"And the Petrillo scoop, a fine one. A powerful man. I've met him; he's tough, so that interview showed me the extent of your promise."

I wanted to plow ahead and ask her for a job overseas, but I restrained myself. She took a moment to take me in, then she became direct—she was a busy woman with important things to do and little time to do them. I hoped I would command such a presence someday.

"What is it you want, young lady?"

Her question almost threw me. I wasn't ready for it that fast, that direct, so I wanted to choose my words carefully, but my mouth ran off faster. "I want to cover what's left of the war."

I noticed Reid's eyebrows rise. "So does everyone else on the staff. What makes you different?"

I felt instinctively that I had her ear. This was my shot, and I took it.

"All men, you mean. Mrs. Reid, it is very difficult being a woman in this job. Everything passes to the men. The only reason I got the Hartford story was because I was the only one left in the room that day."

I noticed her interest perk, and I pushed my advantage. "I'm a hard worker and not afraid of a thing. I want this very badly, and just because I'm a woman doesn't mean I shouldn't have it. I'm as good as any man on the job. I proved it."

Mrs. Reid's eyes were boring into me, and I met her eye contact. She was playing the eye game, and I wasn't going to blink.

"Why does a young woman want to see the horrors of war?"

I smiled. I was filled with excitement as I leaned forward. "I want to experience what men experience, see what men see, write what men write...from a woman's eyes." I fell back slowly, and smiled broadly as my voice became brassier. "Plus, I love the excitement of danger."

Reid continued with her intense gaze, but her secretive smile grew until she pursed her lips and looked away. I tried to maintain my confidence. I think she saw that this was no act. I had shown courage and ambition just by asking for this meeting. She looked at me and began nodding her head. I breathed deeply.

"I hope you know what you're doing, young lady. Hope you can make it. I'll begin the paperwork immediately."

I jumped up and almost cheered, automatically as if my team had scored a goal. In my euphoria, I almost hugged Mrs. Reid, but regained my professionalism in time. "You won't be sorry, Mrs. Reid. I'll make all of us proud."

"I'm sure you will Maggie, I'm sure you will." Her head went down and she began reading some papers, signaling the end of the meeting.

Getting back to the city room kicked me back to reality. When word would inevitably leak out, I would be persona non grata so I just hunkered down and completed some of my assignments, my eyes scouting the room. As the shift winded down, I saw John Webster hang up the phone and a queer expression flashed across his face. He turned and looked toward me. I continued to work in my usual feverish manner, noticing his expression turn from peculiar to subservient wonderment. He rushed over to Engle's desk and said something, making Engle become wide-eyed, then both men looked toward me. Webster said something else and I saw a familiar, angry look on Engle's face. He threw down his pen and marched his way to me.

I could tell he was really fuming, but when I looked up, he calmed himself and looked down at me while I finished my piece. I knew I looked tired as I waited for his ire.

"So you're going overseas?"

Engle was ready to pounce. I had gone over his head, and that was reason enough for him. I tried the proud employee approach on him. "Yes. I'm so excited!"

"I'd like to take you to Bleek's for dinner; you know, for a little celebration."

I knew something was amiss, but it was nothing I couldn't handle. "I'd love to." Engle closed down the shift and took me to the club.

As we settled into a table and waited for the waitress he said, "So, you're leaving us behind for the glamour of war."

I squirmed. The tone of his voice told me plainly that this was no celebration. I scanned the room for a waitress, but they were all occupied.

"One thing you'll be comfortable with is the lack of available showers on the battlefield and plenty of men to go around," he said deadpan.

I felt my blood pressure rise. After all my work, all he had for me were jabs about carbon smudges and sex. He nodded his head and began to leave, but I wasn't going to take it from him. "You low life jealous jerk. Oh! You're like all men: full of it, hiding behind stupid grins and scared of women doing a better job!" I thought I saw a smile on his face as he turned and left, bumping into the waitress who was finally making her way to the table. I looked up at her with my carbon dirtied face and angry sneer. "Double scotch, please—no make it a triple. I'm celebrating."


## JOHNNY

The first time I saw her, she was walking down 54th Street at a fast pace, her hips swaying and blond hair bouncing in rhythm with her stride.

I never followed a woman before, but this one had something that drew me to her, like a wide-eyed tourist to the Empire State Building. I walked behind her at a measured pace, not too close or conspicuous. She intrigued me, struck some indefinable, magical note within me. She was heading in the same direction as me, so I felt less guilty about trailing her.

I lingered so I wouldn't pass her, but she stopped at a newsstand to ask a question. When the clerk pointed to the Herald Tribune building, I realized we were heading to the same place and trembled. I don't scare easily, but this unknown woman made me weak. I saw her smile at the man and it flushed me. She set off toward the Trib building, and I followed quickly to make it in time to hold the door for her.

When she hesitated to read the white lettering on the large glass door, I stepped up and opened it for her. "Please," I stammered, wondering how I could mess up such a small word. She smiled again and my body went limp. She was beautiful, with a cherubic face on a sensuous body. She didn't say anything, just walked in. I followed behind and when she stopped at the elevator, I bumped into her.

"Excuse me," I said and then wavered when she looked directly into my eyes and smiled. Still looking directly into my eyes I could tell by her expression—the raised eyebrows, the growing smirk—that she knew I followed her. I felt a lump grow in my throat. I took pride in being tough and streetwise, but this woman had me feeling stupid and awkward.

"That's okay. It was my fault. I shouldn't have stopped so quickly," she said in a soft, caressing voice.

"You work here?" The whole encounter was new to me. She responded quickly, so I breathed again.

"No, I'm looking for work. You know anyone here that can help me with that?" She looked right into my eyes, and I noticed that hers were as blue as Australian opals.

I regained my composure. "I know some people. I'll show you around."

She smiled again, softening me for her next statement. "I'm looking for a job as a reporter," she said deliberately.

I would have hired her right there. I wanted to take her home with me. I wanted to kiss her, I wanted to do a million things with her, but I had a feeling I'd never pull the card for this inside straight.

"I know some guys in sports. I'll introduce you, and you take it from there. But you have to have a drink with me later."

She nodded. "Sounds fair. I'm Marguerite Hogan." She offered me her hand, straight and forward. I thrust mine out, ready to shake but stopped quick enough to take it lightly with just a bit of pressure. "Johnny Pero. My friends call me Johnny Stone."

"Glad to meet you, Johnny Stone."

I was in love.

I found out later from Sam, the baseball reporter, that she was hired—the war had created shortages of men—and that she was celebrating at Jack's. She asked him to tell me that part, but I didn't get to have that drink.

Don Vito gave me an order to help Luciano's guys on a hit near the docks. It was the same as before, supposedly—Germans infiltrating our ports and sabotaging ships. When Don Vito ordered something, I didn't ask questions, at least not this early along, but it did seem strange. This time there were two guys to deal with. I could see why they needed the extra muscle, because one didn't go down easy. They were big guys who were cautious even after being tempted by our bait of a full palette of stolen booze. The bigger guy, all wrapped in a pea coat, obviously had a gun in his pocket. I had a gun and a knife, but figured we weren't going to get close enough for a knife kill.

They came closer to the pallet, and as I positioned myself sideways for a more difficult target, the smaller one recognized one of Luciano's men. "That you, Sammy? What's —"

Sammy pulled his shotgun from under his long coat and blasted both barrels into the guy's chest, knocking him three yards from where he stood.

His partner opened up and caught Sammy on the chin, blowing a good chunk of it away. Sammy screamed as another shot hit Luciano's other guy in the shoulder. I squeezed off three rounds into the big guy's chest, but he didn't go down. I shot three more times and knew I hit him, but he kept coming.

Luciano's guy, bleeding from the shoulder, shot from behind hitting him in the back. As the brute staggered near me, I pulled my

36

knife and swiped at his jugular. He went down, twitched a few times, and died. Sammy was curled up holding what was left of his chin as the other guy, I still don't know his name, tried to get him to his feet.

"What the hell was that?" I asked. "That guy knew you guys."

"Yeah, what of it? Come on, help me with Sammy and let's get the hell outta here."

"What about the bodies?"

"Leave 'em. We were told to leave 'em for proof?"

"What?" This was really strange. We'd dumped the others into the water.

"Just move. Come on, we gotta get outta here."

He was right. I did as I was told, knowing Don Vito would get the word I obeyed my orders.

I was still cleaning blood out of my fingernails as I rushed to Jack's, but she was gone. I think of that missed connection often now, wondering what could have been and if things would have been any different between us. Maybe we wouldn't have liked each other, since I was disheveled from the hit and preoccupied by the fact that the target knew Sammy. Maybe the magic I had seen in her could have faded. Instead, she kept invading my mind. I kept thinking I saw her on the streets, but it always turned out to be someone else. It wouldn't be safe for me to get careless at work, so I tried to concentrate on my job, but it wasn't easy.

Finally, I felt missing our meeting at Jack's was actually good for both of us. Why the hell would she want to mess around with me, a crook? Things were getting really bloody and I had a lot of cash and our gang ruled the streets, but I could tell she was a class above me. Later I found out from some guys that owed me that she had earned a real education—Berkeley and Columbia, multiple degrees—and I knew she was beyond me. She was refined, and although I knew I was no idiot, I came from a rough neighborhood with immigrant parents, and I didn't finish high school. I told myself that the date would have been a failure. But I still felt like I lost a bet I know I should have won, something I had no control over, so I went on with my business. My work got noticed by some of the guys in control, and they liked me, so I was getting really busy.

Thoughts of her came back to me on a Sunday morning when I picked up the paper. I could see her again, standing in the doorway to the Trib building, but it was different this time. I read about the Hartford fire and ran my thumb over the by-line: Marguerite Hogan. I read it to myself then ducked into an alley and read it aloud, looking for her in every line. I must have read the article twenty times before I realized I was late for a pick up, so I corrected my craziness and went to the bar to get the money.

Nick's was just off 22<sup>nd</sup> and 38<sup>th</sup>. It was a no-trouble bar with Irish neighborhood guys that showed up after work to drink, carry on with women, and get drunk and horny before rushing home. The war had taken a lot of younger guys, leaving broken down four-effers, sidesteppers, conjobs, and chickens. Many times I went in there to collect on gambling debts and found myself swimming in a cesspool of drunks. Tonight the sewer smelled the same.

One Irishman near the back of the room started busting my balls, saying stupid things in a bar full of people. He called me a guinea wop and said I should take my guinea action back to Mulberry Street. I was alone. I wasn't expecting anything like that from this bar, where the good-natured Irishman who owned the place would occasionally share his private scotch with me into the small hours of the morning. I didn't want to know him by his real name—business was better with aliases—so I called him Shamrock and he called me Calabria, but he saw immediately where things were going and distanced himself from me.

The loudmouth continued with his tirade, laughing as he called me a gimp wimp. A gimp wimp? Who was he calling wimp? And I didn't limp and I was generally fearless, except for Lucky Luciano, and that's because when I looked into his eyes they were dead. So I casually walked up to the drunk and asked him if he'd like to play a game of pool. He smirked, blew cigar smoke into my face, and said, "Sure wop. I'll play ye for a ticket outta da neighborhood."

I smiled and said, "Nine ball, okay?"

"T's sure, nine ball."

"Who breaks?" I asked as I selected a thick-handled cue stick, making sure my smile was set.

"You're the unwanted guest, you break." He blew smoke in my face again.

I nodded and smiled, turned the cue around so the tapered edge was in my hands, and swung the butt end fast and sharp into the Irishman's hard face. The cue broke, along with his nose and cheek in one loud crunch. Blood flew onto the green felt of the table as he staggered back into the rack.

Everyone stood motionless as he spit blood and tried rolling his fat body off the table. I cracked him again, this time in the stomach, which laid him back down and scattered the balls. The one ball and the eight ball went into the pockets. I picked up the two and three, took good aim, and threw them in his face. The two caught the side of his head and made a sound like a bowling ball hitting the gutter. The three ball caught his good cheek and made a stomach churning crack. By the time I finished with the rest of the balls his face was unrecognizable. I pushed him to the floor. He landed like he was dead, so I figured that was enough for him for the evening.

I looked up. No one had moved, so I fixed my clothes and walked to the bar. Buying a round for the house brought the place back to life, and they carried the drunk out to his car. That Irish idiot left town after that, or so I thought.

As I was getting ready to leave, a couple who had been obscured by shadow walked toward me. It was Maggie. I froze and a million thoughts flashed through my mind, but she walked right to me and offered her hand just like the first day we met. "You're Johnny Pero, right?"

Holy, I thought, wanting to say "yes," but anxious to conceal my identity. "Uhh, I'm —" I saw the glint in her eyes, the tension around her mouth, and knew she'd caught on.

"I'm still at the Herald." She came closer as she spoke, and I could smell her perfume. I noticed a smidge of ink near her cheek as she continued softly. "Call me for that drink I owe you." She didn't wait for an answer; she withdrew and gazed at me with those eyes and then turned and walked out of the bar, every inch of her working in motion like it did the first day I saw her. Breathing deeply, I looked at Shamrock, saluted him, and took a good long pull on my scotch. Quite a night, I thought as I swallowed, too elated to even taste the scotch.

I phoned Marguerite a few days later at the Trib. "How did you get through to me?" she asked.

"Sports desk," I said.

"Oh, I see. You know those guys, right?"

"Right. So what about that drink? I'll buy." I wasn't about to start letting women buy my drinks.

"Well, I thought for helping me with the job, I'd buy."

She was tough. "I'll buy the first, you the second," I said, just to make it happen.

"Deal," she said readily.

"Deal. Jack's?"

"Perfect."

My friends would have taken her on some glamour date, throwing wads of money around, but I wasn't the type to impress a girl with money. I liked Jack's, and I figured if Maggie bailed on me, I could still get in on a good poker game.

I waited at the bar with Louie and Tommy the Carpenter. They were pissed off about the Feds using us to help them clean the docks of Nazi subversives, but the order came from Luciano so the argument was moot. In fact, we did so well they were going to use our information and our guys in Italy for a large-scale invasion up the peninsula. All of us paranoid types thought the whole thing was bull, just a way for them to get closer to us and nab us on some charge down the road. Paranoia is the internal alarm that keeps guys like me alive, and without it life can be pretty short.

If something was rotten with the deal, I reminded them, Lucky would let us know. But arguing with them was like arguing with a brick. I felt my control slipping, so I decided not to tell them about the officers that came to my house the other night.

The officers had come as I sat at the dinner table with my mom, eating her homemade macaroni. When a loud knock echoed through the apartment, I figured it was one of the guys. I yelled for them to come in, but another knock resounded through the thin walls, accompanied by a voice announcing the visitor as a representative of the United States Army.

My mother, her gray hair pulled back into a bun and her sad brown eyes widening in concern, watched my every move. "Madonna mia," she said in a whisper.

I opened the door to two very straight officers with their hats tucked under their arms. The one with a gold bar on each shoulder spoke.

"Mr. Pero?"

"Who wants to know?"

"Oh, I'm sorry," he said. "We're here for Mr. Pero about the work he did for his country."

They knew it was me, but I couldn't figure why they were on my doorstep. "Yeah, I'm Pero."

The officer continued, "May we come in? If it's an inconvenient time –"

Better now than having to think about it while I ate. "Nah, it's all right, we're eating but it's okay. Come in," I said, and opened the door.

"Ma, these guys want to talk to me. I'll take them in the parlor."

41

My mother's brow wrinkled, but she nodded. I knew she'd cross herself and say a Hail Mary as soon as we were out of the room.

The officers stood in the middle of the parlor. "I'm Lieutenant Crowley," said the one with the bars and then nodded to his left, "this is First Sergeant Leo."

I shook their hands and motioned for them to sit. They went to the burgundy floral sofa and sat in unison like they were sewn together. I sat across from them in the chair my father favored whenever company came. They both refused a drink.

"Mr. Pero," the Lieutenant started, "we would like to convey General Eisenhower's sincere thanks for your help at the docks. You'd be surprised how important this has been for our war effort and your country." Crowley paused to give his statement more affect.

It kind of made me proud that I did something for someone, like when I'd give some money to one of the kids in the neighborhood. It felt good.

Crowley continued, "Mr. Pero, your efforts, yours exclusively, have been brought to the attention of our commanding General." He cleared his throat, leaned forward and whispered, "Mr. Pero, we'd like to further enlist your services." When he finished, he stared at me.

I had played this stare game before, but as I drew a small smile on my face I couldn't help but try to understand what he meant. Curiosity forced me to break the silence. "Whattaya mean by that, sir?"

Sergeant Leo answered. "We'd like you to join a select group of soldiers to help in the war."

I felt my eyebrows draw together. I was the sole surviving son of my family, and besides, I was already a member of a select group: the Mob. "And just what does this select group do, sir?"

The Lieutenant inhaled deeply, and I could see that his next words would be weighty. "You will be trained to be part of an advanced team of men that would relay information and pave the way for the continuation of our attack on the mainland of Europe. You, Mr. Pero, will be a part of history." He relaxed, satisfied with his statement and its delivery.

"How much does it pay?" Whenever important people came over, it was usually about money.

The question seemed to unsettle them for a moment, then Crowley looked directly at me. "Mr. Pero, you will be adequately compensated in the form of annuities paid in whatever name you wish."

I knew the word "annuity" because we had bought some stolen bank instruments a few weeks earlier, and several of them were annuities. Annuities changed into cash real quick.

"Why me?" My paranoia warned me that they knew more about me than they wanted to let on.

The sergeant spoke this time. "You've displayed some exceptional skills with persuasion as well as with knives and defense. You speak Italian, and we need that. We watched your men work at the docks. We know who did what, and you were the most effective. This operation needs men like you." They let the silence linger.

I wondered what they meant by knives and defense. Did they know what I did to the two Nazis after they tried throwing me into the ocean? Did they know I slit both of their necks and watched them bleed out? I didn't remember seeing anyone but the two goose steppers, and then they were gone. It was impossible for them to know about my other jobs, my other marks. I made my bones alone using a gun that blew off half the side of my target Franco Malina's head and ran for miles afterwards, scared and sick. No one saw anything, I was sure. And the most recent, the one I still hadn't learned the reason for.

Maybe they were traitors, I didn't know, but it was better not to ask. There were too many involved on that one. Stupid, but even so, no one saw a damn thing. They were kills, like kills in their wars. I mean, it is war and that's what I told myself to ease the guilt. But I never liked guns after Malina. Knives were quieter and if done right, life eased out less violently than a gun blast.

Standing in unison as if sewn together, they broke the silence. "Think it over, Mr. Pero. Think of what a service you can do for your country. We'll be in touch."

I shook each of their hands, the sergeant's clamping on mine, testing my strength. I saw in his eyes that I passed, then I showed them out. My mother heard the door and called to me from the table.

"Yeah, Ma." I was kind of dazed. They were in and out so fast I had to recreate my thoughts to assure it really happened. Annuities, I thought, that's weird. Why not pay like a regular GI? It must mean something more dangerous than war. I was no greenhorn—I was fighting a war right in my neighborhood.

As I entered the kitchen, I saw my mom was wringing her hands. "Don't worry, Ma, it was nothing." My brain was whirring about seeing the world, being a special soldier, helping win a war in a big invasion. Me, a kid with a tenth grade education. I was excited and confused. The money interested me. It was clean money that I could put in a real bank. Had I known what would happen during the coming years, I probably would have stayed home.

The volume in Jack's dropped significantly when Maggie came through the door. It was hard to believe that the officers had come by just the day before, and now I was meeting a woman who was beyond me in so many ways. Her tight blue sweater and curve-hugging skirt left little to be imagined, and her smile widened as she walked toward me. Louie choked on his drink, but my eyes were riveted to that sweater.

"How are you, Johnny?" she said. Instead of offering her hand, she kissed me on the cheek.

"Oh baby," Tommy chided, and I looked at him as if he was trespassing. He sneered at me then turned back to the bar.

"Great, Marguerite. How about that drink?" I didn't know what else to say.

"Call me Maggie, and I'll have what you're having." She smiled, looking so innocently sexy that I wanted to dive right on her.

"Two scotches, Jack." I nodded to the back where there was a table waiting for us.

I pulled out Maggie's chair and sat across from her, my back to the wall—a habit from my line of work. I had a hard time not staring into her eyes, which were a shifting, bright blue. Tonight they were like a rich autumn sky, a stark blue that spread from the rooftops out across the harbor. She wasn't nervous. She didn't fidget or fuss over things, and her delicate hand was steady as she reached for her glass. Her curious glances showed interest in the surroundings, and her reporter side showed as she leaned into the conversations around her.

When she looked into my eyes it sent a slight quake through my body and I felt my shoulders twitch. I needed to take a hold of myself so I lifted my glass to hers, "Salute."

She smiled and this time I noticed well-placed dimples on each side of her mouth. "Salute," she responded, and we touched glasses.

She spoke first wanting to know about my ins with newspaper and her job but then she turned to more exciting things. "So you're a gangster?"

"Yeah, I guess."

"You guess? You don't know?"

"Yes, I'm a gangster." I didn't want to answer like that, but she was too fast.

"Have you ever killed anyone?"

I thought back to the Lieutenant, caught myself and tried slowing her down. "That's a personal business matter."

She smiled. "Yes, I suppose it is."

I wanted to change the subject. "That was a great story on the fire." After I said it, I felt stupid. How can tragedy be great?

"It was very sad."

"Yeah, that's what I meant."

"Do you read much?"

I didn't like the question but I answered anyway. "Newspapers." Where was this going?

"Books?"

"Mark Twain." I don't know why I said it. I remembered Tom Sawyer as a kid.

"Hemingway is one of my favorites," she said and looked at me through her eyelashes. I sensed it was an act—this woman was anything but shy. "I also like Walt Whitman," she added.

"I don't know him." I was getting out of my league on writers, so I brought her back into my own ballpark by telling her the truth. "I quit school at tenth grade."

"Oh?"

"My dad died, and I had to work to help my mom. I was the only kid."

"How did your dad die?"

"He was a mason. A building collapsed on him."

"I'm sorry."

I took a slug of my drink and she did the same, looking over her glass at me. "I'm over it," I said trying to act tough. She didn't buy it, I could tell by the way she threw back another drink, but her eyes stayed on mine.

"Did you become a gangster right away?" She was right back on it.

I placed my hands face down on the table. "You like the notorious, huh?"

She glanced around the room, then down at my hands and slowly returning to my eyes. "I find it intriguing." She leaned forward, her face propped on her hand, "And I find you sexy."

Damn, was she fast. "Thanks."

We talked well into the evening, having several drinks too many. The summer air was alive, and the sweet smell of street vendors fruit lingered and mixed with the fragrance of the bakeries first run of bread and cakes as I walked her to her apartment in Greenwich. She said the place was nothing grand, small, just a start-up. Her words floated through the night and I struggled not to lose myself in her.

I reached for her hand and she squeezed ever so lightly and moved closer. Near a corner, in the shadow of a building, I stopped and swung her to me her perfume floating pleasingly around us. She didn't resist as I bent to kiss her. She kissed back, hard and passionately, her tongue thrust deep inside my mouth and our lips melded together, inciting me to more movements. She leaned back against the building and pressed her breasts against my chest and pushed her midsection into mine, my hand slipping up her blouse and around to feel her. Her head pulled back, her lips still parted, sighing as she held the back of my neck. I slowly caressed her, as I kissed her neck I unbuttoned her blouse with my other hand and moved my lips slowly down, a light taste of salt on her skin. She thrust her hips forward feverishly and I pushed hard against her. Then she suddenly stopped and said, "Wow."

She grabbed my hand as she pulled away, and buttoned up her blouse. Then she pulled me to her again and kissed me fully, but again abruptly stopped. "Oh, Johnny." She nodded and hooked her arm in mine as we walked slowly to her stoop.

"I'm not going to ask you up. I'm not like that on the first date."

"Will there be a second?"

"Yes," she said, looking up at me with her eyes widened like a kitten.

"When?"

"Tomorrow, I'll cook you dinner."

I nodded, trying to suppress my excitement. "Good, I'll bring the wine." We kissed again, but not as hard because we probably would have been unable to stop. I don't know if that would have been good or bad.

The first time always carries something with it whether you love someone or not. But if it is love, if it turns out to be love, then I think things become real complicated. I never truly loved anyone. For the first time in my life, I was unnerved, but not by some crazy, bloodthirsty gangster. No, the pit in my stomach came from these new feelings I had for Maggie.

\*\*\*

I'd been hung up on a business call on the West Side, and I was running late for my date with Maggie. Some crazy had tried moving in on our betting trade, setting up shop on a fourth floor apartment overlooking the docks. Tommy came with me and many times, when we both had to do a job, my end was keeping Tommy from killing someone. His burly frame, thick in the shoulders and thighs, made him a cinch for breaking people apart. To Tommy, killing wasn't business or the last resort—it was a sport. Anyway, this guy from Missouri thought he would be able to waltz into New York City and set up a horse-betting parlor without any fuss. He paid the police who told us once they had the money. Cops do that you know; they're as greedy as anyone else.

We had to wait for the guy for several hours, and I was getting fidgety because I knew Maggie would be waiting. I said a quick prayer and then wondered if it was right, saying a prayer to help move along a beating. Whatever, it worked. Just after I said amen, the guy, Charlie, turned the corner and went up to the apartment. We waited long enough to make sure he was in his place, then rushed up the stairs two at a time.

Tommy crashed through the door. It was unlocked, but he buried his massive shoulder into it anyway and splintered the hinges from the jam. Poor Charlie screamed and tried scurrying away at the sight of us, but Tommy grabbed him up by the lapels and slammed him into the wall. He crumpled to the floor, and the picture of Rosie the Riveter hanging above him fell on his head. I liked the expedience of the whole exchange, and thought for certain I would be able to meet Maggie on time.

"You can't operate your action in our territory, Charlie. Certain people don't like that, don't allow it. Capisce?" I was trying to be nice. Tommy began to drool and that wasn't a good sign.

"You sons of—" Poor old Charlie never got to finish—Tommy kicked his teeth in with two smashing blows with his triple E shoe. Charlie tried spitting the broken pieces out through the blood pouring from his mouth. He whimpered as he crawled away, but there was nowhere to go. I began feeling sorry for the guy. Missouri, what did they know about New York? I couldn't stop what we started, though, and we had to finish the business. Tommy picked him up by the feet and smashed him through the window headfirst. The glass landed three stories down, and Tommy held Charlie over the ledge by his ankles. I moved fast. It was getting late, and I really didn't want Tommy dropping Charlie to his death, so I squeezed between Tommy's hulk and the window jam and spoke to Charlie.

"There are certain rules in this town and you have to play by them. Capisce?"

Charlie muffled a weak "yes" and I saw some pieces of his teeth fall to mix with the window glass below.

"Are you going to obey the rules, Charlie?" I asked.

I thought I heard a faint, "Yes."

"Okay, the first rule is you have to leave town. Capisce?" I didn't hear anything. I looked at my watch and sighed, then nodded to Tommy. He knew the cue. He released Charlie's left foot, which swung Charlie like a pendulum and he hit an abutment of brownstone from the floor below.

"Yeth, yeth, pleth." Tommy and I looked at each other and I figured Charlie was saying, yes, yes, please. I nodded for Tommy to lift him up. Tommy frowned, so I motioned for him to hurry. I looked around the apartment as Tommy dropped Charlie on the floor. It was a mess with stacks of books and a bank bag on the floor, but what I noticed was two bottles of wine—one red and one white—that looked French. I went to them and sure enough, this Charlie was living the good life. I picked them up and I walked over to him.

"So you understand you have to leave town?"

Charlie nodded.

"Okay. I believe you, but we have to leave one insurance measure."

Again, Charlie nodded and I did the same to Tommy. Tommy walked to Charlie, his legs shaking and body trembling as he tried crawling away. He grabbed him, pulling him to his feet, and drilled him in the gut. As the air rushed from Charlie's mouth, Tommy cranked a good one to his jaw shattering the bone. Charlie sank to the floor, his jaw askew. With my bottles of wine and the bank bag in hand, we left.

We split up at Varick. I gave Tommy the money, counting it first, and then told him to get it to Jack's where the boys were meeting. I took the wine and ran to Greenwich Village.

I was only a few minutes late, and I wanted to compose myself, so I found a small florist shop and bought a spring bouquet for Maggie. I took a breath and went up the stairs.

I didn't expect what I saw upon entering her apartment. There were papers and books everywhere, strewn along the couch and spilling to the floor. Maggie popped her head out of the kitchen and smiled when she saw me. She had a smudge of ink on her cheek, and I couldn't help thinking she looked like she'd just come off the playground. "I worked late and couldn't clean, so I just started dinner," she said, ducking back out again.

"It's okay. I worked late, too." She giggled in response and I followed her into the kitchen. It looked worse than the living room, with stacks of books and papers weighing down the table. The odor from the stove was unlike anything I'd smelled before. "Why did you giggle when I said I worked late?"

Maggie stopped stirring and cocked her head. "Because it's funny to hear a crook say he's working. The flowers are beautiful, Johnny." I held them out to her and tried to say something, but she pulled me to her and kissed me like the other night. It was steamy in the kitchen but we didn't notice. After a few moments, she pulled back, taking the flowers from my hand, and filled a coffeepot with water.

"We won't need coffee tonight," she said, placing the flowers in the pot.

We didn't need to eat, either, not dinner anyway. We could have gone on kissing, but I didn't want the night to end before it began. The beef cooked in cognac was a taste I'd never experienced. The stories of her dad and mom were intriguing to a guy who never went past the bridges. Her father was an aviator in World War I and met her mother in France while on tour. Maggie was born in Hong Kong and lived there for several years before the family came back to settle in California.

"You love and miss them, don't you?" I emptied the first bottle of wine into her glass.

She nodded with a wan smile, clinked her glass to mine, and said, "Salute."

We were in bed before we were half way through the second bottle. We lay there, kissing and stroking one another until our clothes came off. We were left panting and perspiring in the sultry dark. I lit a cigarette and inhaled deeply, letting the smoke out in a blue steady stream.

"Mmmmm, that was wonderful," she said softly.

"Yes," I said. Her perfect breasts and light skin were lit by the glow of the city. She turned to me, took in my body, and began tracing a finger from my neck slowly down my chest.

"You have a nice body," she said and continued downward with the finger. It made my midsection jump, and I quickly doused my cigarette and turned to her again. She was ready with her mouth, and I moved down as she arched her back.

We went on like this for most of the night, falling in and out of sleep occasionally until we heard the rumblings of the morning through the open window. She turned to me and traced a circle on my chest.

"Say, you gangsters know union guys. You work with them kinda, don't you?"

I was a little surprised. I thought she was about to say she loved me or something, because that's how I felt at the moment. "Yeah, kinda," I mocked back. The mocking didn't matter to Maggie and, through the years, I learned that when Maggie wanted something for a story, she got it.

"Do you know this Petrillo guy?"

I stole a glance at her and the wide-eyed look on her face made me smile. I knew Petrillo, but didn't tell her.

"Or somebody that you know who knows him?" she pressed.

"Why?"

"I'm supposed to interview him and he doesn't give interviews."

My paranoid instincts went off. I didn't know if Maggie planned the whole night just to get information from me for an interview. Here I was, lying beside the most beautiful woman I had ever been with, on the brink of falling madly in love, and she probably designed the whole set up. I had been conned, but it was a good one that didn't cost me anything, so I answered her. "I think I can do something for you there."

She smiled and kissed me. "Thanks baby. I knew you'd come through. I'd like to do it soon because I think I'm shipping out next month. You know, cover the end of the war." I took her again, the price for my favor, but before we got back into the heat of action, I made a mental note to contact Lieutenant Crowley. If Maggie was going overseas, maybe I should, too. I didn't want to let her out of my sight.

*** 

52

Crowley was pleased to see me and quickly sent me through a battery of medical tests. I returned to his office where he sat at a long, wooden, army green desk flanked by an Army Air Force and an American flag. He seemed livelier than the first time I met him, friendlier maybe. He explained that a troop ship would transport me and three other men to an undisclosed base in England. I asked him about money and he assured me that they would make first payment prior to my departure so my mother could take care of herself while I was away.

The difficult part was telling my people I was going to war. I thought of every conceivable argument—patriotism, excitement, adventure, and money—but settled on what I learned in the neighborhood: lie. I simply told them that they'd mistakenly drafted me. The guys wanted to contact Mr. Luciano to fix it, but I assured them I had everything under control, and that when I went to headquarters the following week I would straighten it out. I left two days later, leaving my mom with my first annuity and three hundred extra that I'd squeezed from Crowley. He wasn't happy about it, but this was my mother we were talking about, and I wasn't about to leave her destitute.

## MAGGIE

I missed Johnny. I missed everything about him, his coarseness, his ruff hands, his street language, and sound. I tried getting in touch with him several times but he seemed to have disappeared. Just yesterday I thought I saw him turn the corner. I even yelled, "Johnny," chasing the guy. "Johnny," I yelled again and the man turned. I was so disappointed when I saw it was not him. Thinking the worst, I continually checked the ticker for any gangland shootings that might have Johnny's name attached.

One reporter commented on my vigilance. "Maggie, what's the matter, either you're empty on stories or you know something's going to pop. Knowing you, you got something and want to be first at it, huh?"

I didn't realize how conspicuous I was. "Naw, come on. I'm doing my job is all."

"Well, if that's what you say, but slow down. The stories will come."

There were stories but the ticker never mentioned any mob killings, so I checked for arrests at the city blotters, but again turned up empty. Then I figured a guy like him, a guy with an ego, probably saw the Petrillo story and figured I used him. I did in a sense, but it was a piece of luck after an enjoyable evening. It wasn't my main intention to get the interview from him. It was one of my intentions, but not the main one.

I liked Johnny. I wanted to see more of him, but I was swept up in my urgency to get abroad before the end of the war, and I had to forget Johnny to concentrate on my career. I found out from Mrs. Reid that I had a berth on the Queen Mary, which was leaving in three nights. I had a lot to do to prepare.

Soon, Johnny, sorry to say, became a distant memory, until I turned the corner on 40th and 6th and saw him stepping out from Harry Bloom's cigar store. He caught sight of me quickly; he had those eyes that see in every direction. He looked surprised but nowhere near as surprised as me. He hesitated.

"Hi, Johnny?"

He stepped towards me, his eyes quickly taking in everything about me, my Simplicity-patterned navy blue suit whose skirt fell just above my knees, my hair windblown and messy. I wondered if I had any ink stains on my face but I didn't need to worry, Johnny's eyes lingered on my knees, and I liked it.

"You look great, Maggie."

"You mean my knees look great?"

His eyes jumped to mine.

"No, the whole you," he reached for shoulders then pulled me to him and kissed me hard. I knew then, right then under the sign for Harry Bloom's cigar store, that I missed him. I wrapped my arms around his waist and squeezed him to me without stopping the kiss, oblivious to the surroundings. When he stopped he put his cheek in my hair briefly then pulled back. "I missed you."

"I missed you, too, Johnny, really and truly. I didn't think so, but now I do. I'm sorry."

He squeezed his lower lip with his finger and thumb, then shrugged his shoulders. "About what?"

"About, you know, um the —"

He shrugged again. He didn't care. I simply was off track thinking he was mad about the Petrillo thing. No sense in even bringing it up. "You know about, not calling or ..." I shrugged.

"Listen, you want a coffee or a malt? This place has great malts." He nodded at a sign just past the cigar shop that read Tip Top.

"Malts?" I laughed. "I thought you were the tough, bad guy scotch drinker."

He took my arm in his, as if he were a gentleman, except that when we touched it was electric. "Ah, too early for that. You working?"

"Kinda, why?" I knew why, but I wanted a little tease.

We started walking arm-and-arm in the direction of my apartment. "Well it's too early for drinks and you don't seem too keen on malts, so I thought maybe we could take a walk or something."

"Or something?"

He circled his arm around my waist. "Or something."

Johnny never mentioned anything about the mess of my apartment, the clothes spread out on the couch and piled into two suitcases which would never close. He yanked my arm and spun me to him and in seconds we were peeling off our clothes, stumbling towards the bedroom. It was the first time I ever made love during the day, and I soaked in the sunlight beaming through the thin curtains and onto the bed. Maybe it was the mystery of sex or people's objections to unmarried people having it at all, but I always felt it was reserved for the dark. Now, that didn't matter, and Johnny and I melded like never before. The recklessness of war time seized me as I tried to keep pace with Johnny's wildness. We thrashed and ravenously tore into each other, our legs entwining, our bodies slick with perspiration slapping against our flesh. The sun disappeared and the bed slipped away as we catapulted into another place, another world.

Afterwards we laid in bed, both thoroughly exhausted. Johnny grabbed for a cigarette and, leaning against the headboard, inhaled it deeply. "You're leaving soon," he blew a stream of blue smoke into the beam of sunlight. I rested my head in his lap.

"Yes in a few days." Then I remembered what he said the last time we were together, about maybe seeing me in Europe. I pulled my legs from under the sheet and kneeled, sinking into the bed with my knees touching his ribs. "You said something about going there. What did you mean?"

He kneaded his knuckles on my knee then rolled them up my inner thigh. "Oh, nothing, I uh, well, I enlisted." He said this without emotion, like it was the normal thing to do.

"Johnny, what? For what? For me? I mean, don't do this for me. My God, you might end up in the Pacific."

He was very still and quiet. "No, they're sending me to Europe." Then he crushed out his cigarette, turned to me, and grabbed both my hands. "I'm not chasing you," he said. "I'm going because I need to, and you being there and maybe us meeting adds to the adventure." He kissed my ear. "I need to go."

For the first time in my life, I swallowed my questions and realized he was right. At this time, in this crazy world, it did not matter. I crawled on top of him, pressed myself against his chest, and let the light of the afternoon sun wrap us in its warmth.

## JOHNNY

Mother couldn't understand why I was leaving. I didn't want to tell her that I was a mobster without much future. We were about ready to engage in a war with the Profaci mob, and part of the reason was the bar fight with the drunk Irishman. Seems he was brother to a brother who knew someone in the Profaci family and now they wanted payback. If I stayed, their guys would hit me, or my guys if they thought it would save money. I figured with the annuity money these government guys were giving me, this would give my mother the easiest way.

"Perche, Giovanni, perch vai a guerra?"

"Perche ci devo andare, e per tu, e per tu."

She shook her head and sat at the table, burying her head in her folded arms. Then she looked up, tears rolling from her eyes. "Non capsico questa guerra, non capisco nulla."

"Mom." I wanted to speak English because when we conversed in Italian, she would become more emotional. In English she would have to listen more intently and would be removed slightly from her emotions. "These people are offering me good money to do a job for them that will help this country. They want me to go to Italy. I want to see our country, your country. I want to provide for you. Do you understand?"

"Johnny, this is our country now. It is safe here. It is molto danger there now. I read the paper. I know. Money does not matter. My son matters." She said this measurably and with meaning. Her eyes, which carried all of her emotion, always went to the ceiling when she searched for the correct words. My mother is a beautiful woman. I love her dearly, and knowing that I was hurting her, hurt me. I also knew her hurt could be greater if I stayed.

"I know, Ma. I'll be careful. I'll come back to you, I swear it."

She nodded slowly and then made the sign of the cross. "Dio mio, I know you will, my son. I will pray for you. I will tell your Father in Heaven to look after you."

She resigned herself to the fact that I was going to leave. Mothers know things intuitively, seeing into their children's future. I really think she knew something strange happened when the soldiers left the house. I looked at her and wanted to cry, but knew I had to be a man. I hugged her and felt her tremble slightly, then she pulled back and kissed my forehead. "I'm going to make you a big bowl of pasta and my best meatballs. Okay, Johnny?"

"Yeah Ma, I'd love that." Feeding me was her way of showing she would be strong. Like I said, she is a great woman.

I tried to reach Maggie before I left, even after several days earlier while having coffee at the old Hudson Diner I unfolded the *Herald* and saw Maggie's Petrillo story. My stomach turned as I started reading it, then folded it and shoved it away. Just as I had suspected, she used me to get to him. I shook it off. I had to. I sipped my coffee thinking about things then felt that was okay with me, I understood that kind of mind. People use each other all the time, and many times they are unaware that it hurts the other person. I know I've done that, and I've finally realized it's not a nice thing to do.

People hurt easy—we're not as tough as we make out to be. If I had realized this sooner, I probably would have settled down with a nice bride who wanted to be a mother and raised a family. I guess it wasn't in the cards. Several days later I wanted to get an idea about what people on the streets were saying about me since I kept myself away from the mix. My best and most trustworthy source was at Harry Bloom's where I bought my cigarettes. Harry was a street smart, short and squat Jewish man who smoked his cigar to the nub. I loved him. He knew things, I don't know how but he did and gave good advice. "What's new, Harry?" I asked like always and he humphed back like always chewing on his unlit cigar. Then he one-eyed me with his big round brown as he took the cigar from his mouth. "You know what I know," he said sizing me up.

"I've been laid up so maybe you know more."

"You be careful Johnny. You know that. I'll tell you one thing. You get out. Word is you started something and there's this pride thing going on. You know the pride, that's bad."

"Yeah, it really wasn't me though," I wondered if I wanted Harry to vindicate me.

"It don't matter. Go somewhere. You got both sides against you. Go, go to war, it might be safer."

Good ol'Harry, right on the money. He tossed me my cigarettes and I gave him a real good tip, nodded my thanks and walked out the door. The sun hit me right in the eyes and made me turn and suddenly saw Maggie. "Madonna," I thought. She said something and I said something back but I was really taking her in until I focused on her knees just below her skirt line. I never realizing how perfect they looked. I silently thanked the war effort for rationing dress material. God, I felt good she was standing right there. It didn't take long. I don't even remember the words we said but I remember the lovemaking and the sun and her sweet breath and kisses and I could have died there with her in my arms but I knew there was much more in store for me. I don't know how I knew. I just did. Maybe Harry was rubbing off on me. Maybe someone or something guided me into their own direction where I had no control. But I truly hoped I would be steered in Maggie's direction, that's what I wanted most. A few days later one cold morning in April, with the sun still buried in the sea's horizon, I boarded the Queen Mary, bound for Europe away from the gang war brewing, into a huge battlefront and hopefully somewhere near Maggie.

# PART II
## The Way to War

**MAGGIE**

I missed my ship. I couldn't believe it; in my excitement, while packing and phoning friends and relatives, but mostly thinking of my time with Johnny, the hours rocketed by without me knowing. Then, already late, my taxi stalled in a traffic accident and by the time I reached the docking area, the lights of the Queen Mary were slipping out of the harbor. It felt like there were marbles in my stomach as I frantically looked for the dock master. I found him, leaning against a weather-worn building and smoking a hand-rolled cigarette, and convinced him to radio ahead to the Ambrose Light dock.

I grabbed the taxi driver who lingered by his cab, waiting for his fare, and yelled for him to get me to the Ambrose Light dock. He took the turns so fast that they sent me flying from one side of the back seat to the other, and I was relieved when I saw the ship's lights ahead.

About an hour later, the ship docked and dropped a pilot ladder over the side. I ran and grabbed the rope, realizing I had no choice but to abandon my duffel back or miss my chance to go to Europe. The ladder slid across the ship's hull and I hung on for dear life. A voice above commanded me to remain still—which was exactly what I wanted—and then with a jerk, the ladder began to rise. I didn't open my eyes until I felt myself placed firmly on deck.

Scattered around deck were several men and women dressed as I was, in full army uniform, and a ranking officer. My combat helmet fell back as I stood, and in the expectant silence, I knew I had to say or do something. Taking off my helmet, I stood at attention, spitting my whipping hair out of my mouth, saluted the officer and said, "Marguerite Hogan reporting for duty."

It seemed everyone was trying to suppress laughter, but it was difficult to tell amongst the faces of the military and correspondents. A tall woman with long dark hair bent and said to a shorter stout man next to her, "She's too sweet for war." The man responded with a laugh.

"That's Maggie Hogan, and she ain't no nun."

I asked the captain about my abandoned duffel. He looked at me with a stern eye and briny face partially hidden underneath a neat white beard. He shook his head slowly, and then pointed his finger to another man. "Ensign, have someone get the correspondent's duffel, and hurry to it. Welcome aboard, Miss Hogan. The Ensign will show you to your quarters."

The thing about the ocean that impressed me the most wasn't the expanse of water reaching out to the horizon, but the clean night sky. After every dinner, I would climb through the frigid evening to the top deck, where I could be alone with the stars.

The Milky Way stretched into the inky ocean, and the constellations were clearer than I had ever seen. I found Orion and the Dippers, Draco and Pleiades, and for some reason thought of Johnny. He popped into my mind and, though it felt like an intrusion at first, I let the thought linger and it comforted me. I wished he were with me, holding me from behind with his cheek nestled against my wool hat. I felt terribly lonely just then.

Once the ocean air had permeated my layers of clothing, I would return to the cabin I shared with Janet Flanner of The New Yorker. She'd pulled rank and claimed the bottom bunk, for her excellent writing and experience. I was a little overawed by her at first, but my blunt take on our surroundings, men, and writing chiseled away at her superiority until we became friendly. We were females on equal footing in a sea of men.

I sat next to her at the dinner table we shared with four male correspondents who spewed their arrogance like a quickly popped, overly shaken bottle of champagne. It sickened Janet and me, but we played our proper female roles for the first couple nights. But the third night we just couldn't take it anymore.

Janet had dressed in a fine, tight, blue turtleneck, her long, dark hair combed to the side and spilling over her shoulder. She wore red lipstick and blush, making her hazel eyes cast a deeper hue. Her smile was bright and sexy.

I came in my uniform. I liked that it made me look soldierly, and I wanted to impress the captain. I thought he might be good for some information during the voyage, and I noticed that uniforms gave a certain esprit de corps amongst the people who wore them.

I was right. When he came into the room, although his look lingered on Janet, he came to me and graciously accepted my hand with a bright smile. I had a better look at him, and saw that, though he wasn't good looking, he had a command about him, a tough, no nonsense look in his dark eyes. His high cheekbones were rosy from the cold salt air and his full-length beard made his bleached teeth a focal point of his face. Everyone rose when he entered and he motioned with for us to sit, a gesture that meant, "Let's dispense with formality."

The captain sat at the head of the table with Janet to his left. Across from us were the three men, Jake Monroe, Peter Materese, and Gordon Thomas. They were all dressed in dark turtlenecks and smoking pipes stereotypical of correspondents of the day. I knew for certain they would begin the dinner conversation with the egotistical name-dropping that I found so boring. Men who had to parade and swagger about their accomplishments were my biggest turn off.

Jake was a nice looking man, with fair skin and blue eyes but his high-pitched voice irritated me. Peter was the opposite, gruff, burly, and loud. Gordon made me the sickest of all. He was from a well-to-do family and talked through his nose. He was the best looking, but his looks went down the toilet when he opened his mouth.

I was surprised at the fine china laced with gold trim, the glassware from Murano, and the polished silverware. When our drinks arrived, Gordon made himself known.

"Captain, by my calculations we are ahead of schedule."

"Your calculations are correct," the captain said politely. "You people should be in Gourock, Scotland, three days from now."

Gordon nodded his head triumphantly, sipped his drink, and puffed on his pipe. It made me nauseous.

"This is a beautiful setting," I jumped in to get Gordon out of the limelight.

"Yes, it's our peacetime voyage setting, but I thought you fine people would enjoy it."

"Thank you, Captain," Janet said.

"Typical thing a woman would notice," Peter said between pursed lips. I didn't respond, but Janet did.

"I suppose you don't speak of the beauty because you'd rather enjoy the ugly."

"I don't enjoy either in war time. Men are dying," Peter said.

"The battlefield is a very ugly place," Jake added.

"Oh, you've been to battle, Jake?" Janet knew he hadn't.

"Speaking from the words of my colleagues is all. Do you have any female friends covering the battles?"

"That's why we're here," I said.

"Women belong at desks, not on the fields of battle."

Infuriated, my cheeks flushed. "And where does this brilliant piece of wisdom come from?"

"That's a Jake-ism, Maggie." Peter laughed and the atmosphere lightened a bit.

The first course, a light fish cake, came out and the quick waiter who poured the wine diffused the tension. I was famished, so I decided to dive into the fish instead of Jake. Everyone ate in silence until Gordon wanted to hear himself speak again.

"Captain, any sign of German U boats?"

The captain shook his head. "I think the strategy of leaving under the night sky thwarts their efforts. That and luck."

"Sinking this ship would be quite the prize," Peter added.

"With nine thousand troops on board, I believe you are right," said the captain. "But I also believe the Germans have all they can handle nearer home. Things haven't been going well for them."

"I hope we get there in time." As soon as I said it, I knew how horrid it sounded. Jake picked up on it quickly.

"Can't wait to write about kids being slaughtered in battle, Maggie?"

"I didn't mean it like that. I meant it as a story."

Gordon smirked. "I hear you treat stories as a way to get famous. That so?"

"Don't answer him, Maggie. He's playing his role of omniscient journalist, and his degradation of the female reporter helps camouflage his weaknesses." Janet smiled and sipped her wine.

To my relief, the captain interfered. "I think there will be plenty of war left to write about when you get there. We're writing a new history out there, and that will be remarkable for the pen as well."

"Hear, hear." Peter raised his glass for a toast, which served as a peace offering. We all raised our glasses and the rest of the dinner went on without incident.

Obviously nothing had changed, even at this late stage in the war. A woman's right to report on war was still not very popular with our male counterparts or the powers of the military.

Tucked into my bunk later, I asked Janet about their attitude. "Why don't they want us there?"

"It's a male thing. I think it threatens their existence, and they get nervous about it."

"But it shouldn't. If they're good writers and reporters, then they should hold their own, like in any profession." I was thinking out loud rather than trying to convince Janet, who understood completely.

"Exactly. That's why it's a man thing. They threaten easy and they have this thing that women should be dainty little creatures that care for them and cater to them and say yes to them. You know coddle, coddle, coddle. Sometimes they're just so pitiful."

"I like men."

"So I've heard."

I propped myself up with my elbow. "What have you heard?" I watched her eyes and they closed slightly, pensively.

"Word has it that you're loose and get things done by whatever means you have at your disposal."

"Which means my body." I was surprised to see it didn't matter to me. "Janet, I'm as good as any man, and for the sake of myself and women in other fields, I'm going to succeed. And, yeah, I will use everything I've got to achieve that. People talk and lie because they're jealous."

Janet sat up. "I'm going to tell you something, pretty young lady." I looked at her eagerly, my eyes coruscating while anticipating her next words. She smiled at my face. "I feel sorry for the men whose lives cross with yours."

I laid back down. "I do, too."


## JOHNNY

I was in a daze, already adrift in the current, during my last few hours in the States. I moved along, getting my affairs together, and

66

before I knew it, I had boarded the Queen Mary. I had watched the ship come in and out of the harbor many times, dreaming of cruising to some far away island with a beautiful woman. Reality hit me as I walked the gangplank with thousands of soldiers, three of them assigned as my bunk mates in a berth so small we had to take shifts to sleep.

The ship was completely transformed into the Gray Ghost. Where an elegant promenade deck had once been there were canons, machine guns, and anti-aircraft rocket launchers. When I stepped on deck and saw all the soldiers, the emptied swimming pools, berths occupying the lounges and drawing rooms, I realized what had been was gone.

It was the first ship I had ever been on that actually went to sea. My experience with ships was limited to lifting cargo from the docks and scaring degenerates by hanging them from the deck railings.

As we pulled away from the dock and veered eastward, a crown of orange emerged from the horizon but we missed the sunrise as we hung off the rails and watched the skyline slip away. We stopped once at Ambrose Light to pick up a passenger who missed the ship. I figured whoever it was must be pretty important, otherwise the Gray Ghost would never have stopped.

I soon learned to love the sway of the ship as it chopped through the waves. It didn't bother me, but it got to my bunkmate Bobby and two other guys, Stanley and Thomas, who bunked across from us. They all puked their insides out and when they couldn't puke anymore they heaved air, making them sound like squealing pigs. They began to make me sick, too, so I often cut out and went to the top deck to watch the stars.

I didn't know much about the stars, but I was impressed with the vastness of the sky, and the billions of fine points of light filling the blackness made me feel so small. Taking in the enormity of nature, I found myself wondering if anything mattered. I began to question going to war simply over a dame who obviously didn't care for me. I thought we had something, that magic between a man and woman, and I couldn't believe I was wrong. My mind wandered to other things—adventure and travel. I wanted to see the world, so I tried to let my memories of Maggie slip away like the coastline. But still, the idea of her remained.

Midway through the voyage, the boys got their sea legs. Though they looked like death, they began to join me amidships during the early morning to breathe in the good sea air. We walked towards the bow staring down at the steel floor rather than the moving horizon. When we reached the bridge, we'd linger, lean against the pilot house and have a smoke. Having company felt good, and I sensed the beginning of camaraderie like I'd had on the New York streets, a brotherhood that sprung from the danger ahead.

"I was recruited because I fly gliders," Bobby from Detroit said.

"How is a glider used in war when airplanes could knock them out of the sky easily?" I asked.

"I don't know, but they gave me a good deal to do it," Bobby said. "Money in annuities. So I signed in Detroit and took the train to New York."

Bobby was shorter than me, with an almost frail frame. His sandy hair and fair complexion made him look like a schoolboy, but he carried himself like he was completely fearless.

Stanley was the opposite in stature: broad shoulders, thick arms and legs, and about six foot four. He was from Kentucky and could shoot the eyes out of squirrel from two hundred yards. He didn't know anything about annuities, he just wanted to serve his country. "Darn," he said as we all stopped and leaned over the rail. "After a week in boot camp, the brass came to me and said they liked my shooting. Then they corralled me to their office and told me they needed me to win the war."

"You shoot good, huh?" Thomas asked, and it was the first time I heard his voice.

"Grew up with a Winchester and moved on to a thirty aught six," he said with a smile, the wind blowing his jet-black hair into his eyes, the sun soaking into his bronze colored skin. I laughed inwardly, looking at him next to Bobby. Two people couldn't look more opposite in size.

Thomas worried me. He was quiet and with his distant eyes I couldn't quite make him. He blended into a room, and his medium height and thin, lanky look betrayed his grace.

"And you?" I asked him. "Why do they want you?"

He leaned against the lifeboat next to him, looking it over before answering. "Explosives."

We all took notice at that. He was older than us by a few years and had a more disciplined look. "You blow things up?" I asked.

"Yeah. Fires and stuff in the Midwest oilfields and some construction." He was as cool as a Brooklyn icehouse, and I know my guys back in the neighborhood would have employed him faster than a pigeon on corn for his expertise.

These were my guys, my bunkmates, and my troop, as Crowley said. The more we talked, the more I grew to like them, and we had poker in common. When they got over their seasickness, we spent most of our time playing hands of cards for money and smokes. The best game came while the ship's screws churned up the Atlantic in rough seas. Several of the ship's crew joined in and, after several hours, only two of the sailors, Thomas, and I were still in.

We played five-card stud, a game I had grown up playing. Thomas was good, too, the kind of player who bet his hand, knew the cards on the table, and what remained in the deck. The two sailors were chasers, and it would be only a matter of time before Thomas and I had their money, too.

The only problem was that one of the sailors, a red-headed Scotsman who worked the boiler room, was getting very lucky with his cards, even on bad bets. "This is getting too easy. You guys are like kids," he said, punching Thomas on the shoulder. I knew it was getting to Thomas, because every time the Scot ran his mouth, Thomas flinched and hunched his shoulders.

"King bets five dollars, get you freeloaders out," the Scot huffed and guffawed. I caught Thomas's eye. Without having to say a word, we knew the game. It was a bond forged by two players with a knowledge of poker and a dislike for a player. It was a natural understanding Thomas and I had, and we knew it so we went to work dismantling the Scot. My card up was a jack and my hole card was a jack.

"I raise," I said and threw in ten bucks. Thomas knew I had the power so he raised again to get as much of the sailors' money into the pot. Like a sucker, the Scot rose again and his buddy called, then we went the three-raise limit. The next card gave the Scot a queen of hearts and me a four. Thomas dealt himself a seven; the other sailor had no business in the game. The Scot bet a hundred bucks, a good portion of his money.

"I raise one hundred," I said.

"Me too," Thomas said throwing in two hundred dollars with a blank face.

The Scot looked at both of us, grunted, "I call."

It forced the other sailor to drop.

The Scot's next card was another heart, and mine was a four showing a pair. Thomas dealt himself a seven for a pair. He looked at me and saw in my eyes I was still in control.

"Another hundred," Thomas said.

The Scot looked at him. "I raise."

"Me too," I said and smiled. The Scot looked at both of us and called. I think he knew something was amiss. Thomas dealt him another heart, possibly giving him a flush. He dealt me a jack. I had two pair showing, Thomas had dealt himself another seven for three of a kind.

"I check to you," Thomas said to the Scot. The sailor's face lit up like he'd just found a pot of gold.

"Everything; I bet everything," he said, pushing his money and cigarettes into the pot. "Four hundred dollars and forty cigarettes."

70

Then he sat back with a dopy grin, bobbing his head like a blasted buffoon.

I looked at him and smiled back. "I bet it all," I said, pushing my pile of five hundred thirty dollars and sixty smokes to the center.

The Scot's smile disappeared and he sat up, looking at my hand and wondering if I had the other jack. Then Thomas raised another hundred, and the Scot exhaled in a gush. "Jeeze...us Key... rist, what is this?" He looked back and forth at us.

"Poker. A check and a raise," Thomas said evenly.

The Scot looked to the other sailor. "Lend me the difference. I got them." The sailor hesitated, then counted out the difference. He looked at us both as he put the money in.

I motioned for Bobby to come near and then I whispered something in his ear. He went to his pocket and peeled off three hundred in twenty-dollar bills and gave it to me.

"I raise two hundred more." I liked saying it.

The Scot's mouth dropped, and Thomas folded. The Scot's face darkened with anger. "You..."

"Hey," I said quickly, "it's just friendly poker game."

"My ass, you two have somethin' goin'."

I smiled. Thomas sat impassively. The Scot looked back to his bank, who hesitated again and then gave him two hundred in twenty-dollar bills. He threw it in the pot, saying, "I don't got the smokes."

I shrugged and turned over my card: a jack showing a full house. The Scot's mouth began to twitch as I took the money. Then his hand stopped mine with a crushing grip on my wrist. He squeezed and I felt my blood stop going to my hand.

"You owe me smokes, too. Now take your grimy hand off my wrist." We locked eyes in a stalemate. Then, like a flash, I had my knife sunk into the wooden table, flush with his wrist. Real fear crossed his face.

"What is going on here?" Crowley appeared in the doorway and everyone froze. "Pero, get that knife back where it belongs, and you," he pointed at the Scotsman, "get your hands off my soldier."

We hesitated, looking at each other first, then up to Crowley. He had a look of pure meanness, a look I had seen on some of the mob bosses' faces. It meant business. I yanked the knife out and the Scot released my hand.

"Now, what happened here?"

"These guys are cheating."

"That so?" Crowley looked back and forth at Thomas and me.

"No, sir," Thomas said in military style.

"I won the hand, sir, fair and square," I said. My military manner had a hollow ring to it.

"Why do you say they cheated?" Crowley asked the Scot.

He looked to his friends, who shrugged. He stuttered something unintelligible, he scratched his red hair. "It was the way they were betting."

"What do you mean by that? How do you cheat betting?"

"You know, by betting and raising... both guys doing it against someone." He was really floundering.

Crowley shook his head. "Pero, take your money. No more playing on board ship. You," he nodded at the Scot, "you better take up another game. Poker is betting and raising for crying out loud." Crowley left as quickly as he'd shown up. The Scot looked like he wanted to jump me, but his pals dragged him away. I looked at Thomas, who had a tight grin on his face.

"How'd you know?"

"A feeling. I saw it in your eyes."

I liked this guy. I sensed this was going to be fun as I divvied up the money.

The fun was soon drowning in twenty to thirty foot swells, which tossed the ship like a can of anchovies. Although confined to our bunks, I walked up and down the lower decks just to keep my joints oiled and my muscles loose. I can't stand just laying around, and no one seemed to mind since the men outnumbered the beds.

During my turn in the bunk, I listened to the raging storm and thought of Maggie. I didn't want to but, as I lay awake in the late hours, I envisioned our lovemaking, especially our last time during the day. These thoughts turned me on, so I tried to concentrate on her face—her smile and how her forehead furrowed when she was searching for words. I missed her without wanting to, lonely the way only a man going to war can be. I wasn't sure she loved me, but felt she was close, so I used her for my girl anyway. I didn't think it harmed anyone, but the more I did it, the more I wanted to, the more I missed her, and the more I wanted to see her again. Loneliness is a strange bedfellow.

Loneliness also brought my mother with it. I thought of her as much as I thought of Maggie and with her, I was even able to bring in some smells. I would see her at the stove, fussing with the meatballs and sauce, and I swear I could smell the tomatoes simmering with basil and parsley right there on the ship.

My dad came to me in a dream one night when the weather was at its worst and several of the guys were puking. I had covered my head with the sheet to block the ubiquitous odor, and was dozing on the edge of wakefulness when the generator kicked off, cloaking the ship in darkness. In this place between wakefulness and sleep, my dad came to me.

He died before I really got to know him, killed in a building collapse when I was nine, but I was left with some warm memories. He was a small man, with thick forearms and fingers—he was a mason who could lay bricks faster than any guy I've ever known— teased because he was so good. They called him Brickyard because legend had it he could lay a yard full of bricks in one day. He liked his wine and his favorite food was roast chicken with oregano; he could eat two chickens if he was of a mind. I saw him do it once, after a full day of work in freezing weather. He came home and thawed out with wine, then sat down to eat. His cheeks were rosy from the cold and his hair was disheveled from his knit hat. His wool pants were too long for him and he had to cuff them up about eight inches, but he didn't care how he looked. He just wanted to be comfortable and warm while he worked.

The night he came to me, he had on his wool pants and flannel shirt, and his cheeks were rosy, just like the night he ate the two chickens. He stood there for a while, and I tried to talk to but nothing came out when I moved my mouth.

He looked at me and said, "Be careful." Then he turned completely around as if he were doing a little jig and said, very faintly, "Trust your instincts." He sat down at a round oak table and placed his hands face down on it, looking straight ahead, saying, "Fight like a rabid dog if they get you in a corner." A cloud of dust enveloped him at the table, and when it cleared, my father and the table were gone. Then I woke, and Thomas was puking below me.

By late afternoon, the storm had subsided and everyone was walking on the decks to breathe the fresh air. It was my turn in the berth again, but I couldn't get myself to go below, so I made it up to my favorite spot to watch the sea while I drifted to sleep.

I woke to choppy slaps of chilly air on my face. I had slept through the day, and the blue sky had been replaced by millions of blinking stars. I stroked my stomach, feeling tranquil as I listened to canvas flapping somewhere astern and the swish of the waves. A meteor streaked across the sky just as I heard my name whispered.

"Hello, Johnny Stone."

She stood before me like she'd been dropped off a star. She was wearing a military uniform, but her hair was loose and blowing around her shoulders. I froze, my mouth open in disbelief. I shook myself and started to rise when she stopped me.

"Just stay there for a moment, Johnny, while I look at you."

I listened, too stunned to do anything else.

"I saw your name on the roster. It took me a few days to pinpoint your berth. Your bunkmates directed me here."

"Thomas and Bobby?"

"Yes, and Stanley."

"Yeah, they're good guys."

"Funny, I come here at night, too, only I use the stern to watch the stars." She inched closer. "May I sit next to you?"

I was aching for her to sit, to let me kiss her and hold her. I moved to the side. "Yes."

She sat, drawing her knees to her chest, and wiggled next to me so we were just touching. "I missed you, Johnny, especially since our day together."

"I wanted to see you before I left, just in case something happened or we didn't meet for some time. I tried to see you, Johnny, honest. Everything happened so fast, I even missed the ship in New York."

"What, it was you at Ambrose Light?"

"Yeah, silly Maggie Hogan embarrassed to the hilt."

And just like that, she had me smiling. Imagining her unique gracelessness, I turned and hugged her to me. The embrace became a kiss and I knew instantly she had my heart, a good hook right into it. When our lips parted, she rested her head on my chest and gazed upward.

"I love looking into the Milky Way." She caressed my leg when she spoke. "See the constellations, Johnny? Orion, the Dippers, Draco, and Pleiades? They give me such a wonderful feeling." She turned to me. "I get the same feeling when I'm with you. I felt it the last day we were together."

She kissed me again and I lost it. I wanted to make love with her right there, but I pulled away as something nagged at me. She looked up at me and our eyes met. As the cool breeze caressed our hair, I swung her on top of me, her legs straddling mine, and kissed her again, our bodies pressed hard against each other.

Holding each other, we slept for only a few minutes. As the sun crept out of the ocean, we tried to part several times, but kissed again and again, waiting until the last moment when we had to part.

"We hit England tomorrow, so we can have tonight," she with eager eyes and mischievous smile.

"Okay, we'll meet here?"

"Yes, I have dinner with the captain and the rest, and after that I'll be up. About nine, okay?"

"Yeah." The plan made it easier to part, but my time with Maggie compounded the confusion I had been living with. I knew I had to confront her, but wanted our final moments to be precious.

That night I told the boys they could use my bunk and slipped out. They didn't question me, and I was glad to avoid making lies and excuses.

It was the most beautiful night, with a light breeze that blew away the warm air, leaving it cool and fresh. The stars had multiplied from the night before, alive with brightness, and the ocean was calm so the ship rocked like a soft melody.

Again, Maggie appeared from nowhere with a wool blanket wrapped around her shoulders. She dropped it to the deck, sat and pulled me to her. I hiked up her skirt and began reveling in our love. Lit by the stars, we moved with the waves and touched each other like the gentle breeze. It was a perfect moment, a moment to take with us across Europe, loving one another like another day wouldn't come.

When we finished, she sat curled in my arms looking up into the sky. "I know that one," I said, pointing to a red star in the east. "Mars. My dad showed it to me from the Statue of Liberty one night."

"It'll be our star, Johnny."

"What's going to happen with us, Maggie?" It wasn't exactly what I meant to ask, but the words came out on their own.

"I don't know, baby, I don't know." She turned to me. "I have to tell you something. I see other men, but I love you, Johnny. I don't want to, but I do."

"Why don't you want to?" I was confused.

"I don't want to hurt you, or to have this get messy."

"Ah, naw, that's not goin' to happen. No, never, don't worry, I got it covered," I said, but she did have me guessing.

She kissed me. "Thank you, Johnny Stone."

"You're welcome, Maggie Hogan." I pulled her onto me yanking the blanket out from underneath and wrapping it around her. We moved slowly with the same sway as the boat

Moments later, she pulled back and sat up. "But you have to understand, Johnny, I'm still frightened of my duplicities. I mean, I love you, but saw other men to further my career. So, I'm scared of myself, really."

I really wasn't expecting what she said particularly at this moment. "Like you did to me with Petrillo?" She brought it up, so I figured I might as well ask.

She grabbed my arm. "Oh no, Johnny, I thought that too, but I know it's not true. I wish I got to him through someone else. Please don't think that I meant to use you, I love you, truly."

I shook my head; she was really something. "I don't know—"

"Please believe me. This world is a crazy mess, but even though we haven't known each other long, I think we love each other. I don't want it to be ephemeral. I want it to be real."

I saw her lip quiver in the glow of the bow light and held her tighter. "What's that mean?"

"Short-lived, like a flower, like a rose. I love roses."

"It's okay, baby, I'll live through it with you."

"Oh, Johnny you just don't understand. Listen to me!" She turned away and paced towards the stern and then turned and paced back her eyes both on fire and watery. "It's distance. After tomorrow, you'll be gone and as the longer we're apart, the farther we'll be apart. The distance will be a big problem, I feel it."

"Maybe you want the distance, maybe you love people who you know will be distanced from you." I felt her shudder when I said it.

"Why would I do that? It doesn't make sense."

Was I ever in new territory with that one. I'd never been in love before—I wanted to spend every minute of forever with her. So what I said was natural and true. "Maybe you're afraid of love."

It took her several moments to respond. "I don't know, Johnny. That's my honest answer, and I want to always be honest with you."

She was so beautiful, even her contradictions and duplicities, but especially her honesty. "We just have to keep telling ourselves love can bridge the distance." I was unsure if I believed it.

"That's pretty."

"So are you, baby."

She hugged me again. "You're not like other men. Tonight at dinner, the other journalists were awful. I don't understand them."

"Maybe they're jealous of your talent."

"No. They think I don't belong," she said.

"It's a male thing. Maybe it threatens them, you know—more competition and they get nervous about it." It was the only thing I could figure.

"I know," she said. "But I will succeed, no matter what it takes. And you know something else, Johnny?"

"No, what?" I loved listening to her: her defiance and enthusiasm charged through me like ungrounded electricity.

"I love the excitement of danger." She looked up at me, her smile full of impishness and rebellion.

There was nothing I could do, Maggie Hogan was going to break my heart.

Back at quarters, Crowley's voice came from nowhere. "Pero, get your stuff together quick and get above with the others." I looked around and there he was, standing near my bunk. "I don't know what you've been up to, and I don't really care. But now I'm watching. Is that clear?" Crowley's eyes were wide and his face red with anger.

I was shocked he was so mad. "Yes, sir." I grabbed my duffel bag and rushed up to the deck just behind Thomas.

Thomas glanced back as he was going up the stairs. "Crowley did a bed check while you were gone. I covered for you, but he knew. It's no big deal, but I think he's gotta show us he's in charge."

"It's okay. I'm alright," I said trailing him. "And thanks."

"You'll do the same for me sometime."

When we got to the deck, the sun had given way to mist and we were able to see land. "England," one of the sailors yelled from above. I stopped and, leaning over the railing, saw a thin strip of land to the east.

By mid-day, the thin line had turned into a harbor and we were moving into the docks. I smiled, knowing I had crossed the Atlantic, met and made love to the woman who was instrumental in changing my world. I won four hundred dollars and ninety-eight cigarettes and never got seasick. I was feeling pretty good when they dropped anchor. Maybe the next few months wouldn't be so bad.


## MAGGIE

The tug brought us to the Carwell Bay dock just past two in the afternoon on a sunny April day. I was astonished by the pastoral scene—the lush, green hills, and the afternoon sun glancing off the water—which contrasted the frenzied rush on board. It was impossible to find Johnny in the madness, so Janet and I disembarked and took a taxi to Glasgow, where we caught the train to London.

We were staying at the same hotel, The Savoy, and arrived just prior to blackout time. We were both excited about being in

London, but the long journey left us wanting nothing more than a hot bath and a bed.

My modest room was in a section of the hotel that had been shelled in 1940 and had been rebuilt, but still needed paint. It didn't bother me, though, since I spent most of my time at our bureau office.

The office was housed in an old department store, converted into sectional offices for the war effort, and was just a few blocks from The Savoy. Every morning I walked past the rubble of buildings, destroyed by V-1 rockets propelled into the city on a daily basis. I had missed these devilish killing machines, and the whir of their engines whining down before dropping into the city. They had the V-2 now, a silent projectile that snuck into the night and blew away parts of the city.

I always looked to the sky when I walked to the office, wondering what I would do if I saw one of the pencil thin missiles heading my way. It made me shiver just to think about it, but it also thrilled me.

The office was small and cramped but it served its purpose. News from the front came from all kinds of sources: our own correspondents, soldiers returning from battle, and military hospitals. These stories both sickened me and increased my thirst to get to the front before the war ended.

One story I will never forget. Several months into the job, I had been nosing around the hospital talking to soldiers. Anyone capable of talking wanted to with a woman, so there was mutual satisfaction. While speaking with a soldier who had taken shrapnel in his back from a grenade, another soldier rolled to me in his wheelchair. His leg was in a cast and he was smoking a cigar. His face had meanness written all over it.

"Hey, you the lady from the press?"

"Yes, the Herald Tribune." The interruption annoyed me. "Excuse me," I said to the soldier on the bed, who was dozing off from the recently administered morphine.

"How come no one is writing about the valiant effort of our men from the Market Garden Operation?"

"And you are?"

"Sergeant Leo, 82nd Airborne."

Bristling from his bravado, I said, "Well Sergeant, is there something you'd like to say? You were there?"

"Damn right I was there. Me and my men held the bridge at Nijmegen!"

"Is that where you were wounded?" I wanted to zero in on the battle.

"Yes, it was before the crossing of the canal and the fight into Beek and Devil's Hill."

"Devil's Hill?"

"Duivelsberg. A bloody city battle I heard about while I was waiting to get here. The Krauts countered and fought in the streets for more than a day. My men were valiant. New men, just trained."

"Are they still alive?"

"When I left I heard most of them were. They saved my life. Johnn—did—I mean...?"

"Who?" I didn't catch the name.

"A good friend of mine. He took out three Germans pinning me down with a MG 34 that sliced this gam apart."

"What was his name?"

"I can't tell you."

"Because you don't know, or can't say?"

He turned his head away and something clicked in me. Why wouldn't he be able to say the name unless he was under orders? The operation had been over for weeks, so adhering to the communications blackout was pointless. "Was it some kind of secret mission?"

Sergeant Leo turned back to me and said, "No. It was Operation Market Garden. No secret, just damn courageous fighting."

I had stung a nerve, but I decided to back off, filing this piece of information away. "And your men got you out of there?"

"When the war is over their medals will prove it."

"Where are they now?"

"Holding the area. Hitler has to make a move."

"Yes. Would you like to add anything else, Sarge?"

"Just tell them my men in the 82$^{nd}$ are real warriors."

"I will." I pointed to the wound. "How's the leg?"

"I'll get by. In a few weeks, I'll be back with my men."

I decided that I liked him and his gruff manner.

"You're pretty," he said.

"And you're handsome." It made him smile before he wheeled away.

It was the only battle story that ate at me, though at the time I didn't know why. Mainly I filed stories about the people of London, and the nightmares of the rockets destroying the city. The bombs came fast and everyone was beginning to believe Hitler's promise to level the city.

Most of the people killed were women, the wounded soldiers, and the elderly. I wrote a number of stories about the war effort headed up by the women in factories. Everyone worked hard during the day, driven by a sense of responsibility.

One night the sirens sounded just as I began typing tomorrow's story. I jumped up and saw the beams from the floodlights crisscrossing across the sky. It scared me, but not enough to run to a shelter. I watched and listened as I thought of Johnny—what he might be doing, where he might be—and wished he were with me. The thoughts were heartfelt, but the sirens and tomorrow's story, I must admit, made them evaporate. Had I known then that Johnny was fighting for his life just across the channel, my work would have meant nothing.

## JOHNNY

When we reached the docks, we reveled in the feeling of walking on solid ground. Everything I looked at seemed to roll up and down like it had at sea.

Crowley herded us into a truck that had United States Army painted in white block letters on each door and smelled damp. We had no idea where we were going, and the road was too rough to consider sleeping, so we bounced through the hours and wondered about our destination. Except for me; I wondered about Maggie. Where was she?

We stopped several hours later, and Crowley's face appeared in the rear of the truck. "Okay gentlemen, we're home. Let's get moving."

I immediately jumped off my bench and onto the pavement. Thomas came out of the truck next, followed by Bobby and Stanley. We sided together while the rest of the soldiers jumped to the road.

"Attention!" Crowley's order made us take notice, and we tried to stand at attention. Crowley shook his head. "Gentlemen, welcome to Farcham Hunts, the training grounds for the toughest guys in the war." He stopped to see if these words impressed us. I knew they didn't impress me, and I don't think they impressed my buddies. "We will be housed and fed in Cams Hall, just past that rise behind you. I want you to understand that we are guests of these fine Englishmen, and I want you to show each and every one of them the utmost respect. Understand?"

We all nodded, except Stanley who gave a feeble, "Yessir."

Crowley's face turned a deep red and his eyes bore into me. "Understand?" His voice echoed through the compound, and the soldiers who had been led off by another lieutenant all turned in unison when they heard him bellow.

"Yessir," we chimed together, and I guess it was loud and clear enough for his liking because he responded in a softer tone.

83

"Good. Now double time it to the Hall, and by double time I mean run."

I knew then my life was about to be drastically altered by the military.

Our dormitory didn't offer much in the way of comfort. Low beds with thin mattresses were covered by single sheets, and the showers and toilet were outdated.

Crowley slept near the entranceway, and he was always the first to rise and the last to bed. He reminded me of the guys I use to see on the short takes before the main movie, the G.I.s that were saving America from the Japs and the Nazis. He remained distant, demanding respect.

After a few training sessions, he certainly gained mine. He had leather balls and was hard as a rock. He did every conditioning and training exercise we did, including jumping from fifteen foot platforms conditioning our legs for parachute jumps. The guy was amazing. Everything we did, he did twice. Even eating. The food was horrible, but he ate twice. The mashed potatoes were the only resemblance of real food, and I hated them. When I asked for macaroni, everyone sang "Yankee Doodle Dandy" and made me feel out of place. I learned to live without it.

After a week of conditioning, we found ourselves in a slaughterhouse, with real knives being pressed into our hands by Crowley. Six-inch blades, sheathed in leather that attached to a waist or calf belt, which I strapped on near the small of my back. This was the way I wore it back in the neighborhood, concealed but ready for quick retrieval. Once armed, Crowley took us to the side of one of the barns where bulging canvas sacks hung from a thick beam. Crowley placed each of us in front of a sack, and he stood facing us, legs spread and hands clasped behind his back.

"Gentlemen, war is blood and guts—a lot of it. You have to get used to it." He began to pace among the bags. "I want each of you to draw your knives and kill the bag in front of you. I want them dead, killed with as many thrusts of your knife as necessary. You will do this on my order."

Crowley passed through our ranks and turned, now facing our backs. He remained silent for a few minutes, making us edgy. Then he said in an even tone, "Men, draw your knives." We unsheathed our blades, gripping them tightly, watching the bag in front of us. "Kill."

My knife sliced through the bag, puncturing a hole that spewed a stream of blood into my face. I stabbed again, this time making a larger hole that gushed the liquid over my hands and arms and onto my chest. Like the others, I slashed and cut until the contents of the bag emptied on my face and the ground. We looked at each other and smiled at our blood-stained faces.

"Gentlemen, within a few weeks, the blood you spill will be human instead of pig. It feels the same, smells the same and believe me, lads, it tastes the same. We are nearing battle, gentlemen, and I know you will be ready for it." Crowley's tone was even.

The sticky blood wasn't a new feeling to me, but I didn't let on. Judging by the other guys' reactions, it was their first time with this much blood.

We held our briefings in a small room of the main house, covered with maps of Belgium and Holland. This morning's briefing was unusually early and, when we arrived, Crowley was standing behind a mahogany table covered with papers.

Within minutes, Stanley, Thomas, Bobby, and I understood that this wasn't an ordinary meeting. We were going on a training mission to take practice jumps out of a mock airplane. Glancing around, Stanley's eyes showed his pure fear—he didn't like heights, and his legs would get so grasshoppery on the short platform that he was unpredictable at best.

We didn't have a choice. After the briefing, we hiked to a remote area near the compound where a large mock up tower resembling a C-47 transport stood two hundred fifty feet from the ground. I thought for sure Stanley would wet himself, but to my surprise he sucked it up. It took him the longest to get to the top, but he made the jump, his chute opened, and he drifted nicely to the ground without much trouble. He puked when he landed and began hyperventilating, but the lieutenant calmed him down, told him he did a good job, and sent him back up the tower.

We had to make five jumps apiece, which we did in fine form, each job raising our confidence. By the end of the day we felt mean and ready for any Kraut or Hun that came our way. The only question we had was, where the hell we were going to go? We heard the Allies were pushing well into France and up the peninsula of Italy, so it seemed to us that Holland must be the drop spot.

We were still picking stringy, dry meat out of our teeth when the four of us sat down for a game of pinochle. After two games, Bobby and Stanley quit because they couldn't keep up with Thomas and me. Then, before anyone could argue about the game, Thomas brought out a bottle of cognac that he had conned from one of the English.

Thomas was an operator. He had a stash of cigarettes, booze, stockings and chocolates in his footlocker, and every day he would come back with something new. He'd have that schoolboy smile on his face whenever he returned from one of his hunts and spread his loot out on his bunk.

"This is one of France's finest." Thomas poured us each a measure in our mess cups.

We smelled and sipped it, the oak and sting of the liquor clearing our noses, and the warm burn comforting our insides.

"It is good," I said.

"Tastes like earth or something," Bobby added.

Stanley took a deep breath and said nothing.

"They're going to drop us into Holland," Thomas said, sipping his drink.

We stopped and looked at him.

"I overheard it near the mess earlier."

"Overheard or eavesdropped?" I asked.

"What's it matter? It's us they were talking about."

"No matter," Bobby said.

"Are you guys scared?" Stanley's ran his hand through his hair several times.

I shrugged.

"Naw." Bobby raised his chin.

"I am, in a way," said Thomas. "But a little fear is good. Keeps my nerves steady."

"Fear pumps my blood," I added.

"Fear makes me sick sometimes," Stanley said, wiping his palms on his thighs.

"You'll do fine," I said.

"I'm not afraid of that, I'm afraid of dying."

"We're all scared of that." Thomas looked back at him.

"Why Holland?" I wanted to get off the fear and dying subject.

"I heard one of the Limeys say the Germans got these big rockets, V-2's I think he said, and they're lobbing them into London and places."

"That true?" Stanley asked still wiping his hands directing the question at me.

"The way I figure it, if we attack Holland and continue into Germany, my bet is that's where we'll find the rockets," Thomas strategized.

He made sense. I took down the rest of my cognac and held my cup out for more. Thomas poured a round for everyone.

"I hear there is a Panzer Division there, you know, tanks," Thomas added after pouring.

"What are they going to have us do?" Bobby asked.

"Hold bridges," I replied.

"Or blow them to stop a retreat."

I looked at Thomas and realized that was just as feasible.

"Tulips, right?" Everyone looked at me quizzically. "Tulips. Holland is known for their tulips."

"Maybe that is what they'll call the operation." Thomas sipped his cognac.

They named the operation Market Garden, and we were part of the fertilizer. We briefed early the next morning, with nine members of the 82$^{nd}$ Airborne Division. They were seasoned soldiers that had seen action during the invasion, and although they looked our age, they seemed older. It was in their eyes, a mingling of sadness, despair, and loneliness that must come with the horror of battle. I was looking forward to action, but after seeing these guys, I began to understand the ugliness that went with the thrill.

We gathered around a map of Holland with three large, red arrows swooping across it, indicating Arnham, Eindhoven, and Nijemgen. Crowley was in front of the map with a second officer beside him. They meant business and we knew by their looks that things were going to get very serious. I was nervous. Suddenly, I knew I was going to war very soon. It felt like getting the order to make a hit, only this time there was an army of marks.

"Men," Crowley started with a loud, even tone, "let me introduce Lieutenant Colonel Ricky of the 82$^{nd}$ Airborne and his men. Names will be given later and, like you, the names will not be their own."

Crowley paused. I had no idea that I would leave my identity behind when I went to war, and my street instincts told me that whatever came next would be clandestine. What have I signed up for?

"You fine men, and many others from the 82$^{nd}$ commanded by Brigadier General James Gavin, are going to show your loyalty to your country in an operation named Market Garden." Crowley breathed heavily, but his face conveyed no weakness. "You will be part of the largest airdrop in the history of war. You men in particular will be part of glider squadron flown into and near the city Nijmegen." Crowley turned to the map and pointed to the city on the map. "You will be the first drop. Shortly thereafter, one thousand one hundred planes, seven hundred more gliders, and ten thousands more men will also be deployed." As he moved back to the table, he continued, "Your main objective is to secure these three bridges." There was some shuffling and, as if on cue, Crowley stepped back and Ricky came forward.

The square-jawed Ricky looked over the men with cold, dark eyes. His voice was deep and round with a faint southern accent. "What you must do first is set up a position for communication and recon. If at any time during the operation the bridges look like they will fall back into enemy hands, you are to blow the bridges." Ricky looked around the room to see if everyone understood. "If the operation is compromised, the bridges must be destroyed or the 2nd Panzer Division is going to waltz right back into Belgium. Securing these bridges gives us a direct line to Berlin." He rocked back on his heels and looked around. "Questions?"

I had plenty, but was afraid to ask. Thomas wasn't.

"Why are we using different names?"

Ricky smirked. "Show business." No one seemed to get the joke so Crowley bailed out Ricky.

"There are a few men in your group that have other orders and these orders are highly confidential, as are your real names. Repeat: no one is to know anyone by name, nor call them by their real name. You will be behind enemy lines. If captured, you will be designated spies and most likely shot. Your real names will only be disclosed after the battle, in which case you will have died bravely with your real name."

It didn't make sense to me. If I was going to die, then what difference did a name make? I'd want my mom to know it was me dead on the field, not some Jack Smith or something.

There were several other questions, especially about the gliders and the times, which the officers answered, and then we were dismissed. Well, they dismissed everyone but me. After the room cleared, both officers came to me and told me what I had to do. I was one of the guys with the confidential orders, and I really didn't like them.

We didn't get much sleep the night before the invasion. We were on some airstrip northeast of our training camp in the beginning hours of September 17, and the whole scene was impressive. The roar of the planes' engines drowned the sound of human voices, so most commands came by hand signals and yelling into the ears of the next in command. Beams of light from the gas lamps crisscrossed the sky, lighting different parts of the runways for each plane before take-off.

Before we knew it, we stood on the runway about three hundred feet from a large C-47 transport with a nylon towrope attached by a D-ring to the ugliest aircraft I had ever seen. Sergeant Leo, the guy who was with Crowley when they came to my house, and six other soldiers from the 82nd soon joined us. I hadn't seen Leo since he was in my apartment, and now here he was again, standing next to the glider that was going to drop us behind German lines.

We traded operation names—mine was Marble—and I noticed that none of us had patches identifying our outfit. We shook hands and climbed aboard the Waco CG-4A glider. I was glad to see Bobby in the cockpit—it was strangely comforting to know the pilot taking me to war.

I sat with my guys in the narrow tubular steel fuselage, staring at the new guys in silence. We belted ourselves in and felt a slight jar that jerked us against the thin sheet metal of the plane. The tow was beginning. We lurched into a gentle roll down the runway, picking up speed until we felt a lift and the air currents bouncing underneath the carriage of the plane replaced the bumps of the runway. We were in the air and it was my first time in flight. I liked the loftiness that seemed to pump from my groin to my armpits.

The roar from the airfield diminished until the only sound was the drone of our tow plane's engines.

Everything seemed to happen so fast in the military. It was like dropping into a strange place, uncertain of where you'd landed or how you'd get back. I wanted to talk, to replace this unfamiliar and mysterious feeling with my voice and hear the voices of others. I knew we had strict orders not to ask names or tell where we were from, so I tried a different approach.

"This glider seems pretty solid." No one answered.

"Anyone fly with the pilot before?" It was a joke but nobody got it.

"You know what the life expectancy of a glider pilot is?" the anonymous soldier across from me asked.

"Not really."

"Seventeen seconds." It was a sobering answer.

"That so?"

He just nodded.

"What kind of odds does that give us?" I said it jokingly, but the more I thought of it, the more nervous I got.

No one answered.

"Any of you guys thinking about dying?"

"I thought about it," Thomas said, "but I'm not thinking about it now, and I don't want to talk about it, either."

"Let's just concentrate on the mission," Crowley, sitting next to the cockpit, spoke for the first time. His face was set, but he seemed relaxed.

Thomas was right: thinking about getting killed wasn't healthy, so I figured I'd clam up and think about my assignment—the post office at Nijmegen.

After two hours of flying in silence, the gray of the first dawn's light filtered through the cockpit window. As we banked north toward our landing field, Bobby tried communicating with the tow plane pilot, but the communicators didn't work. The drop would be Bobby's call.

He turned back to us, the sun poking above the horizon in a sliver of bright orange, then burying itself into a dark purple bank of clouds. "Get ready for release!"

He turned back and pulled the lever, releasing the D ring and sending the glider sailing upward. My stomach rose to my throat, and I thought of the time my dad took me on the roller coaster on Coney Island when I was five.

The glider leveled, and the silence was complete. It felt nice, gliding in the air in a graceful swoop to the green below, but just when I got comfortable, a series of explosions knocked the plane to the left. The men clutched their helmets and dropped their heads between their shoulders.

I closed my eyes and, when I reopened them, I noticed the soldier across from me had slumped forward. When the plane evened out, bouncing its way through the flak, the soldier straightened, exposing a red stain spreading across his chest. He looked down at it and then directly at me, his eyes wide with fear and surprise. He tried to speak, but the glider shuddered and his face froze. I knew he was dead. He fell forward again and I saw three tears in the glider's fuselage where the steel had blasted into the soldier's body. It could have been me, I thought. Then I prayed real quick and waited for the plane to hit the ground.

It wasn't a nice landing, but Bobby got us down in one piece. We filed out of the glider and I raised my Thompson submachine gun. Crowley motioned for us to get into the pine stand. The lieutenant and Sergeant Leo covered our rear and after a few seconds, satisfied there was no enemy present, followed us into the trees.

Leo pulled his map from his jacket and coordinated it with his compass and the surroundings. "We're not far from the bridge. That means there are plenty of Germans around, so stay alert."

He motioned for us to follow him through the trees to a clearing that opened on another stand of pines. He gestured to spread out and form a line across the field. I didn't like walking into that field, but I had no choice. Midway through, I felt certain the gunfire would start dropping us in our tracks but I was wrong. We made it back into the trees without incident.

We picked our way from tree to tree to the top of a small rise. From this vantage, we could see a road winding into a town, which the lieutenant acknowledged with a nod of his head.

It looked harmless, sitting there in the lowlands, bisected by a canal. Crossing the canal was the bridge we were there to defend—from our hiding place, we could see the girders of the bridge's arc. We stared at it for a few seconds, swimming in our own thoughts. I couldn't believe how quiet and green it was—the opposite of what I envisioned when I thought of a war zone. I could imagine lying down on the grass, but a staccato of gunfire brought me back to reality.

We stayed low to the ground, fanning out and inching our way forward. Rapid gunfire continued to the north, but early morning in the little town was utterly ordinary, and my orders started to nag me. They didn't seem to fit until a loud crack came from the center of town, knocking the soldier next to me off his feet.

We dove to the ground as the gun fired again, kicking up a plume of dirt to the left of my shoulder. I rolled to my right and hit the fallen soldier. I felt for a pulse, knowing there wouldn't be any. I saw the other guys making it to the fringe of town, so I sucked in my gut, jumped up, and ran to the side of a building.

Most of us made it. The sniper took out two guys from the 82nd and now we had only ten left to carry out our missions. Thomas appeared from nowhere and tapped me on the shoulder, motioning me toward an alleyway. When we secured the alley, Thomas stopped me.

"I got the post office," he said.

"Me too." I was surprised we had the same building assignment.

"It's not far from here. Just to the south." He pointed toward the bridge, which was closer than I thought. "Near the bridge. Come on."

We made it down the alley and stopped at the street. The bridge was in clear view and, according to our briefing, the post office was just across the street. There were a lot of German soldiers running around, and gunfire began erupting. We needed to make a move, so we waited for an opening and jumped out onto the street, running into another alley and following it behind the buildings.

Thomas stopped me halfway down the block and pointed to the next door. "That's it."

I recognized it from the photographs they had shown me. I realized they must have shown Thomas the pictures too, but couldn't figure out why they spoke to us separately. Thomas took out his revolver, bringing me back to the objective at hand. "Ready?" he asked. I nodded.

He went through the door first, and I followed right behind. The only people in the small post office were an older gentleman behind an iron cage and a younger blond man that looked like a kid. They both jumped back, frightened by our intrusion, and raised their arms in unison. "Don't move. Don't move." Thomas pointed his gun at one and then the other. They both froze.

I remembered my orders to neutralize anyone in the office. The word neutralize ricocheted through my mind. Why couldn't they say, "Kill everyone?" Why did they make it sound so clinical? I couldn't neutralize an old man and a kid. I started to tell Thomas that something wasn't right when I saw the old man move quickly. Just as quickly, Thomas opened up on him, bullets flashing sparks when they hit the cage. Two hit their mark and exploded the old man's head in a spray of white and red. In my peripheral vision, I saw the kid move, so I squeezed the trigger on the Thompson, knocking him into the far wall. He was dead when he hit the floor.

Thomas scanned the room with his gun, then went behind the cage. There was nothing there. I went to where the kid lay, blood spreading from underneath and staining envelopes scattered on the floor, his eyes staring at the ceiling. Close to his hand, I saw what we were looking for: the igniter. I motioned for Thomas who came over and immediately deactivated it. I looked at the kid again. That kid was my first kill of the war, not a soldier. I didn't like it but I didn't hate it.

Thomas looked out the window to the bridge. Sporadic gunfire sounded above the Germans running up and down the streets and across the bridge. A siren went off and I looked at my watch—it was the hour for the next drop. Thomas barricaded the front door with a desk and sat at the corner of the window. His orders were the same as mine. We'd neutralized, now we had to hold the place while our guys attacked.

Soon shells from our tanks were whizzing into the town, blowing apart German strongholds. The fighting intensified every second, and the air filled with uninterrupted gunfire. Germans in armored cars poured over the bridge, but we stayed put. Shots drew nearer and several rounds shattered the winter. I noticed two Germans signaling toward us from the bridge and figured it was the sign for us to blow it. Thomas decided to take them out, and he fired his machine gun into them killing them fast and clean. It drew the attention of several others, who began firing into the building.

"Why the hell did you do that, Thomas?"

"Boredom. My name is Sticks, remember?" He returned fire through the broken window.

I took aim through the window beside him, feeling like an idiot for forgetting to use our operation names. A deep rumble caused the Germans to shift their focus and start across the bridge. One dropped to his knee, pulling out a stick grenade, but I cut him down before he had a chance to pull the pin. Then I saw one of our tanks pull up to the bridge and fire a round from its canon to the other side of the canal. The blast vibrated back to Thomas and me as more Allied troops filtered into Nijmegen. Fifteen minutes later, the town and its bridge were ours.

Thomas and I leaned against the post office, sharing a bar of chocolate as the battle wound down. "It was the kid." I didn't know why I said it.

"Yeah." Thomas showed no emotion.

"I thought for sure it was the old guy."

"Didn't matter, they both had to go."

"It doesn't seem right."

"It's right. Look," Thomas nodded in the direction of the bridge, "the Germans will counterattack and our guys are going to get killed. A lot of their guys are going to get killed, too. It's war. Everyone is expendable."

"You, too?" It was a mean question.

He didn't hesitate. "Me, too. You, too."

"That's kind of ...I don't know. It makes me feel unimportant."

"You got it. We aren't. War is in control."

Gunfire picked up from the other side of the river just after he spoke. I saw some of our men duck behind buildings, and then a loud swoosh whizzed overhead and an explosion rocked us backwards. Sergeant Leo waved to us to get down, so I grabbed Thomas's arm and dragged him to the ground just in time. I looked for Leo and saw him trapped by a sniper in a tower close to our hiding place. I pointed to the tower.

"Sarge's pinned. I can get to it. Cover me."

Thomas nodded and fired his Thompson at the tower. The machine gun stopped a second, giving me just enough time to cross the street. The sniper opened on Thomas but couldn't hit him, so he swung back to Leo. I saw the sergeant go down, but I kept curling along the building until I got to the tower. The machine gun continued to fire, so that meant Leo was still alive.

The door to the tower swung open easy enough so I was cautious, moving slowly until my whole body was in the room. The stairs were just across from me and I moved to them cautiously. The shots from Thomas's Thompson continued as I started up the stairs. Then I heard someone coming down fast. I waited and the

German ran into my fire, which blasted him over the railing. The fire from above paused, then began again. I continued upstairs, my mouth becoming drier and my stomach beginning to quiver.

The wooden stairway opened on a small landing where I could see two Germans through a small trap door. I had a pretty clear shot, so I pointed my gun and fired. The bullets sparked against hinges of the trap door and found their way to both the Germans. One was killed instantly, the other came forward with a Walther like they showed us in training. But my firepower tore through his chest, knocking him backward through the trap door to the steps just below. There came a calming silence in which I licked my lips, swallowed, and noticed the feeling in my gut was gone.

Remembering Leo below, I rushed down to see if he needed help. Thomas was struggling to hold him still as blood rushed from the wound in his leg. The pain was making him pretty wild, but Thomas and I restrained him until a medic came forward and shot him up with some morphine. He relaxed a bit, then grabbed my arm.

"You saved my life, Marble." He was the first to call me by my operation name. I was surprised he knew it.

"Nah."

"Yeah, don't tell me. They had me. I owe you big time."

"No, you rest. Just make sure my mom gets her money, huh?"

His smile looked like a grimace. "I will. Damn it, I'll make sure she gets every cent."

He passed out. Lieutenant Crowley showed up, demanding that the medic take good care of Leo. Then he turned to us. "The Germans are starting a counter attack. We have to get across the river and secure the other side of the bridge."

"We swimming, Lieutenant?" Thomas asked.

"Boats. We're going to take boats."

I didn't like the sound of it. The Germans were on the other side, and if we went across in boats, we would be the proverbial sitting ducks. "We'll all be killed."

The lieutenant looked at me and nodded his head. "That's right, Marble, welcome to war." He turned back toward the bridge.

The boats had no motors, so we rowed through the artificial smoke created to cover our advance. Just about midway across, a wind began blowing away the smoke screen and the Germans opened up on us with MG 34s.

Two guys in the front of my boat took hits immediately, blasting them into the river, then one of the rowers caught one in the head. Thomas fired, then looked back and forth between me and the water. We went over the side at the same time a 50mm cut our boat in half.

I reached the other side and lay against the embankment, trying to regain my breath, when Thomas surfaced just to my left. We had lost our guns, so I pulled my knife out quickly, a nice issue that cut on both sides like those used at the slaughterhouse. My knife from home was sheathed on my leg to give me additional support.

Our men had taken it bad. I think maybe four of the twenty boats made it, and the river filled with floating corpses. They looked almost comfortable bobbing in the water, and I remember thinking that their worries were finished and ours were just beginning.

Soaked and chilled, I moved mechanically, slithering towards the Germans. Thomas was just behind me when one of our planes passed a few feet from the bridge and riddled the area with gunfire. It was enough to make the Krauts turn the 50mm skyward.

Seeing my opportunity, I jumped up, ran the short distance to them, and embedded my knife into the back of the triggerman. The other German pounced on me, pulling his knife, and jabbing at me. Suddenly he coughed, blood filling his mouth, and fell to my side. Behind him stood Thomas, expressionlessly wiping his knife on his pant leg. I nodded to him and he nodded back.

The fighting continued until nightfall, when we finally rested while holding our position on the east side of the bridge. Bobby and Stanley showed up around midnight, spared from the massacre in the boats.

The next morning, Crowley passed out the patches that identified us as the 82$^{nd}$ Airborne. Then we moved out, heading east towards Ooijolder to meet up with the British at Arnhem.

The fighting became bloodier. We moved into the town of Bleek and took it, but we fought in the streets for two days at Devil's Hill. I saw a lot of guys killed on both sides. Why I made it through, I'll never know. I figured I had a good, strong guardian angel and I thanked him each day.

We didn't have much time to rest, pushing southeast to France and then east to the Ardennes. Word had it that Hitler was going to mount a huge offensive in the area to try and push us back to the sea. I had seen enough for the time being. The guys and I were tired, both physically and mentally, and the pervasive odor of death, its sweet, gaseous pungency was unforgettable.

Then the cold set in. We welcomed it at first, because it dampened the smell like a blanket smothering a fire. But the cold kept coming and coming, seeping into the skin and digging into the bones. It hurt. Stanley, Thomas, Bobby, and I were bivouacked with some of the 82nd guys and our small campfire barely warmed us. We didn't have times for tents or shelter instead we laid and sat in the German trenches just in case some mortar shell whizzed down. We built our fire just at the lip where the mud froze in furrows and clumps. It was at this camp when I received my first letter.

It was from Mom. Using both English and Italian, she wrote that she had received the first annuity and that made me happy, knowing she had money. She didn't say anything about cashing it, but at least I knew it was there if she needed it. The rest of the letter was about praying for my safety and quick return. I kept the letter in my helmet.

"How is she?" Stanley asked.

"It's from my mother."

"Oh, I thought—" "

"Maggie? No. She's not the writing kind."

Bobby, sunk down deep in the trench, perked up and poked his head out from the wool blanket covering him. "I thought she was a reporter. Don't reporters write?"

"Yeah, for newspapers. I think someone like her is too busy." It sounded like I was defending her. I put my hands towards the fire to get the cold sting from them.

"Did you write her?" Thomas asked as he chewed a bar of chocolate leaning against the other side of the trench wall. He always had chocolate. It was a good question. My silence answered.

"Maybe you're each waiting for the other," he said, still chewing. The fire cracked and sent embers into the air along with the smell of pine from the limbs sap.

"No, we talked about it. Everything is okay. Let's drop it." I realized just then how much I missed her and how much I wanted her with me.

"Your mom's okay?"

"Yes Bobby, thanks." The question diverted my thoughts of Maggie.

"My mom's dead," Thomas said unemotionally, pushing away from the dirt with his back and getting near me and the fire.

"I'm sorry."

"Died of a broken heart after my father left with another woman."

"That's lousy," I said.

"Yeah, he was no good."

"You have a girlfriend, Thomas?" I asked.

"Kinda, a couple actually. I'm not the one girl type. Like my father, I guess." He finished his chocolate and warmed his hands near what flame was left. "It's getting cold."

"I'd like to have just one," Stanley's voice sounded dreamy, which was funny coming from such a large guy.

"After the war, you'll be a hero and get lots of gals," Bobby tried to cheer up the big guy.

"I hope."

Crowley shuffled near the fire and we all looked up at him. He looked tired, too. "Leo's okay. I just received word from England. Johnny and Thomas, decorations are in store for you both. I put in for silver stars."

I was surprised, yet I didn't know the prestige of the medal. "Thanks." Thomas remained silent.

"The other good news is we're getting out of here. Orders to spare us from Hitler. Seems they need us in Italy."

"Italy?" Bobby jumped out of the trench.

"We're lucky. The Panzers are moving. This is going to be a brute."

"Then why aren't we staying here?" Stanley asked, pointing at the safety of the trench.

"Orders." It was all he was going to say. "We move out in the morning for Paris. You guys can get some rest. They'll be coming around with more rations." He kicked at the embers. Get that fire going again. Stay warm."

"Paris," was all Thomas said, but I noticed a grin spread across his face.

Nothing like a few hours and a hundred miles to remake a man. From frozen bodies, stench, and hunger to Paris. Oh, it was a mess and the people were hungry and weary of war, but at least it wasn't the battleground. I could actually sleep again.

They put us up in a small hotel in the Latin Quarter, converted to house Allied troops back from the front. It was a quiet place where I sat and had coffee outside, even though it was still cold. I was used to the cold now, so I enjoyed sitting in the open air, looking for Maggie's articles in the newspapers.

101

I was surprised to see her mention some of the Market Garden action. Reading between the lines, I knew she was thirsting to get to the front, and I really hoped it would happen for her. It was partly selfish—the closer she was to the front, the closer she'd be to me—but I scribbled a note to the address in the paper. I never received a response, then for a while her by-lines stopped and I felt like I lost her.

I got lonely fast and started drinking with the guys through the night. Paris was wild, but after a few days of drinking, our raid and what I did came back to me. I felt like I had put the thoughts on a shelf somewhere, forgot about them, then passed by the shelf and pulled them off again. Battle was horrible, but I remember feeling more alive than ever, and I knew it was because I had been near death. I think everyone felt it and it lodged within the soul. Now we let irresponsibility rule the day.

I liked sitting out, watching the French women during the day. One morning, after a particularly long night, I saw one pretty lady turn her head and smile at me as she walked by. The next day I made sure I was at the café at the same time, and the lady didn't disappoint.

I stopped her and found she spoke some English. We sparked right off, making each other laugh and feel comfortable. Her name was Renée, and she had lost her husband in a battle on the African desert. She invited me to her house after our second date and, wanting and needing companionship, I put my thoughts of Maggie elsewhere. It worked for both of us, so I spent a lot of time with her while waiting for orders.

Renée brought in the papers one morning and I began reading about the Battle of the Bulge. We were lucky: we got out of there just days before the bloody fight. I couldn't help but question fate's role in the war—why were we spared the horror, while others were doomed to kill or be killed? I wondered about this while watching Renée dress. There was a heaviness in her movements which betrayed her sadness, but even this couldn't detract from her physical beauty.

Paging through the paper as I waited for Renée to finish getting ready, my eye hooked on a familiar name. I smiled to myself, realizing that Maggie was in Paris, but I slipped into guilt. Replaying her parting words to me—do whatever to survive—I couldn't decide whether or not I was cheating.

Before reading Maggie's column, I looked up at Renée. I liked her, a lot, and I didn't know if seeking out Maggie would be the right thing to do. I could wind up hurting two women I truly cared for. This was a new situation for me.

"You look puzzled, my dear." Renée was half-naked, standing in front of a full length mirror and watching me in the reflection.

"I am."

"*Pourquois?*

"I don't know. Because women are puzzling, I guess." I winked at her reflection in the full length mirror.

"Ahh. Another woman?" She ran her fingers through her bed-tangled hair.

"She's not my type."

"But she must or you would not be troubled."

"I'm not troubled."

"You would not look so if you were not. Is she here, in Paris?" She fastened her bra and turned to me.

"Yes, I think so."

"You love her?"

I shrugged. The only thing that might hurt Renée more than a lie was the truth.

"You made love to her?"

My instincts told me not to answer the question, so I let my silence answer for me.

Disappointment pursed her lips. "Will you try to find her?"

"I think I have to."

Stepping into her dress, she nodded and turned so that I could zip her up. With my face nestled into her brown hair, I could smell the lavender soap I had brought her.

"You must not tell me when you do." She leaned against my hands.

"I won't." I ran my hands over her hips.

"I am going to see my parents on the other side of the city. I will return in a few days." She stepped away from me.

I didn't want her to leave me, but the urge to find Maggie was growing. I was beginning to think I didn't know what I wanted. "I've only got another week."

She kissed my cheek. "I will return to you, Johnny."

"I want that."


## MAGGIE

A rocket blasting a nearby building knocked me from my bed. I scrambled to find the bedside lamp, but remembered we were still in blackout mode, so I drew near the window, gazing out at the orange glow lighting the block. I expected to feel panic or anger, but I was filled with an unusual clarity. The need to experience the war firsthand, to find and write the stories of battle, was growing within me.

I returned to bed but couldn't sleep. Maybe it was my father's blood—his passion for adventure, the contagious excitement in his voice when he told me about the daring missions he'd carried out in his bi-plane—that made me so restless.

When the gray dawn filled my simple hotel room, I began dressing. Thoughts of Johnny, my mental sanctuary, haunted me as I applied my makeup and set my hair. Staring into my reflection, I said "I have to get to the front." The woman staring back at me nodded with determination.

My well-reasoned pleas to get closer to the action were all but ignored by my bureau chief, so I continued to cover the civilian war efforts. But when Parliament denounced a bill from the Auxiliary Territorial Service that would allow women on the front, I really got going.

I was irate when I heard that the men of Parliament had indicated that a woman's place was with her children, and wrote my story with as much anger I could put into words. But when I read what had been printed, my fire had been taken out. It ran with just the facts, and when no one would listen to my ire, I was sickened. Then I was hospitalized with a jaundice that hobbled me into a hospital bed.

My month in the hospital left me frustrated. My room was constantly covered in newspapers, which I inhaled with a new appetite. Reading that the Allies had beaten back the German counteroffensive at the Bulge, I knew the end of the war was near, and I grew increasingly anxious to get back in action. Lying awake just after reading the news of the battle in the Ardennes, I looked up at the gray ceiling and told myself to get the hell out of the hospital, and I did.

I wrote a few more stories the next week and was quickly losing interest in everything. I thought of Johnny occasionally, wondering where he was and what he was doing. One afternoon, I was deep in these thoughts when I returned to the bureau.

The chief greeted me with a surprising, "Pack your bags Maggie, you're going to Paris."

For once, I was speechless. I could only gape while the chief explained that two of the correspondents had been wounded at the front, leaving vacancies in the Paris office. I was a last resort, but I didn't care.

My goodbyes were brief—everyone, including Janet, was already on the mainland—and in a matter of hours I was on my way to the city of lights. It was finally my turn.

# PART III
# PARIS, THE FRONT AND BEYOND

## MAGGIE

My air of sophistication was lost in the commotion in the lobby of the Hotel Scribe. Correspondents from the front were jockeying for cots lining the walls, looking for their mud-caked typewriters, and conning as much vin rose as possible from the bartender.

I was in awe. Most of the guys wore patches on their sleeves indicating where they'd been on assignment: Normandy, Holland, the Ardennes, and Algiers. Not me, I had only my bright yellow patch designating America and London. It was embarrassing, the patch and my neat, clean olive uniform. I tucked my red mittens into my purse to hide my novice dress and tried to conceal my wonder.

Fortunately, Russell Hall from the Trib came to my rescue. Russell had escaped from behind the lines in Yugoslavia and fought his way back to Paris via Greece and North Africa. His stories were legendary, but I was most surprised by his looks. The tall, lanky body, fair skin and hair, and a daring grin made him look like he'd just left school. He was a welcome sight.

"I heard you were sick," he said.

"Yeah, I'm okay now, though."

"Good. Come on, I'll introduce you around." He touched my elbow and directed me to the bar where a loud group of guys talked.

I was surprised when, instead of taking me to them, he stopped me in front of a large gentleman with a full beard sitting with his back to the wall.

"Ernest, I'd like you to meet Maggie Hogan, one of ours from the Trib. Just in from London."

My mouth went dry as the name connected to the face. It seemed like someone else's hand was reaching to grasp Ernest Hemingway's .

"How's London doing?"

"Fine, good." My mouth was full of lumps. I was talking to one of my heroes, and I couldn't seem to say more than monosyllables. I was glad he spoke again.

"The war is winding down. I think most of us are, too."

"Yes." What the hell is wrong with you, my brain screamed.

"You have fun in London?" He was giving me a second chance.

"No. Got jaundice and couldn't drink." I sounded stupid, trying to impress the master.

He nodded. "Tough pill. No need to worry here, the only thing to drink is the water wine they've been pushing."

"Soon maybe, I'll get back into it."

"Good luck to you." He raised his glass to me.

"Thank you."

Russell introduced me to the boisterous guys, and their stories of the front were amazing, exciting and brutal. Once I swallowed my embarrassment over the Ernest Hemingway debacle, I had fun.

I hardly slept that night, gazing out below my window at the city, lit only by the moon. I was lucky to get a room, lucky to be here at all, but as the February cold seeped into my bones, I began to feel frightened and alone. Russell was headed to the front, and I was taking over his assignment covering international news. It was a breathtaking responsibility and I was nervous.

The wind moved the trees, rocking shadows against my window. I watched them, thinking of the many obstacles that lay ahead.

I was young and a woman, two disadvantages in this world which celebrated wisdom and manliness. I doubted whether I would be taken seriously, and I had no clue where to begin. I got into my wool pajamas and laid on the bed, wishing I had something to play my Schubert on, and listened to the wind grow stronger. I drifted to sleep finally and woke a few hours later just when the sun began poking through the window. My thinking continued while I cleaned up. Strategies of how to win favor and do my job filled my mind. They helped give me a line of vision.

When I woke I was determined, fueled by a need to fill my days and banish my loneliness. I was rude at times, and I was seductive. Both worked better than niceties or courteous femininity, approaches which left me running errands and warming desk chairs. The pervasive sexism was starting to make me angry.

I had just about reached my limit with the macho crap when one day, on my way back from the only black market in the city that still had eggs, I rounded a corner and bumped into a rushing soldier. He almost knocked me over, but grabbed me with a strong grip before I fell. Looking up, my mouth formed a disbelieving O. It was Johnny, his eyes filled with disbelief. We looked at each other, frozen in each other's eyes, until we both moved forward in a long embrace.

The kiss felt so good—warm and moist. It took me into his body and banished the cold. Gray winter was replaced with a Paris spring. I could even smell the flowers on his skin. Our lips parted and in his eyes, I saw a change.

"Johnny."

"I can't believe it's you. Somehow you're even more beautiful."

"Oh. No, I've been sick and busy. I'm just in from London for about a week."

"You look great."

"So do you." I meant it. He was a newspaper photograph of soldier, tall and proud in his overcoat, with his hat tilted perfectly to the side. "Where—"

He drew me to him again and kissed me. I didn't want this one to end; I wanted to take him back to my room and never let him leave. "Oh Johnny, I've missed you."

"I've thought a lot about you while—while doing things."

I saw his 82nd Airborne patch. "The airborne?" I never would have guessed.

"Well, we're in Paris. I have a few days, you have a few days. Why don't we have some fun?"

We made a plan to meet the next day, then we shared another lingering kiss. "Tomorrow," I said.

We decided to meet at my hotel, and then we parted slowly, each walking backward a few steps. I felt like a young girl with her first love once again. Johnny did that to me and I hoped I did that for him.

I didn't think the evening would ever come. I occupied myself reading through the releases, several magazines, and newspapers. Like the other correspondents in the lobby, I sipped thick, warm coffee brewed on small gas stoves, the flame quickly extinguished when done. It cooled quickly, so we drank it down and waited for our latest story: a briefing from Eisenhower.

The meeting came at ten o'clock in the Scribe's reception room, and it consumed the remaining morning. I marveled at his brilliance and detail. He gave us every bit of information allowed with a stateliness I had never experienced.

A brief meeting with two people from Mademoiselle magazine followed, and I learned they had chosen me to write feature articles for the periodical. My work was getting around, and people were interested in it back in the States. It made me feel good, like I was really competing with the male writers. The welcome assignment eased my anxiety about seeing the end of the war from the front lines, and I accepted readily.

Finally the electric lights came on, signaling the end of the day. Johnny was due in an hour, so I rushed to my room and quickly got into my bathrobe, grabbed a towel, and prayed no one was there before me. I was lucky, not only was the tub free, there was warm water. I bathed quickly, then dressed in a comfortable wool sweater and skirt with just a touch of makeup and sat on the bed to wait.

My stomach jumped when the rap on the door came. I couldn't believe I was nervous, but I was. I think I was actually shaking and I knew my palms were sweaty. I took a deep breath, straightened myself, then opened the door.

Johnny looked so handsome standing there in his uniform, a small smile that creating a dimple on his right cheek. He handed me a small box of chocolates and, placing the box on the table by the door, I pulled him into the room. I took his face in my hands and kissed him, losing myself in the embrace He pulled back first.

"That's the best welcome I've ever had."

"Let's sit before I get carried away."

The room was small, with a narrow bed in the corner and a wooden chair near the window. I sat on the bed and Johnny pulled the chair closer.

"You're lucky to have a room," he said.

"My paper has been kind to me." I reached out and touched his hand, convincing myself he was real. "What about your room?"

"Shared with one of my platoon guys."

"I can't believe you're here, I can't believe it."

"Geez Maggie, everything seems so strange anymore. I mean the way things happen."

"Tell me," I took his warm, calloused hand in mine. "Tell me where you've been." His eyes widened and I hastily added, "To a lover, not a reporter."

"Holland," he said. He was looking at me through lowered brows, a gaze that was tinged with distrust.

"Market Garden?" He was surprised I knew the name. "I met a sergeant who was at one of the bridges."

"Oh?"

"Leo was his name." He knew—I could see it on his face—but I didn't pursue it.

"There were a lot of guys there. It was my first battle, and it got pretty bad."

"Did you lose friends?"

"No," he said flatly.

"Were you in the Ardennes afterwards?"

"Yes, there too, but not for long."

"You were lucky to get out."

He nodded. "It was really cold—blood would freeze in the wounds. It actually saved lives." His words were measured, his voice softer. "Command pulled our platoon before the Panzers got too close. I heard most everyone that was left was killed."

"I'm glad you're here, Johnny."

"Me, too."

"Let's enjoy our time together."

His eyes were sad, but he smiled and kissed my hand, moving up my arm to my shoulder, neck, and mouth. We became lost in each other for several hours, his strength mingling with a new sensitivity that blanketed me in fearlessness.

Johnny smoked, taking long, deep drags, after we finished. He kept the smoke in his lungs for a few seconds before exhaling it into a steady stream that caught the moonlight filtering into the window.

I turned on my side and put my hand on his stomach, feeling its warmth. "Where are you off to next?"

"Italy. Next week."

"That soon?"

"Yeah, orders came yesterday."

"I want to get to the front, Johnny. I want to experience it for my work."

"It's not what you think. It's worse."

"I know. I'm ready for it."

"No one is ever ready, but I think you need to see horror to write it, if that's what you want."

Johnny, the first man who didn't laugh at my goals, was almost as unconventional as I was. "It's what I want. Everyone else thinks I should stay behind the lines and write the soft action."

He thought about this for a minute before replying. "Don't let people think for you. Most times they can't do a good job thinking for themselves."

His words made me smile, and I was reminded of why I loved him. He was my guy and I let him know it.

He was gone when I woke. I couldn't believe he'd slipped out in the night. When I went to the sink, I saw a small piece of paper propped against my box of chocolates on the little table. I kissed it, then gently unfolded it.

Maggie,

Thank you for the beautiful night. I will stop by in the next few days for a kiss goodbye. Meanwhile, I'll think of you every second I'm gone.

Love, Johnny

His letter was short and to the point, typical of my Johnny. In spite of our short time together, I already understood him better than any man I'd known. We were both very intense people and intensity, it seemed, made up for time spent.

Two days later, I received a message that he could meet again, during the day this time. Johnny took me to a small cafe open to a select crowd. They served cognac and food from the black market––the first real meat and real wine I'd had since arriving in Paris. Johnny knew the people and got us a nice table near a window, next to the small fireplace.

"How'd you know about this place?"

"My friend, Thomas. He's a real operator."

"Give him my thanks."

"I will."

"I'll miss you, Johnny."

"I'll miss you, too."

"What's to become of us?"

He took a sip of his cognac. "We go on our way and hope we meet again."

"But shouldn't we try to meet again?"

"I think if we tried, it would hurt more if we failed.

I hadn't thought of it like that, but he was right. Being separated would be hard enough without trying to guess where we would wind up in the coming weeks. Fate had found us twice, so maybe we were safest in her hands. "You'll be careful?"

He smiled, his dimple showed in the light of the fire. "As careful as I can."

"Do you know where you'll be in Italy?"

"North."

"That's a big area."

"After I'm done, I'll wire you and tell you exactly where and what happened."

I couldn't tell if he was joking, and I didn't want to fall into a trap. "I didn't ask for that reason. I asked because I think I love you."

"I think I love you back, but it's not the right time. Our futures are so undecided."

Again, he was right. His insight, combined with his history, was amazing. "What exactly do you do for Uncle Sam?"

"Is it the reporter asking, or the lover?"

"Both."

He took another sip from his cognac, and I took one from my wine. Our lunch arrived at the same time and I couldn't believe it——chicken breast with greens and potatoes.

"I fight, Maggie, like everyone else." He motioned to eat, closing the conversation.

When we parted, we kissed and embraced. He kissed my nose last, then touched my cheek. I saw his eyes recording everything for his memory, and I did the same. Then I watched as he turned and left, his shoulders straight and his stride strong. He didn't stop to look back. I blew a kiss to his back and turned away. It was time to get back to work.

## JOHNNY

When Renée returned from her parents' house, I knew that she sensed I had been with Maggie. The hurt was written on her face as we exchanged our goodbyes, and when I left, I knew somehow that I would never see her again.

My thoughts of Renée and Maggie had to wait, because Crowley had us on a plane to Rome before dawn. The people were beautiful, but the city had been wracked by the war. The boys and I enjoyed the few days there, eating pasta and drinking wine before we began the briefing sessions.

The new operation was different. We were alone on it, just Thomas, Stanley, Bobby and me, and we were going to be parachuting onto the side of a mountain. An invasion force was supposed to meet us after we had blown the bridge. I was beginning to see why they paid us differently. This was serious stuff. Only Thomas seemed unfazed, and his fearlessness gave me some reassurance.

Next, we flew to Florence and learned the plans had changed. Not only were we to blow a bridge, but we were also ordered to secure another in the same region, thereby trapping any two of the five Italian Fascist divisions in the area. It was a mountainous region near Lago di Garda called the Adige line, which was also the name of the river in the area. I asked if we would have help in securing the second bridge.

According to Crowley, the 10th Mountain Division would be nearby to assist after the blowing of the first bridge, but we were not under any circumstances to communicate with anyone until the bridge was down. They named me platoon leader. It was getting really scary.

The sky was lit by a three-quarter moon when we flew out over the lake. I couldn't help admiring the moon in the mirror-like water, which looked like it had been cut to fit the mountains.

The co-pilot motioned for us to get ready. Thomas jumped first, then Stanley and Bobby, then me. The cold air blasted me in the face when I jumped, but I forgot it when I felt myself ripped upwards by the cord. My chute opened and I began the silent drift down to the mountains below. As they rose below me, I saw three other chutes nearby and they gave me a sense of security. There was peace in the descent, the lake to the west, cradled by the mountains.

The ground came up faster than I expected, and I had to quickly adjust for a landing. I hit a small meadow below a huge crag in the mountain. Snow still clung to the rocky ground, making the landing rougher than usual, but I was still glad to be on solid earth. The rest of the boys had gone down below me in another meadow.

I brought in my chute, unhooked it, and buried it in some brush. Then I oriented myself with the map, realizing the guys would have to come in my direction since the bridge was farther to the east and at a higher elevation than where I had landed. The guys would know the direction and head my way.

At daybreak, the fiery orange sun rose slowly above the mountaintops. I had positioned myself between two boulders with a view of the two valleys where I figured the guys would be pushing. The small village of Dro to my east looked out of place, quiet and peaceful sandwiched in the mountains. I wondered if the people who lived there even knew a war was raging.

Thomas appeared first, pressing out of the northern valley. The rest followed, heading toward me, so I saw no point in revealing myself until they were close enough to hear our whistle signal. Bobby heard it first and whistled back. Within minutes, we were reunited.

According to our orientation, the bridge was due east about one mile, near the village. It looked like some rough going, more snow and what looked like another thousand feet of elevation. We all complained of the cold. For some reason we had expected something warmer but, in the mountains, winter had not lost its grip. The climbing was strenuous, but unless we were completely careless, it wasn't dangerous.

The route took half the day and by noon, we looked down at the bridge. It seemed smaller than in the pictures, an expanse of two hundred feet between two mountains whose summits disappeared in clouds. It was a two-lane road bridge and on each end were MG 34s in sandbag bunkers, four Germans to each. Two remained in each bunker and two were out, patrolling. The two on the far side of the bridge leaned over the rail, looking towards the river below. The other two sat off to the side, eating.

Thomas motioned to me to get nearer. "We've got to get them out. I have to set this plastic on the supports on each side to take it down, and I can't do it with them watching."

"Okay, okay." I motioned for Stanley. "You're the marksman. Whattaya say?"

117

"I can get three pretty quick, but then they'll be firing back."

I nodded. I rolled it over in my head, trying to figure something. Then it dawned on me. "Can you get three on the other side of the bridge?"

Stanley looked over my shoulder with his trained eye. "Two for sure, maybe three. This M-1 can drift at that distance."

"Okay, we figure two. Then take cover and we'll get the rest."

"How?" Bobby asked.

"You, me, and Thomas are going to take out these guys near us when Stanley starts shooting. We'll position to the left of that overhang, there. See it?"

"That's going to be tough," Bobby said.

"We have to kill the guys on the machine guns. The rest we take however we can. Stanley, get to where you gotta be and wait for my signal."

Stanley nodded and disappeared behind us. A few minutes later he waved from above, settled in a crag to our right. We funneled our way to the road, about a quarter of a mile away from the bridge, and doubled back behind the rocks until we were less than twenty yards from the Germans. I located Stanley, looked to see if everyone was ready, then waved to him.

His first two shots tore up the silence, cracking overhead. I saw one German go down before we jumped out and began firing. We quickly disposed of the two on the MG, and the lunching Germans began running for cover. Thomas cut them down as shots from the other side of the bridge struck close by. Two more shots rang out from above, then silence. It was fast and it was clean.

Our orders were to blow the bridge, leaving the bodies to go down with the rest. A good enough burial, I figured. Thomas began unpacking his plastics and Bobby started with the wire detonator. Stanley got to the road in a few minutes and we all walked to the other side, covering Thomas as he set the first charge.

"Fine shooting," I said to Stanley.

"No draft, no drift," he replied, smiling at his good work. "I like this gun." He patted it like a faithful dog.

Thomas set both charges he returned to our position, twisted the detonator, and pushed down. The blasts were small, contained, but loud and thudded underneath. Waiting for something to happen, I looked at Thomas, who had a weird smile on his face, and then I heard a loud groan as if the bridge were trying to speak. Rumbling and cracking began to vibrate the road, and in seconds, the bridge buckled. Both sides gradually, smoothly fell to the river below. Thomas's smile turned into a wide grin.

"Good job," I said. "Now let's go get the other one." We moved south along the river, descending down the mountains toward a lakeside town named Nago. The plan was to secure this bridge and all the other bridges along the Adige River. Our point was the last to the northwest, so any help would come from the east. The plan would theoretically trap twenty-four German divisions and two Italian divisions for our approach. However, I was learning military theory and military reality were sometimes miles apart—what they told us might not be the truth. So we carried out orders like good soldiers and left strategies to the generals.

The enemy put up no resistance. Two Italian trucks passing to the north scurried us behind some hemlocks, but they passed without incident. By nightfall, we saw the bridge in the distance. It looked like another half-day hike, so we found shelter under an outcropping shielded by low growth white pine. We ate k-rations to keep our body temperatures up and drifted off to sleep when the sun fell behind the mountains. I didn't think of the soldiers I had killed, and the cold night banished any thoughts of Maggie.

I welcomed the sunrise, which promised some warmth. We ate more k-rations, then quietly headed for the bridge, wondering what lay ahead.

The Nago Bridge was the same length as the one we had already blown, but the terrain was more open, meaning positioning Stanley was impossible. An armored German Puma sat menacingly at the far end of the bridge, and Italian troops armed with MG-34s guarded the closest bunker. The situation didn't look good, so I motioned the guys away so we could talk.

"Any suggestions?" Even Thomas was silent.

"Okay," I sighed. "I think we have to take out the bunker with grenades. Stanley, you position yourself wherever you can to lob one into the window of the car Take out the driver. Bobby, if he does, you drop a grenade into it." No one looked enthused. "Any other suggestions?"

"Let's use knives," said Thomas. "If we kill quietly, it won't alert the car. Then all of us can go after it."

I didn't know why he hadn't spoken before, but it made sense, though it was riskier for Thomas and me since we'd be hand-to-hand. "Yeah, okay. But you guys stay in the same position. When Thomas and I are done, we'll open up with the MG."

Thomas and I laid our guns on the ground, unsheathed our knives, and slowly made our way to the enemy. Bobby and Stanley circled back to the bridge. The two Italians in the bunker looked bored, and I watched as one of them pulled a deck of cards out of his pack. I heard him say, "Brisko?"

The other replied, "Si. Si."

We waited until they sat, intent on their game.

We slid on our bellies up to the sandbags. The game was going along fast, each soldier beginning to shout at the other, oblivious to any threat. I gave the motion and we both jumped over the bags onto the soldiers. My knife caught one in the back, while Thomas dove on the dealer and buried his knife under the ribs and up to the heart. Both died quickly and soundlessly.

The engine of the armored car roared as Thomas jumped behind the machine gun and positioned it towards the armored car. The gun on the car opened up, but the rounds went above us. They must have seen Stanley firing from above. Thomas fired, drawing their attention, and I saw the gun lower to our position. The bullets hitting near us blew puffs from the bags, but Thomas kept firing until there was a loud explosion and the car erupted in flames. Bobby waited to the left for the soldiers to exit. One escaped the burning wreckage, but Bobby nailed him. The other guy was fried.

I clapped Thomas on the back as Bobby joined us at the bunker, but there was no sign of Stanley. The three of us looked at each other, then ran to his position.

On his back, staring at the clear sky, he looked like he was relaxing after a good day's work, a wry smile on his face. Then I saw the blood spreading down from his neck, and his twitching left leg.

"Goddamnit," I said. The 50mm hit him somewhere in the chest. There was no saving him.

"That you, Johnny?"

"Yeah."

"I can't see. Something… knocked me over. I couldn't fire… anymore."

"It's okay. We got 'em." My mouth was parched and I felt sick.

"Good." He smiled and died. I don't think any of us were ready for it. The first thing that flashed in my mind was that he had never loved someone.

"Never knew what hit him," Thomas said.

"I never saw a friend die this close," Bobby said, his eyes still on Stanley.

We sat together, silent in our thoughts. I knew now that he would never get a girl, and it made me feel worse.

Thomas broke the silence. "Are we going to bury him? It's D-2, so his body will get pretty ripe if it warms up while we're waiting for the troops."

"I want to get him back. Get him to his home area." It just seemed right.

"Why? He'll be just as dead there as he is here." Again, Thomas had logic behind him.

"Because I think that's what he'd want to be," I said.

Thomas shrugged. "It's your platoon. I'd pack him in some of that snow, though."

So that's what we did, separating him from the dead Italians. Then we waited for our guys to get to us, keeping warm as long as the Puma burned, and afterwards moving to the sandbag bunker.

I tried to look away, but I watched as Stanley's skin turned gray then blue from the cold. Death used to get to me—back home, hits used to make me sick—but it was starting not to bother me. The finality didn't frighten me like it used to, maybe it because I was viewing life differently. I don't know. It was almost as if Stanley never existed.

I slept better that night and by mid-afternoon, we spotted troops coming up the valley. They were our guys, no doubt the 10th Mountain Division. They had a few more hours before they reached us, so we relaxed in the sun. The snow slowly melted and Stanley's body became exposed. Another day of this warmth weather and the fresh smell of pines wouldn't be able to mask the odor of decay.

When the column was about fifty yards away, we halted them. My neighborhood instincts told me to be careful, though I had no qualms they were the 10th.

"Who you looking for?" I yelled.

They stopped, and several sought cover, but the platoon leader looked up to the bridge.

"Stony!"

He knew my operation name. I had forgotten we were even using them. "Who else?"

"Crowley said to call for Stony or Emerald."

They were legit. "Come on up guys."

They shipped us behind the lines in no time. We took a Jeep back to Brescia, where we spent two nights before shipping out to

Milano, where we met up with Crowley and Leo. They'd both been promoted—Crowley to captain, and Leo to lieutenant.

Leo had made a remarkable recovery and was going to accompany us on our next mission, a drop near a prisoner of war camp in Germany. They wouldn't tell us anything else. I received a battlefield commission to rank of second lieutenant and got a gold bar. Thomas and Bobby were elevated to Staff Sergeant, and we were all awarded bronze stars, even Stanley whose body they shipped home while we headed behind German lines.

## MAGGIE

To keep Johnny from haunting my thoughts, I drove into my efforts to get to the front. Convincing my bureau chief, Hill, that I was good enough to go to the front was frustrating. The male authority which insisted that I know my female place had me fuming. Even after winning a drawing to see who would parachute jump into the Rhine River region to cover the advances there, my prohibition continued. My optimism was fading and I knew I would soon lose all patience with the circumstances.

I had a blowout fight with Hill when I heard he was about to leave for the front. It came from nowhere and my arguments were pointless. I learned that three other women were going on the Air Force junket with him—Margaret Bourke-White of Time and Life, Lee Miller of Vogue, and Helen Kirkpatrick of the Chicago Daily News—so I based my argument on the fact that women were already going to the front. It didn't matter. Hill made the decisions, and he decided that I was staying in Paris. I was furious—the war was going to end, and with it, my chance for real correspondence.

I had resigned myself to staying in Paris and began a few articles based on interviews with Ambassador Jefferson Caffery when Hill called.

"Maggie, something's come up. I can't make it on the plane."
My heart pounded so hard that I was afraid he would hear it as he
said, "Do you still want to go to the front?"

"Ahh...ahhh..." I couldn't talk.

"Maggie, you okay?"

I swallowed and composed myself. "Yes, I'm fine, and yes, I
want to go to the front, and yes, I love you Russell Hill." My
number had come up, and I was finally going to be rewarded for
my work.

They only gave me a day to prepare and, since I had to travel
light, I had time to finish my stories and write everyone I knew to
boast of my new assignment.

The next day I was on a C-47 with my typewriter, an army-issue
sleeping bag, and two changes of clothes. The other
correspondents traveled just as light. We conversed over the drone
of the plane's engines, but wrapped up in my excitement, I barely
heard the chit chat. I felt a wild rush of exuberant anticipation that
had me soaring in my own skies.

We landed at the airstrip outside Darmstadt and hooked up
with Patton's 7th Army racing towards Munich. My good luck held
out when I met I met Stars and Stripes correspondent Peter Furst.
He was around my age, ambitious and reckless with a face to make
any girl ready to banish caution.

Peter had a jeep and invited me to team up with him. I could
feel the jealousy coming off the others in waves as I threw my gear
and typer in the back. I climbed into the passenger seat as Peter put
the jeep in gear, and then we were off.

My bubbling excitement soon went flat. No number of
interviews with wounded soldiers could prepare me for the war-
scarred landscape, the grotesque positions of dead bodies, or the
sickeningly sweet stench of rot. There was no romance in the
reality of war, I realized as I met the eyes of a man on the roadside,
mutilated by gunfire and the crippling winter. This was not my

father's war. This was the apex of human evil, a self-indulgent force without boundaries or conscience.

Thoughts of Johnny tugged at the corners of my mind, but separated by time and distance, I chose to focus on the present. Peter and I were similar kinds of people—in another time, we probably would have fallen for each other—but here and now we were partners, and we kept our relationship professional.

Peter drove along the front lines and into a town where my first war front coup developed: the story of Dr. Alfred Rosenburg, the Nazi philosopher who contributed to the racial inferiority theory. We stopped in Lichtenfels and discovered the doctor and his wife held up in the Lichtenfel Castle. His friend, Baron Kurt von Behr, had betrayed him, turning over his secret documents and giving up his whereabouts in exchange for some kind of amnesty deal. By the time we reached the castle, the doctor and his wife were dead. They'd taken poison with their last sips of French champagne. The story made the front page back home, bearing my by-line.

Several days later, near the town of Wasserburg, I saw another kind of evil. Approaching a bridge that led into the town, I saw several American soldiers taunting German prisoners. Then, one of the Americans pushed a prisoner off to the side and shot him. The unarmed prisoner looked famished, and I doubted he'd have the strength to do antagonize the Allied solider. The American killed him in cold blood, then met my eyes as we crossed the bridge. His eyes were crazed, and a shot of fear rippled through my core for the first time since I had become a correspondent.

"We have to do something, Peter." I twisted in my seat to look back.

Peter remained silent.

"Peter, stop the car. Americans don't kill people like that."

Peter turned to me, "Listen Maggie, this is war and it's ugly. It makes people ugly."

I couldn't believe what I heard. "But, Americans don't act like the enemy, the enemy—"

"Maggie, forget you saw it." His tone was intractable.

"Bull, I'm going to—"

"No one will listen and your tour here will be finished."

His words fell like a wet blanket, casting a silence like moment following a death knell. I couldn't believe him; I didn't want to believe him. I slouched down in my seat as we motored toward Buchenwald.

Lines of troops, trucks, and munitions moved along a bombed-out road filled with craters and smoking debris. We didn't talk as Peter banged along, avoiding as many potholes as possible. The conversation by the bridge reverberated in my mind as I soaked in the war-time scene. I could do nothing but gape at the mutilated living and grotesque dead—some corpses still smoking from the mortar blast. I was dazed by the horror. I had no idea what I was getting into.

Peter and I arrived in Buchenwald shortly after Patton's army liberated the camp there. I had no idea what lay ahead, and when we pulled through the gates I realized there was no way to prepare for the atrocity that lay within.

Emaciated corpses were stacked like logs in a mill. Many were partially burned from the ovens, others had crushed skulls with mucus and blood frozen to their faces. Vomit rose in the back of my throat as I saw that there were small children in the pile, but I swallowed hard and put the story foremost in my mind. The world must know, and I had the responsibility to tell it. Then, when I thought that nothing worse could happen, a GI called for me to come to one of the cellblocks for a story.

Inside the dormitory, two rows of GIs were lines up against the walls. Screaming and crying rumbled from the far end of the long, narrow building as I followed the soldier through the rubble. He stopped in front of three battered Germans. One GI would periodically lift his leg and smash it into one the three faces.

"Stop it," I yelled. The Americans grew quiet and looked at me, only the sound of whimpering filtered through the silence. One GI got in my face.

"Stop what, lady?" Flecks of white foam formed in the corners of his mouth.

"This," I put my open hand in the space between the soldier and myself. "This cruelty."

"Hear that boys?" He looked around at the others. "Seems we got here a dame with no belly." He got into my face again. "You look around outside honey? You see what these no good bastards did to those people? You don't think they deserve this and more?" He pressed his index finger into my shoulder.

"You have no authority to judge these people." I had righteousness on my side and tried to remember it. He smirked at me and shook his head.

"Lady, get outta here. Go back home and wash your man's clothes. This ain't no place for you."

I wanted to scream at him, tear into him. I felt my cheeks flush, and my Irish pride welled inside. Abruptly, he turned into the cell, grabbed one of the men and, turning to make sure I was watching, smashed his rifle butt into the prisoner's face. I rushed out, hoping to find someone to stop the brutality, and ran headlong into a second lieutenant on his way to end the madness. But for the second time in a matter of days on the front, I had experienced untold ugliness from the supposed good guys.

I wanted to get out. I wanted to file my story mentioning what I had just seen, but Peter convinced me once again that the story would only jeopardize my position on the front. Looking blindly at the stacked corpses, I decided that if I got myself sent home now, I wouldn't be around to find out if more of this kind of abuse of power happened. I needed to stay on the front, to gather information, and I promised myself that one day the public would know the whole story.

The next morning, after a fitful night in the officers' barracks, Peter and I set out for Dachau where the 5th army readied to liberate another death camp. I felt a pang of reluctance, but it was my job, and I was slowly learning how to distance my emotions from the facts. So, although I traveled with some reservation, I looked forward to what the next situation would afford.

## JOHNNY

We parachuted behind the lines along the Danube River between Dachau and Linz. We were there to take out a bridge on the Amper Lager, then liberate a prison camp and find an imprisoned OSS officer. Officially, we were part of the 45th infantry of Patton's 7th Army, but that didn't mean much. We were still going in without any patches and that meant we really didn't belong to anyone.

I slept intermittently. I couldn't help but think about the last operation and how fast everything happened, including Stanley's death. He was with us one day and the next he was gone. Then I thought about me. I chuckled to myself when I realized I hadn't spoken Italian to anyone in the operation—no need to up to this point. I couldn't believe it had taken so long for me to figure out that Crowley didn't want me for my Italian. They'd only ever been interested in my killing, and my orders were always to kill. And these new orders were no different: "Neutralize anyone who threatens the integrity of the operation." Did they mean civilians, women, and children?

A memory of Maggie's face interrupted my thoughts; I wondered how she would react to my job. Hell, I didn't know how I was reacting to my job—was it an emotionless execution of duty, or a courageous role in a righteous battle? I couldn't answer these questions for myself, and I had no idea how I'd answer them for

Maggie. All I knew was that the ghosts of the people I'd killed stayed with me from one operation to the next.

I looked at Thomas and wondered if he felt the same. Bobby seemed too naive to even understand, but maybe it was better that way. Crowley and Leo were professionals; there was no doubt that killing was their business, you could see it in their faces. Now that I was in with them, I wondered if leaving would be as tough as getting out of the mob.

The navigator yelled, "Drop zone. Drop zone." My focus turned from killing to surviving.

The evening drop went smoothly. Crowley led the advance of three platoons with Leo and me leading the other two. We kept close, using our assigned names—I was Stony, Thomas was Emerald, Bobby was Quartz, Crowley was Foxx, and Leo was Sparky. I didn't know the other guys' operation names, and I didn't want to. Less is better.

Our target was one of the main bridges to Dachau Lager, the camp. Though visibility was poor in the misty dark, the charges were set easily. I covered my ears as the blinding explosion blasted the bridge to pieces.

We continued along the Amper, and just before dawn crossed one of the remaining railroad bridges in light trucks and on foot. We were on alert for the enemy, but encountered nothing—it was almost too easy, too quiet. I was on edge, spooked by the whole scene.

As we followed the tracks, we came to a spur and followed that line. Several of the men began wrinkling their noses and gasping at a stench blowing in on the cold breeze from the east. It smelled perverse, like burning flesh and decay.

The rising sun tinted the mist orange, but visibility remained low—about twenty yards in any direction—and the boxcar seemed to rise up like a monster in the fog.

As we neared, we found a line of boxcars emitting a smell that invaded my reasoning. On all sides men were gagging and retching at the contents of the cars: thousands of emaciated corpses, stacked like bricks at a construction site. They spilled from the doors, rotting even in the frigid weather, and their eyes stood out huge in their gaunt faces. Seeing a small girl with long, black eyelashes like Maggie's, I leaned over the side of the bridge and vomited.

Crowley had seen men react to horror before, and he must have realized that hate, the primal call for revenge, would outweigh rationality. Swiftly, he moved his platoon past the death train, and the rest of us followed his example.

Finally we encountered German soldiers and SS Guards, who surrendered without a fight. We led them back across the tracks to a power plant, lining them against a long masonry wall near a coal yard.

I ordered three of my men to hold the prisoners, but when Thomas and Bobby brought more Germans in, I started to worry. The prisoners were multiplying fast and controlling them would be a problem. I looked for Crowley but saw only Germans.

"Hold them against that wall." I tried to fill my voice with Crowley's authority, leaving the three guards with a bi-pod machine gun behind as we moved out in search of Crowley.

We finally met some resistance near a tower. A short firefight left most of the Germans dead, and the rest surrendered. I left these prisoners with Thomas and Bobby against another wall, then headed along a line of trees toward a gate.

The gate was massive, and an inscription—Arbeit Macht Frei— was welded in an arc at its top. I didn't know German, but I had seen enough of the compound to know that what it meant, it was ghastly. When I saw the prisoners—walking skeletons with frost-blackened toes and ears—I pinched myself to be sure I hadn't walked into a nightmare.

The prisoners walked slowly toward the gate and fence, looking at me with bulging eyes. The fear must have been beaten out of them along with most of the life, because they cocked their heads at me and several even attempted smiles. I felt ill again, and battled to remain calm as the rage and injustice pumped through my body. There were hundreds of them, all approaching the gate, pressing against one another as the hum of engines signaled an approach.

Crowley joined, me and we wondered who the hell was coming. A woman, with a fur cap pulled low on her forehead, rode shotgun in a jeep, but our questions went unanswered. Gunshots rang out around the compound, and I abandoned Crowley to charge back to the crematory.

Thomas and Bobby were gone, the Germans they'd been assigned to guard were lying dead and dying. "The coal yard," I said to myself, rushing off to the second group.

From a hundred paces away, I saw the three guards conferring. They'd heard the gunshots in the compound. I pressed forward, seeing one soldier shove his way clear of his companions and take aim at the prisoners.

"No, don't," I bellowed as I ran.

Many of the prisoners had fallen by the end of the first round, but those who remained were standing with their hands raised in surrender. The rebel blasted another round, and this time the other soldier joined in. I ran faster as more prisoners dropped, and the first gunner fired into the downed prisoners. Three remained standing: two with their hands in the air, the other with them crossed against his chest.

I came running, taking out my Browning pistol just as the rogue soldiers mowed down the remaining three prisoners. I had lost control of my men, and I was losing control of myself.

I don't know what I shouted as I fired three rounds at my men, killing the machine gunner and his partner and wounding the third guard. As the echoes of the gunshots faded away, I stood alone amongst the corpses of my men and the German prisoners. The wounded soldier at my feet was thrashing and moaning, and I knelt next to his head.

"Listen, Solider. You're an American. Americans don't murder unarmed prisoners. If this is the last thing you hear, then you can at least die like an American." I paced until I felt calm again, then returned to the prison gates.

By the time I got back, the column had stopped by the gate. The woman jumped out of her jeep before it stopped and, pulling her fur cap off, trotted past Crowley and Leo. I stopped short and ran a hand over my face. What else could happen in this nightmarish day?

Maggie was wearing a leather flight jacket and a fur-flapped hat as she shoved the bolt on the gate and strutted into the camp. I watched from afar as she walked up to a man and kissed him and then the situation deteriorated rapidly. Several shots rang out and I saw several people—Germans and soldiers alike—drop. A horde of crazed, emaciated prisoners were swarming her, while several rushed by her and through the gate.

"Close that gate!" Crowley recovered from the shock of her bravado first.

Leo and three other soldiers from the platoon linked arms and forced the prisoners back into the gate as Crowley shot the bolt, trapping Maggie inside. The prisoners shoved and pressed her into the gate. I ran to help her.

"Get me out!" She was beating her palm against the iron gate, then she saw me. "Joh-" She stopped—even in those circumstances she had the presence of mind to conceal my name.

Crowley glared at her, then at me. "I should shoot you, lady," he said. "You know her, Stony?"

"You could say that."

"Damn right you do. I know her, and I know you know her."

Maggie was smashed into the closed gate and nobody was really trying to help in any way. Someone at the back of the crowd yelled, "Typhoid!" I saw her face turn from anger to terror.

"Please, please let me out." Her body was pressed flat against the gate by the weight of the inmates.

Crowley let her sweat it for a couple seconds, then opened the gate a crack for her to wiggle through. I grabbed her outstretched hand and yanked her to safety. Crowley was so angry, he probably would have slammed the gate back on her if I hadn't been there, but he waited until she was out to shoot the bolt. I could tell, as Maggie looked from me to the prisoners, that she wanted to say something, but I shook my head no, so she backed slowly to the jeep. Crowley followed her in a cloud of rage.

"Thanks, Colonel. And tell the lieutenant I said thanks, too." Maggie forced a smile.

"Get outta here, lady. Now, damn it."

An officer in the jeep ahead of her rose. "I'm General Linden. Stand down, Colonel. This is my command, the 42nd Army."

Crowley saluted his superior and Linden returned it, resuming his confident, commanding tone. "This lady is a correspondent and is to interview VIPs in this camp."

I moved closer, and although still numb from the action at wall, I knew Crowley didn't like where this was going.

"What VIPs, sir?" Crowley asked.

Linden seemed unsure, so Maggie jumped in.

"Schuschnigg and Blum, and Hitler's bomb plot conspirators. I have to get inside and interview. It's the story of the day," she said with her schoolgirl charm.

Her determination was admirable, and my love for her shone through the evil running through the compound.

Crowley's patience with the situation was waning, and he looked ready to just walk away, but the general wasn't ready to butt out.

"Sorry, you got enough for today. We got things to do. You get outta here," Crowley said.

One dazzling smile from Maggie reinforced the general's machismo. "That's okay, Colonel, I'm taking over command here."

I had to chuckle. Obviously, this idiot didn't see that we weren't wearing patches, which meant we were the command in cases like this. It was either that, or he was ignorant, but either way it posed a threat to prisoners and soldiers alike.

"With due respect sir, my command is from a higher source than you and, until I hear from that source, you are out of line," Crowley said flatly.

Linden became furious. "I'm taking over, here and now." Linden's eyes bugged out.

"I'm sorry, sir," Crowley responded, and then pointed to Leo. Maggie seemed to recognize Leo, and I saw her raise her hand to point at him before remembering her surroundings. "Leo, get the lady into her jeep."

Leo took Maggie by the arm, and she looked at the general in outrage.

"Take your hands off her," Linden ordered. Then he smacked Leo on his arm. Leo loosened his grip on Maggie and everyone froze. Slowly Crowley pulled out his .45 and seeing it, the rest of us charged our weapons. The general backed away from Leo, regaining his composure, and staring directly into Crowley's face.

"I'm gonna have your career for this, Colonel," Linden said, looking for Crowley's command patch. Realization crossed his face finally, and he grew purple with anger. He motioned to the 42nd to move out.

Maggie sat still, looking directly at me with my gun pointed at the jeep. I lowered it, but she continued to stare at me. Then Crowley yelled to us, "Secure the perimeter!"

I walked up to Crowley. "I want to get back to my men. There's been a problem back there."

"More?"

"Some guys lost control. I lost control."

He nodded at me and said, "Okay, get back to your men," then turned back to the prisoners.

Linden's jeep was idling near the coal yard—he must have been following the tracks out of the compound when he'd spotted the scene. To my relief, Thomas was standing guard with another soldier, and we exchanged terse waves as I trotted into the area.

Linden was looking at the dead men—Germans and Americans lying together in a heap—and Maggie had just jumped out of the jeep. Another correspondent climbed out of the vehicle and stood behind her.

"What's this?" She stepped towards Thomas and directed her question to him. "What happened here?"

Thomas didn't answer, and Maggie looked at the general and back to Thomas. She slammed both hands to her hips. "I'm Marguerite Hogan with The Herald Tribune and the people back home want to know what happened here." She paced and stared right into Thomas.

Thomas remained stoic.

"Answer the lady, soldier. That's an order," said the general.

Thomas saw Linden's star and, feeling as if he should say something, began to weigh his words carefully. I skidded to his side and Maggie raised a haughty eyebrow at me. I wanted to reassure her, to explain, but she stood stiffly, with her arms now crossed in front of her chest.

"Sir, my orders are to guard the dead. Theirs and ours." His face was as placid as a mask.

"How did they die?" Maggie asked craning her neck right into him.

Thomas looked at the dead, then turned back. "Looks like they were shot.

Maggie's eyes grew wider as she stepped forward, her hands balling into fists at her side. She was scary.

"Who shot whom?"

Thomas didn't like the question, so he did what he was supposed to do. "You'll have to ask command, ma'am."

Linden got out of his jeep and leaned into Thomas's face until their noses almost touched. "And who is your command?"

Thomas looked straight ahead, unaffected by the closeness of the general's face. I was just about to bail him out when he said, "As you are well aware, Sir, I'm not required to say."

135

"What? Why?" Maggie raised her palms to the sky.

The other correspondent pulled Maggie back by the arm. "Come on. This isn't our battle," he said to her. I was glad he was there.

But Maggie wasn't giving up. She held up one finger in the international symbol for wait and said, "You executed these Germans?"

Thomas didn't answer, but watched as Linden circled him, then walked to the dead Americans. He addressed me, "Who killed these Americans, Lieutenant?"

He pressed his hands to his temples when I remained silent, and I could see a vein pulsing in his forehead. "Have it your way. Good. I'll have you all court marshaled!"

Maggie stepped forward again and dug her index finger into my chest. "Did you kill these Germans?" I couldn't respond, so I just stared into her face and tried to tell her silently that I loved her.

"I just came from Buchenwald, a camp like this. And there, too, our men acted like the enemy. Now tell me, damn it! Why are Americans acting like the enemy?"

"We're fighting a war, miss, and it isn't pretty," I said.

Her face softened for a moment. "Is that true, Lieutenant? Is it true you acted like soldiers, like American soldiers?"

As I spoke, I knew I could be ruining any hope of a future for us, but I spoke unflinchingly. "Soldiers carry out orders to achieve an objective. The objective here was to liberate this camp. That's what we've done. That's the truth, and you can write that." I turned from her. "Excuse us, but we have a job to do."

Her face was unreadable. "General, I want to know what happened here, and I want my interviews of the VIPs."

The general, motioning everyone into the jeep, had about enough Maggie Hogan. "Furst!" he yelled to the other correspondent. "Get your passenger in the jeep and meet me at headquarters."

Furst grabbed Maggie by the arm and steered her to the jeep, where reluctantly she climbed in. She never looked away from the horror, or from me. When she finally turned, I thought it was probably the last time I'd see her.

## MAGGIE

I looked at Peter and in a whisper asked, "What happened?"
He drove on without answering.
"Those Germans were executed, weren't they?"
Finally, refusing to meet my gaze, he spoke. "Forget it Maggie, it's war and bad things happen."
"What's that supposed to mean? I want to know, the people want to know, damn it."
"They can't. Don't you get it?"
"Yeah, I get it. There were dead prisoners and dead Americans. I figure a couple of our guys got shot, so their buddies executed a bunch of prisoners."
Peter heaved a sigh, then pulled to a stop at the side of the rode. When he turned to me, his eyes were glinting with a grim menace. "This is too big to write about. Write about the camp and the people there and what happened to them. You saw them. They were tortured and killed like animals—worse than animals. I've been at the front a very long time, but never saw such horror. You know who did that? The Germans. They're monsters and they deserve whatever they get from our guys. Don't you get it?"
I closed my eyes and pinched the bridge of my nose. When I spoke, I measured my words carefully. "Peter, war does not give anyone the right to judge whether one should be executed. The law does. Our law. What happened there, what our men did, was no better than what the Germans did to those people. We reduced ourselves to their level."

He surprised me by nodding. "You're right, Maggie. We don't have that right, nor did those men. But, the circumstances here were enormously unusual—unprecedented in human history, maybe."

"Then I can write it from that angle."

The lines around his mouth softened. "You're still so naive."

I couldn't stand it when people said that, and I was ready to lash out at him, but I took three deep breaths and let him continue.

"They didn't have patches."

"So?"

"They were volunteers."

"So?" I was losing patience with this conversation.

"They have orders, and I mean orders from the highest command, to do a job. No one has any authority over them other than the highest command."

"I don't get it."

"They don't exist." He said this between clenched teeth.

"But—"

"Maggie, no one will ever let a piece of information about those men and what happened get past your typewriter. If you try and you're really lucky, they'll just send you home. Sometimes worse can happen."

An explosive understanding ripped through my gut, and I slouched in my seat. As Peter pulled back onto the road and gunned the motor, trying to catch up with Linden's men, I wondered who the all-powerful "they" were. My emotions roiled inside me, mingling with the horrors I had just witnessed and Johnny's betrayal. I felt sick.

Pictures of the dead Germans slumped against the wall, their bodies riddled with bullets, kept flashing through my mind, spliced between memories of Johnny—his eyes wide and foreign, scary like something evil had crawled inside him. His men with guns aimed at the dead; our own men dead next to the guns. No matter how I tried to train my thoughts elsewhere, on the terrain or on the sound of the jeep's engine, the visions kept up their insane parade. I tried rearranging the sequences, masking the action by covering it with the barbarous acts of cruelty heaped on the prisoners, but the truth wasn't going anywhere.

We didn't reach the camp where the press center was located until late evening, and the transmitter had been shut down for the night. We made our weary way to the barracks, where Peter immediately crashed onto a cot. As his breathing slowed and deepened, my mind continued to whirl.

Maybe it was some kind of cover job—a passel of dead Germans and two dead Americans looked awfully strange, and even the general couldn't get a straight answer out of Johnny and the other soldier. Johnny's presence on the scene was another puzzle: I didn't want to believe that he could be a part of...whatever that was on the coal field, but the way he looked through me just seemed to confirm his involvement.

I knew the truth. The American soldiers had executed those Germans. And if it had been done in retaliation to some aggression, Johnny would have said so. Our men were no better than the Germans we were fighting, and what did that say about our justice?

"They don't exist." Peter's words rang through my head. "No one will listen, no one will let you write what happened." I didn't know how or why they would stop me, but I knew there had to be a way to tell the story, to explain that war, the evil war within, where men take upon themselves the role of God, had reached into the souls of our soldiers. War had sent shoots of evil into their hearts, choking out the righteousness and decency, blacking out the good. The people deserved to know that war created monsters and they were not just Germans.

I watched the sunrise, splashing the war-scarred earth with beautiful, cleansing rays of light. The sky was a stained glass mosaic of vibrant colors as the gray dawn retreated and the deep blue of day came on. It seemed so peaceful. Peter startled me from behind.

"Let's get some coffee before we file," he said. He was too kind to come right out and say that he wanted to keep an eye on my story.

The coffee was strong and bitter, making me shiver as it went down. "You got it straight about what you're going to write?" Peter asked bluntly.

"I know what I want to write."

"No one knows the whole story of what happened except those soldiers at the wall."

"Then I'll report about what I saw afterwards, unarmed dead Germans all in a row." Peter didn't move a muscle. "And two dead Americans lying just in front of them."

"Forget it, Maggie. Write about the liberation that will make you famous, not about an incident you'll never be able to prove."

"I don't want to prove anything, just tell the truth."

"Damn you Maggie, there is no truth in that pit of hell. You saw it. You saw the horror. Just forget the wall…"

"You could corroborate my story," I said, raising my eyebrows to underline the challenge. He winced and mulled over my words. I could practically hear his thought process chugging along.

He shook his head and two lines formed between his eyebrows like single quotation marks. "I didn't see anything, Maggie. Just brave Americans liberating a death camp. That's what I saw and that is what I am going to file."

"Not me."

He rose and his tone was filled with derision. "You do what you want; it's your career and it's going to be a short one." He shook his head as he walked away.

Everyone from Engle to Hill had tried to tell me that the front wasn't a place for a woman, that I wouldn't understand the horror, that some things would go unsaid. This was one of those things.

I got up from the table, leaving my coffee, and walked to the transmitter. Peter stepped out of the tent when I got there, and held the flap for me to enter, his face devoid of emotion His meaning was clear: I was on my own.

I stepped in and formulated the story in my mind. Then I did what I never believed I would do, and betrayed my urge to write the whole story. Laying truth aside all for the wrong reasons seemed absurd, but I wasn't willing to be yanked from the front after all of my work. I felt like the world was watching as I consciously and deliberately left out a part of history that I had seen with my own eyes. Fear and selfishness won the day.

I wrote of the liberation, giving the 42nd Infantry credit for being there first. I mentioned the 45th Infantry and the fighting, but I made it look good for our men. The liberation and the end of the misery for those prisoners was a wonderful day in history, and I never mentioned Johnny, his troops, or what I knew they did. His army didn't exist. The story hit the Herald on April 30 and the reality of my name under a major headline erased most of my bitterness.

Peter left for Italy the next day, and I missed him immediately. We said our goodbyes over a bottle of Riesling from the region, and I told him that my story had focused only on the liberation. He smiled and relaxed—he must have felt that I'd done the right thing.

Neither of us wanted to part. Our shared experiences had given rise to a mutual, professional respect that I had never shared with anyone. But he remained solid in his beliefs and cautioned me again to be smart about what I wrote for the papers, to wait until it was safe, even if it took years. We parted with a warm embrace and a firm handshake, and I never saw Peter again.

Ten days later, the war ended. I was at General O'Daniel's 3rd Division Headquarters in the famous Ribbentrop's Castle atop a mountain overlooking the Salzburg valley.

That evening I chatted with some of the correspondents and officers, hoping to distract myself from the recent past, but I couldn't get the realization of Johnny's involvement out of my

The

head. Though I didn't want to believe it, the evidence was against him. Trying to preserve my love, I began rationalizing his actions—he deserved the opportunity to explain it all in his own words, I told myself. Unfortunately, getting that explanation wasn't possible at the time. Concerned for his safety, I wondered if General Linden had actually court marshaled everyone, so I cornered General O'Daniel and badgered him for information.

We were drinking a twenty-year-old French cognac from the castle's cellars and looking out a window to the valley below. The wind was light and fragrant, making me feel good—human again—for the first time since I'd come to the front. I sat across from O'Daniel, close enough to ensure that our legs would occasionally brush. "Have you heard anything on the Dachau court-marshal, General?"

He sipped his cognac, breathing in its rich aroma. He placed his hand palm up on the table and said, "Nothing like a victory brandy. Mmmm. No, well, yes. It's a non-issue. Nothing went wrong. In fact they decorated all the bastards. That Patton, he's something."

I wasn't giving up, so I put my hand on top of his. "But it came out that they executed those Germans. And what about the two dead Americans, isn't that cause—"

"No Americans were killed during the Dachau liberation. That's what the report says. Let it be, little lady. That's war and it's over now. Enjoy it." He took another sip of the cognac. "You get yourself to the balcony when it's time."

I retracted my hand and shook my head. Peter had been right all along: if I'd filed the story the way I wanted, not only would no one believe it, but I would have no way to prove it. I felt sick over the madness of it all.

I thought, after the trial, I would finally be able to write the truth. But there was no trial, no guilty or innocent, just decorated soldiers. I would never believe that the confusion and insanity of the day caused me to misunderstand the events. I knew I had to accept it for the moment, but I promised myself that it wouldn't rest for long.

I pushed away from the table and my eyes caught a beautiful blonde man dressed in English Army summer clothes—knee-length khakis and short sleeved shirt. The man's grace and confidence diverted my thoughts as I gathered my bag and thanked the general for the lovely evening.

Pretending to be rummaging in my purse, I orchestrated a collision with the handsome British man. At first he was taken aback, but he quickly regained his composure and smoothing his clothing said, "I'm terribly sorry; please excuse my clumsiness."

He was gorgeous, with a sophisticated London drawl, and a smooth worldliness that held me transfixed. Then I realized that I had seen his face before. It all fit—his accent and his style—he was reporting legend George Reid Millar. The same George Millar who, after joining the rifle brigade, was captured, then escaped across France only to return by parachuting back into the occupied zone to help with the resistance. Obviously he had started writing again, and now he was rubbing his elbow, smiling and wincing down at me. "No, no it's my fault."

"I'm George Reid Millar, and I'm looking for some of that French cognac. Can I refresh yours?" He held his arm out to me.

I hooked my arm into his. "I'm Maggie Hogan, and you sure can."

We wove through the officers and other correspondents, stopping briefly at the bar. He handed me a drink with a slight nod and we clinked the glasses together in a salute. I watched him over the rim of my glass as he relished the alcohol, rolling it on his tongue. "There is only one taste better than a good French cognac."

"And that is?"

He put two fingers under my chin and said, in his smoothest accent, "I think we both know."

I had to come up with a snappy rejoinder before this guy overwhelmed me completely. "That's obviously just a man's perspective."

"Is there another kind?" He slid his hand around to cup my neck.

I decided to let him have this win, but filed his attitude for a future skirmish. His hands were surprisingly soft, and as his index finger ran down my neck I realized it had been a long time since I'd been properly kissed. I ran the tip of my tongue over my lips, "None I can think of at the moment."

As George leaned in to brush his lips against mine, a commotion broke out and everyone rushed for the balcony. As much as I wanted to share a passionate kiss—to pour my relief, my anger, my worry about Johnny into one perfect kiss—we were reporters, and our inquisitive natures urged us to follow the crowd.

The marble balcony was large enough to hold all the guests looking out over the Bavarian valley. A few thin clouds scudded across the satin sky, stretching from horizon to horizon as though basking in the sudden peace. A tremendous boom erupted over the valley, causing more than a few of the guests to jump. More flashes lit the sky, followed by a continuous barrage of red, white, and blue explosions in celebration of the end of the war. It was exactly midnight, and the blasts continued for another thirty minutes. The war was really over. It was a victory, but in the back of my mind I couldn't help but feel a little lost.

A gentle breeze blew through George's window, which showed a panoramic view of the mountains' crags. We kissed in the blue moonlight filtering through the thin white curtains. Pressed against George's lean body, I was able to begin blocking out the horrors of the past weeks. His touch was delicate, electrifying my skin and urging me to forget my worries about Johnny and truth. When we made love, it was honest and tender.

After the war, George and I made the most of life together, and I was able to cloak the memories of Johnny in the carefree fun of the moment. After several weeks, I was able to bargain for a black sports model Mercedes, a car owned by a German officer confiscated by the Allies. I used some money and charm, and in a few minutes it was mine.

George and I spent a lot of time in the car, driving through the beautiful, rolling hills of French vineyards, their leaves luscious against a cloudless blue sky. George never asked to drive, but rode next to me with his head pressed back on his seat, enjoying the rides.

Finally we arrived in Paris, where thoughts of Johnny came back like a fever. No matter how hard I tried to forget him, his face and his work nagged me, and my conscience tingled over my involvement in the cover up at the coal field.

I didn't know if my feelings for George were strictly physical, like the beauty of the landscape, but our thoughts were always geared to our work rather than to our feelings for each other. Maybe that's what Johnny provided that I was missing—the separation between work and pleasure. But still, I was frightened to re-examine my feelings for Johnny, and even more frightened that I would never see him again.

## JOHNNY

When our command arrived the next day, we moved back to headquarters. We were supposed to wait there while the inquiry into the incidents during the liberation took place.

I felt awful, with a hollow gnawing in my gut. I wanted to forget, but the memories surrounded me on all sides. No amount of distance or time could make the shootings—not to mention seeing Maggie again—go away. I had nothing to do but wait for my punishment. I didn't even know what they did to guys like me, but

I knew that if I'd pulled this kind of stunt back in the neighborhood, it would mean the slow end of old Johnny Pero.

I sat on my helmet across the street from the headquarters building, waiting for the news. When I saw Crowley coming my way, I rose and saluted. I searched his face for a clue to how it had gone, but he was expressionless as ever.

"Relax, Johnny."

I cracked my knuckles—relaxing just wasn't a possibility.

"Come on, let's walk," Crowley headed toward the hotel we used as quarters. He talked, staring straight ahead as if he were talking to the air in front of him, his words forward and direct. "They're going to decorate you and the men. All of us. We're all getting bronze stars and a citation for bravery. The men killed in action—and that is what happened—will also get medals posthumously. That's what command wants. The day was glorious; the liberation, history. We freed the world from Nazi tyranny, and that's the whole story as far as they're concerned."

He stopped and turned toward me, putting a heavy hand on my shoulder. I could hardly believe what I was hearing, much less understand it, and Crowley's words weren't doing much for my conscience. He must have sensed my confusion and disgust. "Put this away, soldier. Don't let it eat at you—it's done, finished. War makes things like this happen, uncontrollable chains of events. You got yourself caught in one and now you have to forget it. Otherwise, you'll be haunted the rest of your life, questioning, wondering. I need men who act and fight, not ones who dwell in the past. You understand that, Johnny?"

His eyes flickered to the sky, but his hand remained on my shoulder. I swallowed, trying to let Crowley's advice fill the hollowness I felt inside. Then I thought of Maggie. She knew something, and with her knack for digging, the truth would surface. "What about the reporters?"

"Forget her too, Johnny. Your work doesn't mix well with hers."

"But she—"

"She, nothing. It won't get out. She'll be told to button it."

I knew Crowley was right. I had to start thinking like him, to forget and move on. "Yes, sir." I could hear the military influence in my tone.

"Good. Remember, there's more than just me in on this. I could do so much for you but you gotta do the right thing, or it can get quite dangerous. Understand?"

I looked him straight in the eye and firmly replied, "Yes sir!" It was good enough for him at that point, but he really had me thinking. Crowley dropped his hand and we resumed our walk. "We've got new orders to search out and capture or destroy the Nazis who haven't killed themselves yet. We start in several days. Command is expecting a surrender any day now, but we'll go even if that happens. Orders are to neutralize anyone necessary."

There was that word again: neutralize. I wondered if we were any different from butchers with animals. Don't wonder, I told myself. Obey. "Is my mother getting her annuities?"

Crowley smiled, showing a broken molar. "That's my boy. She sure is, son. And she'll get more if you stick with me."

It started to rain. I needed a drink, so I met up with Bobby and Thomas in a pub filled with guys from our company. There was no mention of the incident—it was as though it had never happened. I drank until the bar began rocking like the deck of the Queen Mary and the colors faded to gray.

Thomas must have carried me to my bed, because when I woke the next morning I was back in my bunk smelling of beer, schnapps and piss. My pants were damp and heavy around my crotch, and I knew I must have peed myself in the night. I threw water from the basin in the bathroom on my face, and Thomas hurried me out the door and down to command headquarters. The rest of the company, including Crowley and Leo, was already there ready for a new day's briefing. Crowley looked at me and shook his head. I was pitiful, but I evened out and corrected quickly.

After calling everyone to attention, Crowley addressed us.

"Men, we've got cleanup work ahead of us." He clasped his hands behind his back and paced the front of the room. "We got word Krauts high command agreed to an unconditional surrender yesterday, but the war isn't over for us." He paused and looked at us to see if anyone had anything to add. Not only did we all keep quiet, but most of us hardly looked like we cared. I don't remember hearing about the surrender through the night, but maybe that's why we got so sloshed.

"Good," he continued. "Like I said, we're gonna mop up. Each unit will have a tank and a specific, assigned territory. You will attempt to capture certain German criminals. If they don't cooperate, you neutralize them and whoever else they want to take on their one way journey to hell. Then and there, on the spot. You are volunteers and will act as such." He stopped pacing and put his hands on the desk. "Questions?"

Ordered to kill again, even though the war was over, made me feel uneasy. I fell in like a good soldier, but I wasn't sure exactly what that meant to me anymore.

"Good," Crowley continued, "Your orders will be given inside as you are called." He pointed to a room on his left.

Several days later an M4 Sherman tank, operated by a seasoned crew who saw combat from the Bulge, accompanied me, Thomas, and Bobby. No names however, except for one guy they called Bo, who didn't seem to care about much. He liked me because I was Italian like him, and he didn't hold anything back when he talked about the action he'd seen in North Africa. He sounded like he had marbles in his mouth and sometimes stopped mid-sentence, lost in what he was talking about. No doubt it was the effect of howitzers blasting away above his head during battle. Noise like that rattled the brains, and believe me, Bo's brains were rattled. He was as solid as brass, though, and a guy you wanted on your side.

The first two Germans we encountered surrendered easily. We pulled the tank in front of their safehouse, they hung a white flag, then filed out. We took them into custody and moved to Nuremberg and the next criminal stronghold. Thomas had command of our platoon and, after every assigned capture, immediately radioed in to headquarters to ask if we should continue. He got the go ahead every time. There was no stopping us.

We reached our last mark mid-afternoon on the third day of the operation. The setting was peaceful, and the house was pretty and neat. The tank pulled within fifty yards of the little house and lowered its gun barrel for a direct shot into the door. Thomas called out in English for everyone to surrender, but no one answered. He tried again in German, but the only answer was from the birds chirping in the trees.

We waited a few moments, looking at each other and shrugging our shoulders, then Thomas rolled his eyes and laid several shots across the masonry below the left window. Finally, a white flag waved from a window making everyone breathe easier. The door opened slowly and a middle-aged woman appeared with a young female child clinging to her leg.

"We want Herr Mueller, now," Thomas yelled to her.

"No," she replied.

That got my attention.

"He's in there?" Thomas tried again in German but she shook her head and went back into the house. Thomas fired into the wall of the house again, but no one reappeared.

"He's there," Thomas said to me, pointing at the house.

"We don't know," I said.

Thomas fired again, then the hatch of the tank opened and Bo's face popped up. "He in there?"

"He's there."

"We don't know."

"I can put a blast to the left side."

149

"Do it," Thomas said.

"No! There's a woman and kid there, Tom." I put my hand on the barrel of his gun.

Bo poked his head out again. "What?"

"They're not coming out, and we have orders," Thomas moved his gun out from under my hand.

"I can take out the left of the house," Bo repeated.

"Do it, then."

Bo ducked back into the tank and fired; the roar of the gun made me turn away and, when I turned back, the right side of the house was lost in black smoke. Shooting erupted from inside the house. I dove to the side of the tank, hearing Thomas yelling to fire. The tank roared again and tore a hole through the center of the house, and within seconds a gush of hot air preceding a storm of fire. No other shots came from the burning house, and the woman and child never reappeared. It just burned in a nightmarish, crackling silence.

We waited by the tank until the fire had died down enough for us to risk taking a look. Shuffling through the debris with Thomas, I found the blackened remains of the woman and child, fused together in a last hug. Near the back of the house, Thomas found two men—one without legs, and the other without a head—burned beyond identification. One of the corpses clutched an SS issue knife, so we decided they were the guys we wanted and moved on to the next, and the next, and the next, killing whenever necessary, though the war was over.

I became callous to it, the killing of innocents, I mean. It felt like it was getting easier. I buried the shame for the child and her mother and the killing of my men. I wanted to go home, but moved along like a mechanical piece of equipment, turned on and running until turned off. Finally, the action ended for us, and they sent us back to Paris.

Renée had moved out of her old apartment, so I filled my time with drinking, gambling, and French women who were trying to land an American husband. Waiting to get shipped home, Thomas and I made good money on the card table, which got us even more attention from the women.

Then one night, through a cloud of cognac and wine, I heard a laugh from a dark corner of the bar where we had been gambling. The laugh rang a bell in my heart—it was Maggie, I knew it—so I left Thomas to pick up our winnings and wove my way to the back of the room.

Seated as a small table was a pretty blonde. I stared at her and she smiled at me, giving me a tiny wave. It wasn't Maggie, but the smile and sarcastic wave brought back all the memories of her. The hurt started again, and though I realized it had never really left me, it was more intense now. I couldn't smile back at the lady and I think I frightened her with my stare, because the English soldier she was with got up and asked if I had a problem.

"No, no problem. I thought she was someone else."

"Well mate, there's plenty to go around. Forget the one you lost; it isn't healthy dwelling."

"Yeah, sorry."

The post-war world had changed for me—the hurt drained the color from life, and nothing I did eased my pain. It wasn't until I ran into Renée near a restaurant we had both enjoyed that I began to get some relief. She had moved to a new apartment near the Seine which had the same simple elegance as Renée herself. Although the pain for Maggie continued, Renée became my safe haven, and I couldn't imagine being with anyone else.

I proposed to her near the river in late June, with the sun beating down on my neck and the sounds from the Seine floating up to us. When she said yes, her eyes were soft and her hug was warm. I didn't know if I loved her, but I wanted to. She filled some of the holes left by Maggie, and I promised myself that I would do whatever it took to make her happy.

Several days later, we received orders to ship back to the States. The debriefing and discharge would take place in New York, and Renée would join me in July. The war was over even for me now, and I was going to see my mom with my new wife. I felt I had lived a lifetime in a few years, but I knew instinctively there was more to come, more than I really wanted. I felt an unseen energy that frightened and excited me.

## MAGGIE

I pulled my sports car to a stop between the vegetable and fruit carts in front of our hotel. I got out of the car, smiled, and threw my arms in the air as if encompassing all of Paris. I loved Paris—its look, smells, and bright sun. I was wearing George's bagging soccer shorts, and I loved them, too. He leaned against the car and opened his arms to me, watching my excitement

Wrapping my arms around him, I sighed, "It's so beautiful."

We took in the sights, walking hand-in-hand like young lovers, stopping to gaze at the sights and the colorful people who were immeasurably happy that the war was finished. We lost ourselves in the joy, and kissed in front of the Notre Dame and the Champs Élysées as though the city were ours.

We strolled to the Seine with a picnic lunch of cheese, fruit, and wine. Settling on a grassy spot, I couldn't think to ask for anything more in life. I leaned over to kiss George and caught sight of a soldier holding hands with a woman. I paused mid-lean—it was Johnny. George followed my eyes.

"You know him?"

I shook my head. "No, I thought I did. But no. He's someone else." I pressed my lips against George's cheek, but the romance was gone for the day. I felt faint, and my stomach soured.

I did my best to exchange the passion of the past for the beauty of the present as we filled our mornings with work. I noticed at times that George was drifting from his work, his typing paused and his gaze turned toward the window. I didn't know what he was thinking, but it didn't matter much. After seeing Johnny again, the relationship between George and I was drifting. I thought only of work, and fervently cranked out stories for both the *Herald* and *Mademoiselle.*

A week after seeing Johnny beside the Seine, George and I were in a small, quaint restaurant in the Latin Quarter. It was perfect for lovers, run by a French family who had helped George escape from behind enemy lines. I couldn't help but think of the little café Johnny took me when we were in Paris. It was late and the place empty, but we enjoyed the peace.

After finishing our meals, we decided to have some fine cognac. The warmth of the brandy made me feel contemplative, and I began staring at George. He reached across the table to touch my hand, a questioning look on his face.

I ran my thumb over the back of his hand. "Did you ever write something that wasn't true?"

George remained silent—he knew better than to answer.

"I mean, not lies exactly. Maybe more like camouflaging the circumstances, or using them in slightly different way."

He answered cautiously. "Do you mean lies or metaphor?"

I sipped my cognac to gain a little time to think, then said, "Untruths, or maybe omissions is a better word."

"You're gonna have to give me more, doll."

I chose my words carefully, "We're you ever told not to write about something?"

George lightened up—he knew where I was leading him. "By my editors?"

I took another sip of cognac for courage, then swallowed hard. "No, I mean by the military."

George's answer was quick. "No, and if they did, I wouldn't listen."

I wished I hadn't started the conversation.

153

George leaned forward, journalist to the bone. "You mean your great country suppressed one of your stories?"

I held up a warning finger, "I didn't say that."

George raised his eyebrows and didn't speak, forcing me to continue. "Suppose something very sensitive at the time required, you know, tact?"

"Tact or censored?"

I had to think on that. "Is censoring wrong during war?"

"Censoring is wrong anytime."

"What if your career is on the line?"

"You Americans are always ready to put career ahead of integrity," he said harshly.

Pulling my hand away from George's, I felt hurt and angry. "Maybe that's because we find that success is the best way to help the world out of its many messes."

"Right, right, America the Savior."

"We won the war for you, didn't we?"

He didn't like that. Our walk home was silent and tense—it was our first real fight, and we were both mad. We got back to the hotel and into the large four-post bed and slept, tired from the day.

I woke in the dark and rolled onto my side, facing George. He was covered by a sheet and dimly lit by the moonlight that poured in through the open window. He was staring at the ceiling and didn't acknowledge me.

"I want to stay here forever," I said, fingering the cotton sheet.

He didn't answer, so I reached out and ran my fingertips over his bare shoulder.

"Whattaya think we get married and live in Paris for a while? Then we can go on safari in Africa or something." I don't know why I said it or even if I meant it. Maybe it was just a test.

George still didn't answer. I tapped him with my index finger. "You okay, honey?"

George nodded then took a deep breath. "I've been thinking that maybe I want to get out of the paper business. Write a novel instead."

I scooted closer to him, laying my head on his shoulder. "That's a great idea. Paris is such a wonderful place to write."

He didn't move to hold me when he said, "I was thinking of writing it back home."

I pulled back slightly, unsure of where he was going with this.

"I haven't been back in a long while, and I'd like to see it."

I thought about this a minute. I didn't know if he was including me in these plans, or what I'd do with myself in rural England.

"There's not much news for me to write there, George."

"No, that's certainly right."

I rolled onto my back, sunk into thoughts of the future. I wanted to hold him to me, to hold on to Paris, but on some level I knew it was already over.

The next day broke warm and clear, the summer sky a brilliant blue. George and I decided to stroll the day away, to think and talk about the day before. We walked down Rue Mattin, lost in our separate thoughts.

Our short, intense love affair was drawing to a close, and we both knew it. We kept our distance from one another, sharing terse snippets of conversation and brief moments of physical contact. I didn't want to speak, knowing what was coming, and I don't think he did either. We stopped at a rail overlooking the river, taking in the glory of Paris.

Finally I couldn't keep my inquisitiveness down any more, so I started to feel things out. We had been trying, and failing, to find a place to live in Paris, and I thought that was neutral territory. "It was a terrible flat."

"Ghastly. I don't think there's a good one left in the city with all these Americans."

I didn't like the condescending way he said 'Americans.' "Oh, something will turn up."

George turned towards me and took my hands in his. I knew what was coming. The second man I'd ever really cared about was going to ditch me. I wasn't ready to be alone between worlds; I wanted an anchor and I'd thought George and Paris would be perfect. I wanted to plug my ears and hum like a little girl, but I told myself to be tough.

"Maggie, I want to go back to England."

My throat constricted and I swallowed hard. "With or without me?"

He had to think about it, which made me furious. It was out of character for him—he always had a quick quip ready—but it gave me hope.

"If you wouldn't mind living in a small country village, then by all means, with you."

The dirty, rotten Brit. He knew good and well that I would be left sitting at home doing needlepoint and gossiping with the neighbors while my glorious husband penned the next great novel. I closed my eyes, regaining my composure, and then looked up at him through my eyelashes.

"George, honey, why don't you go on to your cozy little English village and write your novel, and when you're finished you can stick it up your royal ass." I yanked my hands from his and stalked away, making sure George had plenty to look at while he watched me walk away.

I expected to be sad, heartbroken really, but I was just angry. He was so selfish. I couldn't help but compare him to Johnny. I told myself he'd never compromise me like that, but then I remembered Dachau and realized he already had.

I was all set to be fed up with men entirely when it hit me: it wasn't them. It was me, my insatiable ambition. I wouldn't, maybe couldn't, let love interfere with my career, and I was beginning to dislike myself for it.

That afternoon I moved out of the hotel room I'd shared with George and went back to the Hotel Scribe with the other news people. The lobby was still bustling with correspondents, many of whom were passing around bottles of cognac and wine.

As evening drew on, I found myself in a straight-backed chair with my own bottle of sorrow, dimly lit by the flickering electricity and small kerosene lamps. I felt drunk, hell I was drunk.

I spotted Russell Hill walking to me from across the room. I knew I looked awful, but I didn't care.

Sitting down next to me he said, "Hey kid, I've been looking for you. You okay?"

"Men are pigs," I said, staring into the darkness of the room.

"Ah come on Maggie, that's not fair."

I shrugged my shoulders in response, passing him the cognac. He took a good pull from it, but when I reached for the bottle Russell wouldn't let me have it.

I slumped back in my chair and when I closed my eyes, my head spun. It was good he didn't give the bottle back. "I got back a few weeks ago and was staying with George in a place on the other bank." I rubbed my eyes with my knuckles and whispered, "He left for England."

"George?"

"Yeah. I thought maybe we had something."

Russell looked a little awkward, then he leaned forward and patted my hand. "Maggie, what matters is your work. You know that."

I nodded vigorously and grasped his hand. "I know that, but it's convincing the men in my life that's the trouble."

"Your work is more important than any man who is threatened by it." He pulled his hand from my grasp and wiped his palm on his thigh. "I got news," he said.

"I like news."

"I was just assigned Bureau Chief for Berlin."

I rolled my eyes—this was supposed to cheer me up? "That's great. I'm happy for you."

Russell handed me the bottle, saying, "And you're coming with me."

I narrowed my eyes at him, not trusting my own ears. I waggled my finger at him. "You better not be messing with me."

"It's already cleared with home office. You're my assistant."

I jumped right on Russell's lap, knocking the bottle to the floor. "Ooooohh, you darling man!" I grabbed his chin and laid a kiss on his lips. If he kissed me back, I never felt it. I was going to Berlin.

\*\*\*

Berlin had been ravaged by bombs and artillery fire, like many of the great European cities. But with one big difference: the soldiers. There were four main groups walking the Berlin streets: the Americans in their jubilance of victory, the English in their proper gait, the French in their secretive style, and the Russians proud in their new power. The four super powers vying for attention in the defeated city created a sense of danger blowing in the wind.

Exploring the Russian zone, I could see the first signs of domination in the suppression of the press. It gave me a premonition that something terrible was coming—there were things we weren't allowed to write about, and the rumor of a newspaper reporter in the Russian sector brought raised eyebrows and dark looks.

It was censorship, to be sure, but I couldn't help wondering how much experience I already had with this from my own country. Though it scared me, I traveled to the sector several times trying to get a sense of what the people were experiencing. On every side I found faces of fear and walls of silence. It intrigued me, and I wanted to dig for more, but the story of the century was unfolding only a few miles away.

In a Nuremberg courtroom the Nazi war criminals—
Ribbentrop, Keitel, Goering and the others—sat at their defense
table. The room was jammed with reporters, soldiers, and
dignitaries from all over the world, and seeing these men, stoic and
at their ease, was bizarre after my experiences at the camps. I didn't
understand how they could sit there with such cold, faceless
dispositions. Yet sit they did, and listened as their crimes were
enumerated in several languages.

I sat in the press box of the International Military Tribunal with
other reporters only a few paces from the criminals. Images of the
death train and the ovens clicked through my mind when Goering
began his testimony. And with the ghastly images came the
sequence of events dealing with Johnny. I didn't want to think of
him in the same context as these men, but it kept flashing through
to me. I kept shaking my head to clear away the vision of Johnny
standing in front of the dead Germans at the wall, and told myself
it wasn't true.

It wasn't until Goering spoke that I fully realized the difference
between these men and Johnny. Their prideful arrogance and
unscrupulous abuse of humanity overshadowed the events at the
wall. And through his words, I saw suddenly and vividly that
whatever Johnny did at the death camp was precipitated by the evil
created by these men in front of me. I knew clearly that he had
acted and reacted with moral integrity.

To this day, the rationalizations of the Nazi murderers mystifies
me. Although the cool, detached argument of Hermann Goering
made me sick, his demeanor during the argument commanded a
fearful respect. He stood proudly when his name was called, and
his defense captivated me. Every pen in the room was stilled as he
spoke.

His cadence was even, almost otherworldly, and his words were
deliberate. He quoted Churchill when he said, "In the struggle for
life and death, there is no legality." He spoke tersely of a Germany
left crippled by the sanctions of World War I and the hope of

raising his country to relative prosperity. He rationalized his deeds with an air of superiority and a voice steeped in self-righteousness, and with every word I understood more that Johnny had been a victim of this man's wickedness. I was filled with a desire to find Johnny and apologize for misjudging him, but I continued to listen.

Even the presiding judge, Associate Justice Robert H. Jackson, seemed to suppressing rage as Goering continued.

"I have already told you that I did not want war. But I have always believed in the proverb, 'He who has a strong sword has peace.'" Goering clasped his hands and shifted his weight.

"Do you still believe that?" Jackson asked.

"When I see the international complications that exist in the world today, I am surer than ever of that opinion."

I could tell that Jackson wanted to go for his throat, but only shook his head in disgust and disbelief. His face echoed the sentiments that most felt throughout the courtroom. The Court and history proved the men were war criminals, but I wanted more. I thirsted to know what made these men turn to genocide, and I couldn't shake the idea that war itself was the criminal. The longer it raged, the more the veil spread. Realizing what I had seen in Berlin, I knew the war had not ended but rather mushrooming its way east.

***

Just after the trials, I arrived in Poland for my next assignment. My contacts suggested staying at the Hotel Palonia, an old, elegant building that was beginning to show its wear from the cold and poverty. The cold in Warsaw crept under the skin and pressed its fingers into the bones. The snow, piled and crusted on the sides of the streets, stood as sentinels against the lamps, blackened by the car exhaust and wood stove smoke that blanketed the area.

When I stepped from the car, I hugged myself and jumped up and down to encourage my circulation and buried my face in the collar of my fur coat. The vacant lobby of the hotel was moderately warmer, but I kept my hat and coat on. The brown light buzzed overhead, and I felt like I was at the bottom of a beer bottle. The desk clerk, a hard looking young man with vacant eyes, didn't move or acknowledge my presence, so I pulled off my hat to show my hair. Still he wasn't fazed, so I unbuttoned my coat and walked slowly to the desk. I saw a thin, evil smile flicker across his face.

"English?"

He shrugged. "Some, not good."

"Room?"

He shrugged his head no.

"The American Embassy referred me."

I wasn't even sure he understood me, so I leaned across the desk to get closer to his face. Finally, he noticed.

"I can sleep anywhere." I winked at him and, even if he didn't understand my words, my meaning seemed to be universal. He straightened and raised his chin, trying to look superior and prudish. I almost laughed out loud.

"Your car?"

I wanted nothing more than to grab this punk by the collar and shake him, but I chose a different tack. Hunching down, I pulled my coat up and moaned piteously. "It's so cold."

He softened. "Madam, we have no rooms. I can maybe make space here, in the lobby."

I looked around the lobby and wrinkled my nose. I had tried the straightforward approach, the sexy approach, and the pitiful woman traveling alone approach. I was wracking my brain for another angle when a man came down the stairs and entered the lobby. He wore a black cashmere coat, open, and his hair gray and full.

"Excuse me, my name is Stefan Morawski, I've caught the tail end of your conversation."

"Marguerite Hogan. Yes, I need a room. I was sent by the Embassy." I offered my hand and he took it delicately.

Dropping my hand and turning to the clerk he said, "Sir, two aides have just left and will be gone for several days. Give Miss Hogan their room."

The petulant young man wrinkled his nose but obeyed, shuffling through some of the room boxes. He turned back and forced a smile. "Room four-oh-three is vacant for four days. Miss Hogan can have this room."

Instead of thanking the clerk, I turned to Stefan. His face crinkled at the eyes as he smiled broadly at me. I thanked him with a nod and a lingering gaze—I felt the flicker of magic created when a couple connects, and it made me think of Johnny. I quickly cleared my head, then tossed Stefan one more reckless smile as I went up the stairs to my room.

The room was gloomy and bare, bathed in the same weird brown glow as the lobby. I put my typewriter on the narrow table under the bare window, and thought of the gentleman in the lobby as I started writing.

Shadows darted outside the window, finally breaking my concentration. I leaned over my typewriter, closer to the window, to see what was creating the distraction.

Rats, the biggest I've ever seen. I tapped on the window, hoping to shoo them away, but they ignored me and continued their hurried journeys. There was nothing I could do, so I resigned myself to the fact they were going to be my roommates. I sat back in my chair and had just started typing again when I noticed that one of the rats had crawled onto the windowpane and was staring into the room. First it startled me, but he kind of reminded me of someone. "Ah, I see Herr Hermann Goering has come to watch me."

The following day, Stefan stopped by the hotel to ask me to go for coffee. He took me to a small, one-room café which turned out to be a regular gathering place for journalists in the area. The air was thick with cigarette smoke and the only light was filtering through the ice-caked front windows. Despite the dreary atmosphere, everyone was in high spirits, drinking vodka and eating smoked salmon and mushrooms sautéed in butter and garlic. Thoughtfully, Stefan had arranged a translator to help me with interviews, and we found her quickly, seated alone near the back of the café.

She rose and shook my hand, "I am Anna." She had a carrying voice that belied her size. Wrapped in a blue ski jacket, with a fresh flush on her cheeks, she looked like she should be in class somewhere, not pouring out glasses of vodka.

Stefan and I sat, and we each exchanged brief outlines of our recent pasts. I was surprised to find out that Stephan was actually from the United States and seemingly a true Polish patriot.

"So I figured I owed it to my old country and left America to come back," Stephan said with an air of dignity. The more he talked, the more I saw his aristocratic blood in his air of superiority. His words stopped our brief introductions and he continued to wax idealistic about Russia and Poland coexisting in peace. What I had seen and heard so far made that seem unrealistic to me—I could feel an atmosphere of terror lingering like the ether after a lightning strike. It was difficult to explain because it was new, but it was there and it was frightful.

"But you can't believe the Russians will allow Poland to choose their own government." The Russians were riding high from the victory of World War II, and they were too belligerent.

"But I do. This country will evolve into a socialistic democracy." I could see his faith in his smooth brow, and his tone was as earnest as a dreaming child.

Anna swallowed the shot of vodka she'd nursed since we began talking, then poured another. "That's shit of the cow talk."

Anna used American expressions to exaggerate her points, but she generally used the wrong words so I corrected her. "You mean bullshit."

She shrugged.

"Everyone is allowed here, even American bankers," Stephan said.

"But the elections are rigged by the Russians and they use terror for implementation." I knew it was true, and so did he.

"That is not so."

"It is so. I've seen it and heard it. They are pigs, Russian swine!" The vodka was getting to Anna, and her carrying tone carried danger.

I pressed a finger to my lips and shushed her, looking around to make sure no one was listening to our conversation. She rolled her eyes—either she was unafraid, or too stupid to care that she could be overheard.

"Ahhh. It's true what I say. They will get us all eventually."

I was beginning to see defeat in her eyes and the sound of uncaring.

Morawski took a sip of his vodka and said, "Time will prove me right."

I wanted to believe him, but I had seen too much already.

We talked and drank, and after a few hours our conversation grew louder and more heated, so we decided it was time to go. Separately, we found our ways out of the café and back to our rooms.

I typed my stories at night with the company of the rats. Amazingly, I was always able to discern Herr Goering from the others. They were like humans in that sense, each with their own peculiarities, their own looks. Although Goering was the only rat to paw at my windowpane, he had other distinguishing features as well. His eyes were set closer together and several whiskers were missing near a scar that ran the length of the face. His nose protruded farther than the others' and of course, his size indicated he was the leader. Watching him watching me, I couldn't help but wonder whether size and strength was the universal qualification for power.

\*\*\*

Whenever Anna and I traveled outside Warsaw, we attached an American flag to the radiator of my car. She rode in the passenger seat as we motored toward Krakow, where Anna had set up a meeting with a young Pole in the People's Peasant Party, adversaries to the Communists.

The medieval city was still charming, despite the evident remnants of war. The narrow streets were difficult to negotiate, so getting to a particular part of the city took time. I found the place I was looking for near the city's center—an old apartment building where the freedom fighter lived. Anna and I got out of the car and looked to see if anyone was watching before we hurried inside. We had to take more and more precautionary measures now that I had been labeled reactionary. Apparently, the government didn't appreciate my take on their failures to put an end to Communism.

The stairs to the second floor flat creaked under our footsteps. Anna knocked at the door and a young male voice responded in Polish. She told him who we were, but before he would open the door he made us promise not to use his name. Of course, we agreed, and it was a promise I wished I could keep. The one room apartment was very Spartan, equipped with a small gas-cooking stove, a table with three chairs, and a single cot. I was shocked to see the young man's face, his left eye closed to just a slit and cheeks swollen and raw. He moved slowly, gingerly from the pain, and his fingers crumpled as if they had been crushed. He motioned with his bad hand for us to sit.

"Thank you for coming." His voice was labored.

His gracious manners surprised me. I nodded to him, but was beginning to wonder if I should have come. I took out my pad and pencil slowly, knowing that by doing the story I would be putting this young man's life in jeopardy. Anna sat between us to translate.

"The story of my suffering will help our people who are dying at the hands of the Russians." He must have read my reluctant body language.

"Even if your name is not mentioned, they will know." I wanted him to tell us to leave, to kick us out and forget he'd ever heard my name, but he didn't.

"But it will buy me time. This is very precious in this country." He looked at me when he spoke, but his words were filtered through Anna's strong voice.

"The police did this to you?"

Anna sighed, and said, "He says, 'They took me at night and blindfolded me and put me in a room for many hours until I did not know if it were day or night.'"

I put aside all feelings of guilt and wrote his incredible story. If I hadn't experienced the horrors of Dachau and the arrogance of Nuremberg, I wouldn't have believed it. But now, knowing just how much damage one man could do to another, I listened and recorded with measured understanding.

Anna translated for me, her English a mixture of high and low grammar. "Then two men came and, without a sign, began smashing my face with something hard and long. I could feel my face bones breaking. When they finished, they took the blindfold away and this was difficult because the blood had stuck it to my skin, so they yanked it and as they did, it tore the flesh from me. I could not see, but then a light flashed on, through blurred vision I saw a desk and two chairs. They placed me in one chair and the bigger man stood behind me while the smaller man sat across. I remember his face. It was a face of a rat."

I stopped writing, momentarily had a vision of my window and Herr Goering, and then shook my head back to the present.

"The bigger man opened the desk drawer then placed my right hand in it. The rat-faced man nodded and the big man slammed the drawer shut, crushing my hand. I passed out then."

I stopped writing and gasped, more to myself than to the two people with me, "My God, what is this place?" I asked a few more questions, but I already had my story. I was going to tell the world what fear and terror was doing to these people. I wanted to let them know that in the midst of their peace, a silent war was progressing in Eastern Europe. There were no guns or bombs, but the fabric of these courageous people, people who had survived the Nazis, was being slowly worn away.

I wrote the story and filed it that night. Several days later, I met with Anna at the café. When I got there, Anna seemed already half in the bag and had more vodka waiting in front of her. I sat down and as soon as I did, she shot down another vodka.

"Have you heard anything? The story has been out for close to a week." I moved the bottle of vodka away from her.

"I've heard nothing. It does not matter, he did it for Poland. He knew the consequences." She was already drunk, her words slurred.

"I'm worried about him," I said.

Anna pulled the bottle back to her side of the table and poured herself another shot. "You worry too much. Say, this Stefan, you are sleeping with him?"

I cocked an eyebrow at her, surprised that she would ask me something like that, and didn't answer.

"He is a very handsome man," she added. She gave me a tight smile.

"Yes he is."

"And a good way to obtain certain information, huh?"

"Hey, that's low."

Anna didn't know that particular figure of speech, and rather than try to explain it, I tried a more forward approach. "I enjoy men for themselves. Any information I get is an extra benefit."

"As long as it is not the prime motive. Then you would be no better than the rest, like them."

I knew what she meant, but I didn't know if it was true or not. The information I got was used to help people, to tell them the

167

truth about events, not harm them. It helped formulate opinions and create understanding. It wasn't much of a distinction, but I knew there was a difference.

Just then, Stefan himself walked in, looking grave. Casting a cautious look around the café, he sat.

"The man you interviewed is gone."

The sentence was short, simple, and it pushed my stomach into my mouth. Anna looked down and then drank more vodka.

"Pigs," she spat.

I was speechless, overcome with guilt.

"They came and took him away a few hours ago." Stefan spoke quietly, but didn't hold anything back.

"Maybe—"

"They took everything. They made it like he never existed."

I sat back and looked to the ceiling, trying not to cry. "It's my fault. I did it."

"He did it, Maggie. He knew what would come of it." Anna's tone was anything but reverent.

"These are dangerous times, but things will get better," Stefan said.

"Bull." Anna was getting better at Americanisms all the time.

"Amen to that," I said. Things were getting much worse.

Stefan disappeared a few days later. Anna told me that she had heard that he'd married a pretty Polish woman and was studying Marxism.

After his disappearance, I continued to write. It was apparent now that the Russians were smothering the Poles with Bolshevism. The election was rigged and the Communist Party gained control. It was inevitable and just a matter of time until this new evil would eliminate the last few bastions of free Poland.

A few weeks later I was walking back to the Hotel Palonia through the frigidity, when I saw Stefan walking my way. His head was down, fighting the wind, and he didn't notice me until we were within touching distance. He sensed a body nearby and looked up, probably to avoid running into me, and recognition flashed across his face.

I waved slightly to him, but he ignored it. I had opened my mouth to speak to him, but as he neared he gave me a nearly imperceptible shake of his head. It was some kind of warning, and though I slowed and tried to meet his eyes, he walked past without any further sign of acknowledgement. I continued on my way, suddenly impervious to the cold, wanting desperately to turn and yell to him, but I chose to heed his silent warning and continued to the hotel.

A familiar despair—the same I had felt when the young man disappeared—began to crawl over my skin. I shook the snow from my coat and hat, and looked back to the door, hoping Stephan had followed me back to the hotel. But I knew he hadn't.

I looked around and saw that the lobby was empty except for the desk clerk, who saw me and turned from his mail. He'd decided to like me now, and had managed to find me a long term room after all.

"Ah, Miss Hogan. A call from your bureau to get in touch as quickly as possible."

I didn't want to be bothered, but whenever the bureau phoned it meant important business. "Can you ring them for me, please?"

"Certainly."

Feeling frustrated and confused, I plopped myself in one of the chairs near the fire, letting the heat warm my body as my thoughts whizzed along. I couldn't make sense of any of it—first Stefan walked by like he didn't know me, now a call from Berlin. Nothing seemed real except the cyclical nightmare of Poland, and I was becoming part of it.

"Miss Hogan, I have them."

Mechanically, I rose and took the phone. "Yes, Russell. No, I'm fine. What's up? No, I'm standing. It's been a long day, just tell me."

I was in no mood for games, but Russell's next words evaporated my fear and pumped me full of elation.

"Me? A woman? This is unbelievable. I never expected it. Okay, just let me say a few good-byes and I'm there. Oh, Russell, just what kind of pay does the Berlin Bureau Chief get?" I couldn't believe it, me Bureau Chief of Berlin. I was moving up in the world and what I had just learned would have tremendous value for my next assignment.

All that was left was to say goodbye to Anna, then I'd be leaving the country that, in a few short months, had managed to turn me into a silent, suspicious person. Now, with my new job waiting for me in Germany, my buoyancy was starting to return. I had phoned Anna earlier and she said she would come to the café right away, but she was already two hours late.

As I looked from my watch to the wall clock, worry and fear enveloped me. I poured a shot of vodka and took a sip. I knew something had happened, but I had to go, so I scribbled a note and handed it to the attendant, but I knew it would never get to her. I never saw Anna, or Stefan, again, but I was able to find out what happened to Anna.

Another correspondent who had known her found out and gave his account of what happened. It seemed a Russian soldier defected and told the story of how he and two other armed Russian soldiers accosted her. They had stopped her on the street, and she had challenged them with her look and stance. They didn't speak to her, but when she tried to pass them one of the soldiers stepped in front of her. The other two flanked her. Anna must have known she was in trouble, because she kneed the front soldier between the legs. He doubled over momentarily, and the other two were just able to grab Anna when she tried to run. This correspondent told me that she'd wrestled with them until one of the soldiers smashed the butt of his rifle into the side of her head. When Anna collapsed, the soldiers carried her into the alleyway nearby.

The Russian had told the correspondent all of the details, how the alley had been dark and littered with garbage, how Anna recovered enough that it took two of the soldiers to hold her while the other ripped open her jacket. When she spit in the soldier's face, he slapped her. Then raped her. Then the others did also.

Just before the last soldier finished, Anna slumped against the wall, pulled a knife from her blue jacket and stuck the long blade into his ribs. In the chaos that followed, she lashed out at the other two Russians and caught the leader in the throat. The other responded quickly, grabbing Anna's wrist and twisting until she dropped the knife. The soldier with the slash across his throat got up from his knees, grabbed his gun, and fired point blank. The Russian told the correspondent that they left her to die in the alley.

## JOHNNY

I couldn't look away from New York, rising from the ocean in a spectacle of gleaming metal. The rolling in my stomach had nothing to do with the motion of the ship—I was anxious and felt like an alien in my own country. I couldn't understand how a few months away could make me feel like I didn't belong anymore.

The debriefing took place in the same building where I had volunteered. I sat in the back of the room with Thomas and Bobby, listening while Crowley praised our courage and dedication to duty. Then he tried to make us hitch up for another tour. Several guys did but not me—I was done with the killing. Life in the mob taught me a long time ago that people got killed whether the bosses called it war or not. Bobby followed my lead, but Thomas didn't have anywhere to go or anyone to meet him when he got there, so he signed up for another round.

As I filed out with the rest, Crowley motioned for me to come over. I told the guys to wait for me, then followed him into his office. I figured he wanted to talk me into another tour, but I had thought about it on the way home and realized that the military was too rigid for me. Besides, Maggie was history now, so there was no need to chase her around the world anymore. Besides, I had Renée now, and I wanted to make a life with someone who put love before work.

Crowley sat at his desk and leaned back in his old chair. Though his body language was relaxed, his face was pinched and taut. He motioned me to sit. "No formalities, Johnny. You're a civilian now. I wish I could change that."

"Sorry, my mind is made up."

He nodded and turned his chair toward the window. Gazing out of the window he said, "Roosevelt passed a bill last year that allows veterans like you to go to college for free. The government picks up the tab. Fine man, Roosevelt. I wish he had been able to see the end of the war."

He looked back at me, then pulled a packet of papers from his desk drawer. He tossed the packet my way. "It's all right there. You've already been admitted to college in North Carolina. It's military in a sense. Teach you more along the same lines you learned in England. It's the best in the world and will probably get better." I wondered what that was supposed to mean. All I'd learned in England was how to kill, and that was all I was trying to get away from now. "What's it for?"

Crowley sneaked a thin smile. "Security for our great country." He let that weigh on me.

"We just won the war; who would threaten us now?"

Crowley's tone became patronizing. "Johnny, this country, any country will always be threatened by someone. It's man. He's a warring creature. He'll fight, even if he knows he can't win. He'll fight and die, and take as much of the enemy with him. You know that. You saw it."

He was right, I'd seen it in Europe and on the streets. "Tell me more."

"You'll be educated and trained, then placed in a job. At times, you'll be offered assignments which you will be free to accept or decline. You can bet that they'll be dangerous assignments, though." His words came out rapidly, as though he wanted to say it all in one breath.

A hired gun, I thought. "What's my end?" I felt sinful, evil as if I was betraying someone but I had no idea whom.

"Annuities like always. But these will be larger than you're accustomed to."

"Whew. Just like that, huh?"

"Just like that."

"North Carolina?"

"A proper Southern school. It's a fine military school."

"I want to think about it. Talk it over with my mother."

Crowley stood. "Very understandable. I'd want it no other way. One other thing. There's a bonus when you sign. A good one."

"I'll let you know."

I met the other guys outside, and I quickly found out that I was the only one who had gotten the college deal. The fellas wanted to get a beer, but I had to see my mom. She was so close now, just a few blocks away, and I had to stop myself from running to the apartment building.

The door was locked, so I knocked and waited, listening impatiently to the shuffle of her feet coming to the door. I'll always remember that long moment, with my heart beating in my ears, then she opened the door and let out a small gasp. She waved her hands in front of her face, her eyes filling with tears as I stepped across the threshold and folded her into my arms.

"Ma, I'm home."

"Johnny, Johnny. Figlio mio." She wept into my shirt front, pulling back every few seconds to look at me. She touched my face as though she couldn't believe it was me.

I laughed, clutching her small frame and holding back my tears. Lost in the joy, I hardly noticed when she sat me down at the kitchen table and poured a glass of wine, thought about it, and poured a second for herself. We touched glasses and smiled.

My mom made my favorite for dinner—pork sauce with meatballs—and it was incredible. It always amazed me how she could concoct such delicious food in so short of a time. She was a miracle, and I felt comfortable for the first time since I'd shipped out. Watching her, I saw signs of how she'd aged in the few months we'd been apart. Her skin hung loose off her jaw and her eyes were sunk deeper under her brows. They were vacant again, like they had been after my dad died, and I couldn't help but feel that I was partly to blame. I made her sit and eat with me or she would have fussed through the meal—getting me things, asking if I needed anything else. I just wanted to sit and talk with her.

"You have a girlfriend, Johnny?"

"Yeah Ma, a French girl."

"Ah that's nice. Perche French, they have much emotion?"

"No she's nice, Ma. You'll like her. She is coming to meet you."

"Johnny, no!" She laid her hand on my forearm, "Not to marry?"

I took a sip of my wine and looked at her out of the corner of my eyes, trying to anticipate her reaction. "Mmm hmm."

She pulled her hand back and pursed her mouth like she wanted to scold me. She was going to pretend French wasn't a good choice, but I could see by her changing expression, her mouth curving up slightly and her head tilted to the side, that she was happy for me. "Ah, baccala America, baccala the war."

"You'll like her, Ma, I promise."

"We will see, Johnny, we will see."

"Any news from the guys?"

She turned her eyes away and returned to her plate of pasta. "Too much trouble, Johnny. It was good you went to war."

"What happened?"

"Fighting here, just like there. Tommy dead. Killed by guns."

"No." I rested my forehand in my palm, my face flushed with guilt. I had betrayed my buddy, my partner, and I couldn't help but wonder if Tommy would still be alive now if I hadn't left. I thought back to the time we cured Charlie, and I got the wine for Maggie's dinner. Maggie again. Jeez Tommy's dead and I'm thinking about Maggie.

"His mother is dying from the grief."

"Damn."

"Stay away from them, Johnny. They no good."

"I know, Ma. I'm gonna go to school, maybe."

She put her hands on either side of my face. "School, my baby? Your father would be so proud. A doctor."

"No, not a doctor, maybe a teacher. We'll see."

"Bravo, Johnny." She got up and wrapped her arms around my head, squeezing my face, then made some espresso.

It felt good, seeing mom and having her cooking. We chatted about the neighborhood, who had babies, and who else had died. I helped with the dishes, then told her I was going to see my friends. She looked tired and didn't put up a fuss, just kissed my forehead and patted my cheek. She stopped in the doorway to her room and smiled at me and, for a moment, I saw her youthful beauty again. I was sure glad to be home.

Walking into Jack's was like walking into a film reel of the past. Nothing had changed, even where the guys sat, except for Tommy's absence. They saw me quick. It was their job to know who came and went without looking up or giving notice.

"Johnny!" Louie was the first to jump and come to me. The rest followed. "Give the war hero a drink. No, drinks for everyone. We're celebrating." It seemed like Louie was in charge and the wad of bills he pulled from his trousers made it clear. "Get over here!"

By the time I had finished shaking hands all around, a scotch was ready for me. I settled into the vacant place, Tommy's old place, next to Louie and everyone starting talking at once. Questions about the war and what happened, why I hadn't gotten out of it flew past me.

"Quiet," Louie shouted and silence dropped on cue—they followed his directions like he was the director of a movie.

"You heard about Tommy?"

"Yeah, my mom told me."

"Irish. They got him. Had a small war after you left. Nothing like you seen, that's for sure, but a war just the same. They lost more than us. Tommy got it and a few new guys, young ones in their teens."

"How?"

"The guy you beat up was connected to someone. It was all revenge, but we made peace."

Being separated by an ocean didn't matter: I'd still caused the death of another one of my men. I took a long swig from my glass and Louie noticed.

"Easy there. It wasn't your fault, Johnny."

"I started it. It was my fault, and I wasn't here to help. Maybe if I—"

"No, no, no. Don't think that way. You been to war, you know how it is. It's the same. We have enemies, the enemies have enemies, and they're us. People get killed, it's simple math. Besides, Tommy got careless."

It didn't make me feel any better. I motioned for another drink and Louie paid again, ignoring my attempts. "How?"

"He showed up at the wrong place alone. An ambush. Didn't tell anybody. They got him good. Machine-gunned. Never knew what hit him."

The urge to kill the bastards that did it flashed through me. "Who?"

"The Irish. I told you. Anyway, I took 'em out personally. There were four of 'em. I got 'em all. The big guy made me captain."

"Well congratulations, I guess."

176

He smiled and ran his hand over his greased hair. "Yeah. Speakin' o' the boss, he's gonna wanna see you. Put you back to work. Lucky's been deported ya know."

My mind was elsewhere—on college, on my mom, and on Maggie for some reason. Maybe it was the bar or Tommy or both. "No, I didn't know."

"Yeah, government wouldn't let him stay. They yanked him from prison for his help on the docks. Don't matter, he's still runnin' things."

"Yeah, I'm sure."

"So whattaya say?"

"What?"

"Meetin' with the boss."

"Jeez Louie, I don't know. I might not be staying."

"Whattaya mean? This is your home. We're your family."

I wasn't in the mood. I was getting tired and the booze hit me fast, making it hard to think clearly. I knew these guys well enough to know that I didn't want to say the wrong thing. "I might go to school."

Louie almost choked. Then he whooshed a huge laugh. "Hey guys, get this. Johnny here is going to go to school be a doctor or somethin'."

"Yeah, right."

"School? War teaches you to be soft?"

"He's foolin' ya, Louie," someone yelled from the corner.

I stood up and my head rushed.

"Where you think you're goin'?" Louie grabbed my arm. I looked down at his hand, then into his eyes, and he released me.

I sat back down. "I'm not right yet. I want to go home."

Louie nodded his head. I never realized before, but it was large and the gray hair made it seem bigger. His stomach had grown and hung over his belt—he was a big man now. "I understand. But don't be stupid. You got some responsibilities here. You left quick and people didn't like it. Capisce?"

I sort of understood, but nothing was setting right with me or making sense. "I got drafted."

"Bull. We found out. I don't care you went. Ya know, serve your country and stuff. But don't lie to me, Johnny. We got eyes everywhere, remember that."

He was right. I could have been a world away, but to these guys everything and everybody was right next door. I knew that; I was one of them.

"I helped you when the talk turned to the wrong side for you." Louie was trying to make his tone seem light, but his heavy hand landed on the bar with surprising force. His meaning was clear: I owed him. And owing Louie meant that everyone associated with me owed him. I didn't like it—I didn't want to owe anything to anyone, but especially not these guys.

"Capisce?"

"Capito."

"Good. Tomorrow we meet Don Vincenzo. Eight o'clock, no?"

I nodded. "Yeah, okay."

"Good. Now go, get some sleep. Rest up and be sharp for him."

I rose and after Louie shot a warning look around the bar, no one tried to stop me. As I walked out, I heard Louie call after me, "And tell your sweet mother I give her my best."

I hated when they said that.

Eight o'clock came around too fast. A restless night of sleep and a full day of errands with my mom had left me groggy and, before I knew what I was going to say, I found myself seated at Don Vincenzo's desk.

He was dressed in a dark silk suit and tie. He looked like could have been a doctor except for the *malocchio* that made him look in two directions at the same time. I couldn't help but wonder how he could aim a gun with an eye like that. He was a big man, broad shouldered with thick arms and wrists. He gained his reputation for meanness by beating several people who betrayed him to death. He killed maybe ten or twelve people, and most everyone in the neighborhood feared him more than the devil.

Louie sat behind me, which I didn't like but couldn't do anything about, so I kept my antenna up. I didn't have a gun—I didn't think I'd need one—but Louie's position made me wish I was armed. If they wanted me out, it would be the classic pop in the back of the head. I had to remind myself that I didn't do these guys bad harm. I showed a little disrespect by leaving, but it wasn't a capital crime. Even though I didn't think so, I kept alert.

I had to kiss Don Vincenzo's ring before sitting to pay my respects to him and his position. It made me feel like an idiot. I didn't respect anyone anymore, except for my mom, but I did what I had to do.

"Johnny, you did good in the war. I am proud."

"Thank you, Don Vincenzo."

"Two silver crosses, a bronze star, and a distinguished service cross, eh?"

At first I couldn't believe he knew all of that, then I remembered who I was talking to. "Well, they gave out a lot of medals."

"You're too modest. I like that in a man. Your mother, she is good, no?"

There it was again: using respect to instill fear. "She's fine, thank you. She's glad I'm back."

Vincenzo laughed and his whole head shook. "Aren't we all, aren't we all? Louie, get us some brandy."

That was a good sign. Nothing was going to happen—it was strictly talking tonight. Louie opened the handsome cherry wood liquor cabinet, took out a bottle, poured three glasses, and handed ours to us. Vincenzo raised his and we did the same. "Salute to the safe return of Johnny, the war hero."

"Salute," Louie echoed.

"Salute." The liquor was good, warming my throat and stomach.

179

"So now you are home, what are your plans?"

Here it was, right to the point. "I think I'm going to go to school."

He didn't seem fazed by my answer—I guessed Louie had already told him. "I see."

He used the silence, his unnerving stare and his tapping fingers, to create uneasiness. I knew the game though, and waited him out. "Johnny, you have a place here with us. A good place. You are brave and intelligent. You can do powerful things with me, with us."

"With all due respect, sir, I know that and I would like nothing more than to be part of everything again. But my mom, it would kill her. She wants me to continue with school. I want to do that for her." I hoped the dutiful son act would work.

"Does she know?"

"Sir?"

"Does she know what you do for the government?"

I should have known that he would know, but I didn't like it. "You mean for the Army?"

"Johnny, don't try to be clever. I know what you do, where you will go, what you will become. Is killing for the government any different than killing for me?"

Oh, wow. Man-o-man. I hadn't thought of it like that. How did he know?

"Have you already forgotten that we know how to get information? Johnny, you see, already the government has clouded your brain. I know where you were trained and where you will be going to be trained more. School? Yes, military school to make you their assassin. Does your mother know this?"

"No, sir. No, she doesn't."

"I didn't think so. Nor will she. It is our secret, eh?"

"Thank you sir."

He pointed his finger at me and looked into me with his evil eye. "What you did was wrong. Leaving after beginning a war. If it weren't for Louie here, things would be different, capisce?"

"Si, capsico."

"I'm not going to stop you, Johnny. But if you go, you must understand you go without my protection. If someone wants you for past affairs, do not come to me. Your mother also. You are both alone. Your freedom to work for them is my gift to you. But no protection and don't try to work against us. That would not be good, for you or your mother, eh?"

He was letting me off. He was awful—the threats weren't even subtle anymore—but he was letting me go. I rose and nodded.

"I will not work against you, Don Vincenzo. I will stay clear and I will watch out for my mother and myself. I thank you and my mother thanks you."

He smiled and made a generous gesture with his hand, as though I was being too kind. I couldn't tell if he was pleased or barely containing his anger. I hoped I would never find out.

"Louie, show Johnny out, then come back."

Louie stepped outside with me. "You're lucky, Johnny. Something's up for sure. He wouldn't do that for anybody. You be careful now."

"Thanks, Louie." He nodded and slipped back inside.

I needed a drink, so I went to a bar where no one knew me and drank until the early hours.

181

# PART IV
## New Fronts

### JOHNNY

My mom died quietly in the night a few days before I left for North Carolina, after we dined in an upscale restaurant on the West Side. She looked so frail across the table from me, her hands shaking as she held her utensils, and her eyes cautiously glancing around like she felt she didn't belong. We didn't really, but I wanted to celebrate everything, and I thought she'd enjoy one fine dining experience in her life. And we did. After calming her and reassuring her that no one would tell us to leave, she relaxed and we ate roasted duck, drank good wine, and laughed. Her happiness glowed. Her son home, the rackets now in the past, and school in the future. I saw a light in her eyes for the first time since my dad died.

"Your dad would be proud of you, Johnny," she said with a soft smile, her voice wavering a little.

We took a cab home and I could see her excitement during the ride. Her grin widened with each passing block, and by the time we reached our place she looked and acted like someone who spent her lifetime riding in taxis.

In the apartment she turned to me, her cheeks flushed from the wine and the ride. "I knew you would turn out to be a good boy, Johnny. Now if we only can get you a wife."

"Mom, I told you Renée will be here soon. As soon as she gets clearance."

"Ah, we'll see."

I don't think she wanted me to marry Renée. That was fine—I knew she would change her mind once they met. But I couldn't deny that I had my own worries. The delay of getting her here confused me. I fixed everything for her before I left, and I figured it was a rather smooth process. I couldn't help but think that maybe it was Renée. Maybe she didn't want to come. But I would have expected her to write and explain, though. Maybe I just wasn't going to have any luck with women—first Maggie, now Renée.

Mom kissed me good night and thanked me for the wonderful evening. She smiled on her way to her bedroom, and I'll never forget the smile. It was warm and loving, a mother's smile that came from the heart, satisfied her child was happy and his life was comfortable. She hummed a tune, and I thought she must be thinking of Dad.

She never woke from her sleep. After nine o'clock came around, I knew something was wrong. It was too quiet and though I anxiously waited to hear some movement come from her room, the apartment was completely still. The morning whistles and traffic were distant, like they were unable to penetrate the closed windows, but sunlight filtered through the curtains, dust dancing silently in its path from window to floor.

I stood up from the kitchen table and walked into the light, listening. Its warmth reminded me of the sun at the bridge where Stanley died. I winced and my hands clinched robotically when an icy surge raced through my body. I looked towards the bedroom door and just knew. It seemed like the short walk from the ray of sun to the bedroom took hours. I opened the door without knocking. I knew no one would answer.

Mom lay on her back, with morning sun from the small rectangular window splashing on her face. Her arms were relaxed at her side, and her smile was smaller but still there, frozen forever. I stood, looking at her for a few moments. For the first time I realized how beautiful she was: the cut of her cheeks, the curve of her lips. I made my way to her and felt her hand. It was already cold and I swore under my breath but unsure to whom, maybe to myself. Maybe just to the room. That's all that was there: the room, my mother's body, and me. I kissed her forehead.

"Say hello to Dad for me. Tell him I miss him and you know I miss you already. Goodbye, Mom." I hoped she could hear me, but I just didn't know anymore.

The letter from Renée came three days after I'd buried my mother. Her father died and she could not leave her mother. I felt angry at first, convinced that she was lying and inventing wild versions of what had really happened. I didn't want to believe the simple reality, a truth that I should have been able to understand.

I drank, visiting bars away from neighborhood, away from anyone I knew, but there weren't any answers in the bottom of all those bottles. I came close to phoning Louie and finding comfort with old friends, even thought of ditching school and returning to the reckless life. The mob was a family, anyway, and the life had its glories and benefits.

The craziness ended the morning of my binge. I woke next to a woman I didn't know and left without trying to find out. I stopped for coffee at a small diner and picked up the paper, not paying any particular attention to the stories until Maggie's by-line riveted my eyes to the bold type. I put my coffee down and just looked at her name, which rang like a bell in my mind.

It was like clean, rushing water, washing away everything but her: following her to the Trib building, the night at the bar, the dinner in her messy apartment, making love in Paris, even Dachau. The diner disappeared, and in the moment I knew that if Maggie

185

were close, we would be together. I brought the paper closer to me as if it would bring Maggie closer.

She reported fascinating stories from Berlin. She wrote about the Soviets, the struggle for land, and the Russians digging in, thrusting forward their chests and telling the world to take notice. They were standing toe-to-toe with the west. Maggie's words came off the paper and into me. It was like we were just talking, alone before bed or walking the Paris streets. I could almost smell her perfume and hear her laugh and get serious and then reckless in one breath of words.

I stopped reading and closed my eyes. God, I missed her. I didn't realize until now, but pangs of hurt crept inside me from somewhere. I began to suspect that the pain had always been there, no matter how I tried to stay angry with Maggie, or replace her with a less complicated woman. I didn't know if it was the loss of my mother or Renée's ultimate rejection, but I knew I wanted Maggie. I missed her so much that it made my muscles cramp, and I knew that I loved her.

I finished my coffee and folded the paper, tucked it under my arm, and went to the bus station to inquire about trips to North Carolina. Then I went home and started packing. The only way to get Maggie back now would be to show her that I was worthwhile, not just some reckless soldier or ex-street crook that crossed paths with her.

\*\*\*

I hustled doggedly, knowing I had enough time to enroll in the first semester of classes, so Colonel Crowley set up everything and registration went smoothly. I had no problems with the classes and was surprised at how easily things came to me. I breezed through three years, studying mostly, and gained enough credits to graduate early.

In my spare time, I read the papers. I had the Herald mailed to me, and I read every one of Maggie's articles. Some scared me; I worried about her being alone in Berlin while two world powers feinted, positioned, and pivoted themselves like two prizefighters for a confrontation that would be like none other.

A few weeks into my last year of school, I received word that Crowley wanted to meet me in an office at the school's administration building. I'll never forget the day, clear and bright, the sun low in the sky giving no warmth. Winters in North Carolina were cold, but nothing like I was used to in New York. There was no zip to it, no hurt. It chilled my face and made me walk quicker, but there was no need for gloves.

I felt good that day. The Herald had come early and I read Maggie's articles. They were nice ones, nothing to worry about. It sounded like she was having fun with the job and the writing, and just knowing she was happy made me smile. I didn't feel quite right about the coming meeting with Crowley, and questions filled my mind as I walked from my dorm to the administration building.

Crowley sat behind a desk in one of the dean's offices, and the first thing I noticed was that he wasn't wearing a uniform. I had never seen Crowley out of uniform and it threw me. He looked uncomfortable in the crewneck sweater that seemed to dig into his skin. He jumped up when I walked in and greeted me with a firm handshake.

"Good seeing you, Johnny," he said with a grin that looked sincere. "Sit, relax, this is informal." He made a gesture to his clothes as if to prove his words to bogus for a guy like him. It didn't matter that I wasn't working the streets anymore, the instincts didn't wither away. Informal maybe, but certainly serious business.

"I see you are a straight A student," he patted a folder on the desk. "Great work. I knew you had it in you, son."

"Thanks."

We both sat. "I'm not going to beat around the bush with you, Johnny."

He never did. I didn't even know if he knew how to mince words. "So, what did you want to see me about?"

He looked at me and nodded his head. "That's why I like you Johnny. You're direct. Someone who wants to know the score right off. Me too. I'm like that, too."

"Yes sir." I don't why I said that—it came out naturally. Crowley had that in him, an air that commanded a sir.

"I said no formality. You're okay, Johnny." He paused and rapped his knuckles on the desk. "Okay, here it is. You've been reading about Berlin?"

"Yes." Interest grew in me.

"Tough situation over there, Johnny. We need men there to help." He looked at me, waiting for me to comment on the statement. I just moved my hands in a questioning gesture.

He continued. "We need men to gather information, you know, behind-the-lines information."

There were no lines and he knew I knew that. "You want me to spy? You want me to become a spy?"

"Well, spy, that's a...a papers and a book term. No, we call them agents."

"Agents? Hmmm, I see. You want me to be an agent in Berlin?"

He nodded and peered unblinkingly into my eyes, yes.

"And what does an agent do?"

He tugged on the neck of his sweater and tossed me a friendly grin. "He gets information. The information we need is about bombs. Nuclear bombs like the ones we dropped in Japan."

Man-o-man, I felt like I got nailed with an unseen left hook. "I don't know, I don't know how—"

"We'll teach you. One job only. We drop you on their side and you meet someone with a little capsule with information on it called microfilm. Then all you have to do is get back to our side."

"Colonel, I don't know German, I don't know Russian and I look Italian. They'll spot me, arrest me, and put me against a firing squad or into a prison and that will be that. Oh, I've read about Berlin and it's cold there."

"You're good, Johnny. Intelligent." He pointed his finger at me, wagged it a bit. "That's right, but no need to speak any language. Your contact speaks English. After the drop and the rendezvous, you'll be transported back in a cargo truck headed for West Berlin. It's already been cleared by the Russians."

It didn't sound right—Russia wasn't letting anything in or out of East Berlin. "What kind of cargo?"

Crowley cleared his throat and scratched his nose. "Bodies. Some of our boys from the war unearthed last week. The Russians agreed to let us have the remains. They'll be coming in coffins and there's an extra that's empty. That'll be yours."

He shocked me, not by what he wanted me to do, but the way he said it. The words came from his mouth like it was a routine operation, something that happened every day. Great. I'd always wanted to be dropped from an airplane in enemy territory, pick up information, crawl into a casket, then get transported back to the free world. But there was the chance I could see Maggie. "How much?"

His grin widened—he knew me well enough to know that I wouldn't be asking if I wasn't going to do it. "One trip, ten grand and credits towards your degree—operational credits. You'll have your degree, be finished with school. Then, if you like, you can be on the government's payroll. But, I'm getting away from myself. First things first. Yes?"

He'd come to my mother's funeral and after paying his respects, shot me a look that said we'd be meeting again soon. Now here he was, knowing I had nowhere to go. Besides, my boredom with college life grew stronger every day, I could use the money, and I wanted to see Maggie. "Yes."

Crowley stood. "That's my Johnny." We shook hands.

Things happened fast after the handshake. Crowley had me flown to an Army base in Alabama, where we met briefly. I sensed tension in him, something I had never felt from him, and I didn't like it. He told me a gentleman would arrive soon and he would be left alone with me for a few minutes. He was a German scientist they had bought after the war, who was instrumental in building the V-2s that bombed and killed civilians in Allied cities. Now he worked for us. I guess he was still doing the same thing, building rockets to kill people, but Crowley painted him as a patriot—a brilliant rocket engineer that would get the United States into space. I don't think he believed it himself.

"He's a good man from what I know," Crowley said.

"Was he a Nazi?"

"No, yes, but he was forced to be."

"Ah, I see. He had no choice."

"From what I understand, his passion is building rockets, to help mankind ultimately."

How absurd, I thought. I knew Crowley didn't believe a word he was saying—his eyes had gone shifty, and he wouldn't look at me. This German guy, whoever he was, had killed our people, innocent civilians and our friends, but now it didn't matter. His worth to us erased his past. Now everybody who could help was an ally.

"So this information I'm after is for space rockets?"

Crowley squirmed and his eyes glanced to the side, and then came back to me. The truth came out. "No, Johnny. I'll tell you about the information, but I can't tell you who your contact is. Even I don't know that. The German will. That was the deal. If our guy isn't going to be compromised on the other side, the fewer people who know him, the better."

"So, I'll be getting what?"

"Information to make rockets go from continent to continent with huge payloads."

My lack of emotion surprised me. Maybe I just didn't understand the consequences. "I see."

Crowley let it go. Maybe he didn't get it, either. He rose and walked to me. "War is changing, Johnny. We're getting to a point where both sides wage it from control panels. It's becoming a game of nerves and mass destruction scenarios. People don't matter."

"They never did in war," I said this more to myself, but Crowley heard it and knew I was right.

"I'll get the man."

I sat and thought about the words. It was killing again, maybe not directly this time, but the information I would get would kill people thousands of miles away from any front. Big rockets, bombs like the ones used in Japan. The door opened and interrupted my thoughts.

There were no introductions. The sergeant who escorted him to the room gave a quick look around, saluted me, then left. The scientist stood passively, looking at me without emotion or discomfort, looking me up and down and trying to get my measure.

He didn't look like I'd expected. He was just beyond a medium build, with skin held tightly to his bones. His brown hair was thick and brushed back away from his face, making his forehead look larger than it was. His bushy eyebrows stood out starkly like lichen on a cliff.

"You are patriot for your country?" His German accent made his consonants sharp, but his voice was gentle.

I didn't know what he meant by that, and I didn't like the question. I decided to remain silent.

"Yes or no?"

He was trying to direct the conversation, much like the bosses in the streets. I could play the game. "Yes, a patriot of sorts, and you?"

"A patriot of course, why would I be here otherwise?"

"A patriot for what country?" I stifled a smile.

His lips quivered and his craggy brows drew together. "An honest man, no?"

"To myself."

We sat across from one another, and he folded his hands and placed them squarely in the middle.

"You come highly recommended, do you know the danger involved in this operation?"

"To myself yes, to the other no."

"That is fair."

"I play fair, most of the time."

"When don't you play fair?"

"When I see other people cheating."

"Then what do you do?"

"Depends how far in I am."

"Say you are in far."

"I cheat, too."

"Ahhh. Good. A realistic man."

"And you?"

"Practical, like yourself. To further my goal, I use what I must."

"And your allegiance?" I wanted to nail him and I did. He paused, looked at me and then turned his gaze to the ceiling. His hands unclenched and then folded again.

"History will no doubt form that opinion."

"For all of us, I guess."

"Yes, for all of us."

I let the silence hang, forcing him to meet my eyes. When he finally did, we knew the score and felt the power shift toward me.

"The man you will meet has a scar over his left eye and it runs to his cheek." He motioned the direction and the place with his index finger. "You are to say to him, 'Paxter sent me.' He will respond, 'Paxter is dead.' You will say, 'He has risen.' Then he will give you a small tube. Do not open it. Put it away and leave. Do not look back. The rest will be told by your operating command. Questions?"

Yeah, I had questions, a million, but I knew they wouldn't be answered. "No." He stood and offered his hand. I shook it.

"Good luck." His eyes showed nothing. He was tough to read.

"Thanks."

He turned and knocked on the door. The soldier opened it and he exited, leaving me alone with my thoughts of Berlin, my assignment and, of course, Maggie.


## MAGGIE

Measuring the first few weeks in Berlin, I found myself so elated, that rather than talk I paced the floor of my office with a huge grin spread across my face. My new assignment carried immense responsibility but had more intrigue and excitement than I could have imagined.

I rented a house, an elegant one-floor structure that had been inspired by Japanese design where all the rooms flowed from one to the other. Large glass doors in the two main opened to a terrace which overlooked a small lake lined with conifers and wild flowers. It was an area of Berlin that seemed untouched by the war, like it belonged anywhere but nestled into the center of the battle-worn city.

I learned soon that American money went a long way in present Germany, so I had the means to hire Katrina, a housekeeper and cook. I adored her. She had a Russian background that helped with many of my stories, and her expertise in quick haute cuisine for impromptu gatherings gave us quite a reputation. My house became the place to be after late nights of filing stories, thanks to her magic cooking. But maybe the best thing about her was that she knew how to keep things to herself.

Regardless of my title, my gender continued to impede my ability to get stories. Left with few other choices, I decided to use it to my advantage, throwing parties and getting friendly with the kind of men who could provide me with good information. Unfortunately, a diplomatic housekeeper wasn't enough to keep my reputation from growing behind my back. People had labeled me a whore when all I wanted were inroads into stories.

I had no choice but to evaluate myself and my men. Since my relationships with Johnny and George, no one was really important to me. Not in a romantic way, anyway. And I realized that the only man I'd ever been with who couldn't further my career was Johnny.

And as soon as I allowed him back into my thoughts, Johnny consumed them. My feelings for him had nothing to do with ambition; our relationship was never some clever ploy for information. It was love, true love, and it thrilled me until the memories of Dachau returned to shade my opinion of him. I don't know if I was relieved or not, but I dove back into my work and forgot about love and the gossip. My responsibility as bureau chief became my first priority.

Pouring back into my work couldn't have happened at a better time. I sensed something big was going to happen. It was the same anticipation I felt as a kid when I knew my birthday was coming. Everything in the city cried that some kind of action or event reverberated in the air like a squadron of B-29s on a bomb run hidden in the clouds.

My instincts were right: within the next few days the story of the Berlin Blockade broke.

I was sitting in my office, a comfortable space with a large oak desk and sturdy bookcase, when the phone rang. I'd just finished a piece on the new guided missiles and was feeling pretty good, with the afternoon sun filtering through the big window and warming my neck.

The call came from a stringer of mine, relaying information about the Russians and the initial stages of the blockade. According to him, General Lucius D. Clay refused to forcibly leave the city and had resolved not to retreat from the Russians. He played this new game of steel nerves and cold war masterfully and was instrumental in keeping the West Berlin intact.

"You don't say… When?" The stringer provided names that got the cogs of my brain clicking back to Poland and some dealing I had with Defense Department people, a guy name Thomas something and his superior, Hales.

According to the stringer, Major General William Hales was the man who had key information about the approaching history-making event. Getting the story meant getting near him.

After hanging up the phone and grabbing my jacket, I went to the house and, with the help of Katrina, arranged for a dinner party with Hales as my prime guest.

Twenty people attended the party, all dressed in elegant evening wear. The officers wore their dress uniforms, and the women— some wives of the officers and some Embassy staff—were elegant in long dresses. I felt beautiful in my low cut black dress, and I'd worn my hair in a high, tight twist. I liked it that way because I thought it made my eyes look bigger and bluer.

Excitement over the expected but unknown confrontation permeated the air, and questions and theories dangled from everyone's lips. Three young German men were pouring generous drinks, and after greeting several guests, I spotted Hales on his own by the terrace doors. I wove through the crush of people and waited until he spotted me a few feet away. I let him close the distance between us, feigning surprise.

"Are you having fun, Major?"

He smiled, gazing first into my eyes and then letting his look slip down. He was a handsome man, more than I hoped. His dark hair and broad shoulders moved with a confidence that I'd come to associate with powerful men. He was smiling ruefully as he pulled his eyes back to my face, and I knew that, whether he liked it or not, I interested him. He was right to be worried. After all, his job was to keep secrets, mine was to uncover them.

"What everyone has said about you is true." His tone was slick, and it was easy to see how he'd made a living out of choosing his words.

"Oh?"

"Your elegant home, your parties, and of course your radiant beauty."

I smiled modestly and took him by the arm. "Let me show you the terrace."

The June evening was comfortably cool, and the terrace overlooked the candlelit path down to the lake. As we stood in the peaceful beauty, I squeezed a little closer to him. He looked down at me, and I hoped the gentle breeze would catch the scent of my hair.

I turned up to him and said, "Not bad, huh?" I trained my gaze on his mouth, parting my lips invitingly.

At first he didn't move, but then he nudged me teasingly with his hip, trailing his hand over the small of my back. He sounded like he was choking when he said, "I'm losing control."

I knew it was my turn to tease, so I pulled away slightly. "I never met such a handsome hero." What began as an act, a practiced manipulation to get information, was beginning to feel real. He was so confident, so capable of matching me.

He smiled like he thought I was cute and ran his hand up my spine. "I'm not a hero yet. Not until we are able to feed Berlin."

His touch just then truly made it genuine. It was no longer a play, the intensity of the moment ratcheted the fervor, but my purpose tenaciously subdued my emotion. I pulled his hand from my back and traced a vein with my finger then slowly looked up at him. "I beg to differ. General Clay has advised me that your airlift plan is brilliant and cannot fail."

He sighed pulled his hand from mine and slid both softly up my arms and squeezed my shoulders gently. "Best laid plans and all that, dear."

I needed just a bit more, but my restraint trembled like my body. I craned my neck towards touching his cheek and whispered in his ear, "I'd love for you to show me more."

Katrina arrived at that moment and I wanted to kill her, but I found a way to use her intrusion as an advantage.

"Miss Hogan, dinner is very close to being served."

We both turned to her and I said, "Thank you Katrina. We'll be right in. And please make sure the major is seated next to me."

Katrina nodded and Hales allowed his arm to wrap around my shoulders when I turned back toward the lake. My plan called for either a little more information or a little sugar before supper, but the purring of an airplane's engine turned our attention skyward.

I played Major Hales slow, partly because I didn't want to fumble and lose my best source for the biggest story in years, but also because he roused something in me. His handsome looks, gentleman's air, and his intelligence added to his charm, and his power attracted me.

Several days after my party, we had dinner. He hesitated when I phoned—I thought for sure I was losing him—but I convinced him that dinner was going to be more pleasure than business. He was probably too sharp to really believe it but, like most men with other things on the brain, he headed into my lair. It turned out we enjoyed each other's company.

Katrina prepared a lovely meal and left us to our after dinner cognacs in the den. We sat close to each other on the couch, our bodies barely touching at the shoulders, elbows, and thighs. The warmth of the evening mingled with the heady wine, making me as eager to touch and taste him as he was me. I knew, I felt it—there was that certain magic in the air when two people feel natural together—but I couldn't lose my connection to the story. I went carefully ahead, balancing my ambitions with my passions, but I was too slow. Hales had my measure, and he came right at me.

"So before I lose control of myself with such a beautiful woman, what is it you want to know?"

I wasn't used to being on the receiving end of questions like that, so I floundered a few seconds before getting my bearings. "Wha—, uhhm, no. Well, you certainly don't pull punches. Aggressive nature I take it?"

"I was center on the West Point football team. I snapped the ball, and the first person I saw, I floored. That was my job. Still is."

"I see. Well, consider this woman floored."

"Hardly."

I liked him—his style and his rugged looks—so I let him continue. I already knew he was going to tell me as much as allowed, I might as well get out of his way.

"General Clay knew me through football, so my position with him gave me access. Then he liked my plan."

"Are you permitted to tell me the plan?"

"Only on one condition."

"Yes?"

"I get to kiss you when I'm finished."

I took advantage of the opening and kissed him first—a long, passionate one—and he responded quickly. Hales knew the game, I didn't have to hold out on him.

"Consider it a deposit," I said. "I wanted to start, so you know what you have waiting for you when you're finished." I ran my finger along his jawline.

He ran his fingers over my forehead and through my hair, telling me about the logistics of the airlift. It was beyond amazing. He had given General Clay a year's worth of exact numbers of planes, feet of aircraft runway material, drop information, and everything else they needed. When he finished we kissed as promised, and I allowed myself to swim with its tide.

On June 26 the lift began with seventy C 47 and C-57 aircraft carrying two hundred twenty tons of food and supplies a day to the East Berliners. It was food for two and a half million people—not enough, far short of the four thousand five hundred tons needed—but they didn't give up. Another airport was built in France, and an addition seventy-five Skymaster planes were acquired. It was an amazing sight and a deafening roar when the planes flew overhead. To me, all evidence of the plan carried a sense of superiority and a feeling of comfort: the man responsible for this humanitarian effort was my lover, and I was proud.

There were several blackout periods, which helped the aircraft on their daily flights, so I typed by candlelight. I listened to Mozart piano sonatas and let them drown out the clatter of the typer as well as the droning airplane engines.

I saw more of Bill. In fact, we became an item in military and press circles. That didn't bother me, but the fact that he was married with three kids did.

The marriage was suffering and, according to Bill, in its final stages. I didn't have a reason to disbelieve him, and as much as I hated the knowledge that he had a wife, I couldn't stand to be alone. I liked being attached to a man, a strong one like him. Sometimes I wondered if I was using him as a replacement for Johnny, but the thoughts confused and hurt me. I tried to live for the moment, like Johnny did, but he never seemed to be far from my head or heart. I craved Johnny's touch, but I had more to discover, more to claim, and I was as ambitious as ever, so I sunk back into my work.

Bill and I didn't just make love: we made adventure. I really didn't know everything about his intelligence business and didn't ask, although it took horses to hold back my curiosity. But I held fast and accompanied him on several information gathering raids. The trips had an element of espionage in them—for Bill, anyway. We would dress in old, worn clothes and mingle with the activists in the streets and squares. I used the information we got for my stories, and Bill used it to further his intelligence.

On one of our day raids, chaos and mayhem shattered our usually peaceful encounters. We were in the middle of a large crowd gathered at the Brandenburger Tor, the stone gate at what was once Berlin's main street. Though we couldn't have known it at the time, the wall separating West and East Berlin for years to come would soon stand in this area, a symbol of the Cold War era.

On this particular day, there was a crowd of Germans demonstrating against the Russians. Bill and I were amongst the crowd, dressed in our raid clothes—old ragged shirts and trousers—and had become squeezed into the center of the mass, which had taken on its own life, dragging us along with it.

Several West Germans began hurling rocks towards the Russians and, at that time, they controlled the West German Police. Then, an East German boy climbed up on the Tor, wrenched down the Russian flag, and threw it to the crowd. The Russians fired a volley of bullets over everyone's heads and, maybe inevitably, a riot ensued.

I lost my hold on Hales and the crowd pushed me in the other direction, making me fall to the cobblestones. I had no control, and I was trampled and dragged along until someone pulled me back to my feet. My hands and face were scraped and bleeding, and my trousers had been ripped to reveal several lacerations from broken glass and rough cobblestones. Back on my feet, I saw Russians with Tommy-guns firing into the crowd. Several Germans fell writhing to the ground. Instinctively, I ran with the crowd until a strong hand grabbed my arm. It was Bill, who pulled me to him and rescued me from the crowd and the bullets.

We had taken Bill's motorcycle to the square and he got us to it quickly. Turning me toward him by the shoulders, he kissed my bruised cheeks. "You okay, kid?"

I nodded, but actually, I felt awful. He helped me up onto the cycle, then drove us out away from the riot and toward a hospital.

They admitted me immediately. In addition to the cuts on my face and legs, a rash was developing on my arms that concerned the doctors, so in I went.

I was able to run the office from my bed, but things began piling up since I preferred doing the writing assignments myself. I didn't like delegating them to other reporters, but I finally had to resign to doing just that. Missing scoops made me anxious, and I vociferously read every bit of news about the airlift and the blockade I could. I read about the new espionage agents used by the East and the West and how some agents, used by both sides, were called double agents. This fascinated me, and I wondered what kind of man would do work like this. They would need nerves of steel.

I'll never forget the Sunday morning before I left the hospital. My rash had slowly disappeared and my energy neared its normal stage of overdrive. I walked as much as possible through the corridors and only lay in bed when I knew my body required sleep. That Sunday I had walked the corridors to the lobby and even ventured outside. The sun was warm, and it felt good to finally breathe fresh air instead of the stale, recycled hospital air. The breeze blew a clear, cool autumn scent which I drank in like a fine cognac. I needed to get back to the office, to my work, and get on with my life again. I was ready.

I walked back to my room and began leafing through a magazine, paying more attention to my view of the grounds than the glossy pages. I drifted a bit, then something caught my eye in the doorway—a shadow. It startled me at first, the rays of the sun silhouetting the person and obscuring his features. From the size, I could tell it was a man, and I thought for certain it was Bill. I was about to call his name when the shadow walked into the room and stood near the bed, out of the sun's rays. My stomach dropped into nowhere and my heart leaped to my mouth. I didn't know whether to scream or cry, and could only manage a hacking, "Oh," of surprise.

There, standing in my hospital room with a bouquet of red roses, stood Johnny in full uniform wearing lieutenant bars.

Neither of us spoke for a few interminable seconds, then he broke the silence.

"Hello, Maggie."

I wanted to cry, but I held back. I wanted to run to him, to hold him and kiss him, but I didn't know if I should or what would happen if I did. I knew then I loved him, but I didn't know why or even if I wanted to love him. But I did know I wanted him here in the room with me.

"Hi Johnny."

He moved closer and handed me the bouquet. I brushed back a tear, and I think he saw it.

"You okay, kid?"

I nodded, but I still wanted to cry. I must have been holding it all inside with my energy and worry. I gathered myself and took the flowers.

"Yeah Johnny, I'm fine. You?"

"Well, I'm well."

He looked wonderful: lean and hard, but slighter than Bill. His eyes were darker, deeper than I remembered, and he had this air about him that was new to me. He seemed to know everything that was going on around him, but his knowing smile was still soft and warm. Holding me at arm's length, the bouquet between us, he peered into my face and his gaze seemed to penetrate into my soul. It reminded me of the look he had at Dachau.

"You're in uniform and ranked," I said, trying to get a hold of myself.

"Yes."

I couldn't stop staring at his mouth. "Let me put these in water," I fumbled.

No chance. He took them from me and, laying them on top of the magazine, drew me close and kissed me. He actually dipped me like they do in the movies, and I drank from his lips unendingly. All our past kisses poured from our hearts and to mix with this one, forming a moment that sent the past to another world and replaced it with blissful timelessness. I loved this man and I knew he loved me. I wanted to move him right onto the bed, but the nurse stepped in as I pressed hard to his body.

"Playing house?" Her tone was poisoned—she knew Bill, and her words reminded me of him. I pulled back and collected myself, totally unsure what I was doing.

"Are you ready for lunch, Miss Hogan?" She sneered, and I knew she would run her mouth at the first opportunity.

"I am really ready for you to leave me and the lieutenant alone."

The nurse smirked, looking Johnny up and down. "Very well. Let me know when you are ready." She turned abruptly and left. I didn't know if I was glad she'd interfered, but she did and the moment was gone.

"Sit with me, Johnny. Tell me what you have been doing and why you're here. Tell me everything. I missed you so much."

He pulled up a chair and smiled as though he didn't know whether to believe me.

"How did you find me?" I put a hand on his knee.

"You're famous back home, Maggie. Everyone reads your stories and when I got here, everyone knew you too. You're easy to track."

"You look great."

"Thanks Mag, so do you." It was the first time he ever called me Mag.

"Oh please, I'm a wreck. Look: rashes and cuts and scabs." I showed him my arms and felt a little embarrassed.

"Nothing but battle wounds. I heard what happened. You look beautiful now, like always."

After so many months suppressing my thoughts about Johnny, it was taking everything I had to keep myself from jumping into his lap and kissing him. I wanted to take things to their natural conclusion, but I didn't. I didn't know why, I just held back. "How are things back home?" I knew immediately when he dropped his eyes.

"My mom died a few years ago."

"I'm sorry."

"It's okay. She died peacefully in the night. Happy, knowing I was going to college."

"Oh?"

"Yeah I went on the GI Bill and now I'm working as an officer for the Army."

"That's great, Johnny. You're stationed here?" I saw him hesitate. "Listen Johnny, the past is the past. I don't know what happened, I think I know why. War makes people do terrible things. I know you. I know you are good, so for now, let's leave that behind us. I'm not interested in a story. I'm interested in you."

He flashed a smile at me and covered my hand with his own before answering, "For an assignment. I have a job actually, teaching in a two year college in the Adirondack Mountains when I return."

"Teaching?" My reporter side wanted to ask about the assignment, but I didn't.

"Yeah. Imagine that: me, a teacher. I promised my mom, so I followed through. Surveying. Found out knowing my numbers had a benefit. Crazy, huh?"

"You are something, Johnny. That's wonderful. Your mother would be proud." The look of pride on his face made me love him more—he was my man, I just couldn't figure out how to stay with him. "So you here for some time on this assignment?" The time frame didn't bother me much.

"Well, I'm leaving tomorrow, but I should be back within a week. Then I have a two week leave. I thought maybe—"

"Yes, the answer is yes. I should be out of here in a day or so, then back to the bureau."

"Good. Good." He stood, giving my hand one more squeeze. He really looked marvelous.

"Don't leave yet, Johnny."

"I have to, Maggie. I have a briefing soon."

204

I rose with him and pressed myself to his body in a warm hug. Cupping my face, he raised my chin and kissed me hungrily. Feeling his solid body bent over me, I didn't want to let go. Finally, he pulled away.

"I have to go." He kissed my nose.

I nodded and touched his lips lightly with my fingertips. "No danger?"

"No." A quick answer, nothing revealed.

"You'll see me as soon as you get back?"

"Yes." He pressed a last kiss to my forehead and I closed my eyes, unwilling to watch him leave. When I opened them, he was gone. If not for the roses on the table and his taste on my lips, it could have been a dream.

About an hour after Johnny left, Bill came to my room. I don't know if my conflicted emotions showed, but I tried to remain calm. Though inside I was roiling with duplicity and my understanding—or should I say misunderstanding—of love, I tried to face Bill with a smile.

Bill was dressed in his uniform, carrying a dozen roses. He saw the others and raised his eyebrow in a silent question. I got up and gave him a hug. He hugged back then kissed me lightly on the lips.

"You're such a darling. Another admirer of mine brought some earlier, one of the boys from the bureau." I felt a twinge of guilt as I told my first lie to Bill. I put the flowers in my water pitcher and filled it with water.

"How you feeling?" Bill asked, running a finger over Johnny's roses. I knew he didn't believe my explanation.

"I'm great, I'm bored, and I'm angry!"

His eyes widened and he seemed to smile against his will. "Pity the man who has wronged Maggie Hogan."

"Rumor has it I'm being replaced." I began to pace the room. "I just received a call. I'm due out of here tomorrow, and I'm just hearing this. I'm really mad." The call really had come, just after

Johnny left. One of my contacts in another office let fly with what she heard.

"Don't listen to rumors, Maggie. You're too good to be replaced."

"Maybe. But what happens if I get the axe and they ship me off somewhere else?"

He shrugged and sat on the bed, patting the space next to him. "Then you decide."

Damn him. Instead of sitting, I grabbed both of his arms and shook him with all my strength. Surprise flashed across his face. "I mean about us."

He squirmed but remained calm. He was married, a real hard-core two-timer, and I wasn't feeling much different.

"I'd find a way to get stationed near you."

I wasn't sure whether I believed him. I didn't believe myself anymore. "What about your wife?"

He didn't miss a beat. "You've defeated her for my love."

I still was unsure, but I slowly relaxed and allowed myself to sit. "Can you get to Tokyo?"

"Tokyo?"

"Listen, things are winding down here and a war is brewing there. They're going to send me to Tokyo. I can just feel it." All my instincts were telling me it was the truth.

"Jeez Maggie, I don't know if I can swing Tokyo real quick."

"Ah come on, a big intelligence guy like you? There's plenty of spying to be done there." I tried to lay my head on his shoulder, but he shrugged heavily. "Why is it whenever I'm happy, the world turns on me? It's as if I'm designed to be sad."

He pulled my head down to his shoulder and stroked my hair. "Honey, listen, you're one of these people driven to success. It's a difficult and sometimes lonely road, but you're on it. You're going to make it to the end, and I'm gonna be there with ya."

This made me smile, but I needed more. I pulled back. "Do you believe in absolute truth?"

"About what?"

"Truth. Tell me what you feel about it. Is it absolute?"

He stood and turned toward the window. "No. Truth is relative, it varies from one framework to another."

"Then there is nothing perfectly true, nothing pure?" I didn't like hearing it said out loud, but I was beginning to believe it. I didn't know if I was talking about love or the censorship after Dachau or both.

"Yeah, but what about the Dachau story I told you about? Will you be right there for me then, when I tell the truth about that?" I don't know why I put him up to it. Maybe I wanted him to say no so I could run to Johnny, or maybe I wanted him to say yes so I could write the truth I'd buried under several years of ambition.

"What do you mean?"

"Dachau, the shootings? Remember?" He was stalling and it reduced him in my eyes. He knew the score, I had confided in him after making love a few weeks before I was injured.

He walked to the window and put his hand on the sill. "I told you before and I'll tell you again: forget that story. The war is over and there's no merit in it."

"There's no merit in the truth?"

"Don't confuse truth with goodness."

"What do you mean by that?" I knew what he meant, but I wanted to hear him explain it. It was a creed we both lived by, but I was beginning to find guilt in the principle.

"Knowing the truth doesn't always equate to well-being. There is a time when truth can and should be told, and that time is relative to the situation."

"So you say it is good to lie?"

"No, and you know it. One doesn't have to lie when hiding the truth."

"Omission is a lie."

"Omission is a strategy to maintain good."

If I hadn't done everything he talked about, I would have thrown him out of the room. I lied, I omitted, I refrained from being truthful. I wasn't a good person at all, and neither was Bill. My thoughts turned to Johnny, and I wondered where he fit into all of this. He knew the truth, but simply lived with it. Trying to imagine the implications of Johnny's path made me realize that it was all so very complicated.

I looked at Bill and wondered if I loved him anymore. I thought maybe I would work better in Tokyo alone. Be on my own again; but I knew I needed someone. Someone to hold, someone to talk to, someone. I never liked loneliness. I loved Johnny. Did I love them both but in different ways? I wanted to tell the truth, and I wanted to know the truth about everything, but knew it wasn't about to magically and gracefully materialize in some wonderful anointing today or maybe ever.

"Okay Bill, I get it. I'll wait before I write the truth but so help me God should another dilemma force my hand, I'm going to spill my guts."

"Fair enough and wise."

I wanted him to leave. I wanted to speak with Johnny, so I kissed him absently and told him I was tired. He understood, made some nice comments, and arranged to pick me up in the morning.

After he left, I phoned all my contacts but there was no record of Johnny on any of the hotel registers, and my military people had never heard of him. Bill would know, but I couldn't very well ask him, so I figured there was nothing to do but wait and let him find me. I told myself it wouldn't take long. I didn't know how wrong I would be again.

When I went to the bureau, the orders were already there. I was to report to Tokyo within the week. With barely enough time to get my things ready, I arranged to have everything shipped when I had found a place. I stalled as much as possible, hopefully waiting for Johnny to knock at my door. I made Katrina horribly nervous pacing the rooms; picking up the phone and then replacing it roughly back on the cradle. I had no one to call who could help.

The day finally came and with it the news that Bill had arranged for a transfer, too. He would even be flying with me. I had to resign myself to the fact that I wouldn't see Johnny. I wrote a letter and sent it to the bureau office just in case he stopped there. I wouldn't let him think I'd abandoned him again.

## JOHNNY

I traveled as a civilian with an allowance for clothes. Having no idea what the weather would be like in Berlin, I picked a medium weight tweed suit that would be fine in warm or cold weather, several pairs of trousers, a sweater, and three long-sleeved shirts. From New York I took a freight steamer with a cargo hold full of canned juices and flour for the airdrops.

My cabin was small and bare, but I didn't mind. I spent most of the days on deck, watching the ocean and the waves. The kelp beds were moving up and down with the rollers, stretching to the horizon in long straight lines. It looked like I could jump from the ship, land softly on the shiny green bed, and be absorbed in its comfort.

I dined with the captain and the first mate, then climbed to the top deck and watched the stars like I did on my first crossing. I wished on them every night, wished to see Maggie, then sank back and lost myself in their vastness. One night, a particularly dark one that exposed the Milky Way with dazzling brilliance, I thought of my mom and dad and wondered if they were together up there somewhere. It made me think of love and death. I wondered if two people loved each other throughout their lives, if the love would continue when they left the earth.

It must end, I thought. Love ends between two people while they are alive, why wouldn't it end when there is no life?

I didn't know the answer, but I wanted to. I wanted to understand how powerful love could be, to understand why some loves left, never to return, and others were so strong that they tore hearts apart and fueled passions to unruly ends. The stars didn't give me the answer; they only blinked at me, hanging in their endless black sea. A shooting star streaked from the north and tailed its way across the sky. I wished on it then headed to my bunk.

The ship docked in England where a twin-engine Army aircraft transported me from London to Berlin. I was then driven by jeep to headquarters, where a Lieutenant's uniform waited for me. I figured I was back in the military now, but in what capacity I didn't know. All I had was my rank and my assignment, which was nebulous at best.

I didn't understand why I had to return from the east in a casket. Even if they searched me at the checkpoint, I was sure I could hide a file as small as the one in the assignment. I learned later that the Russians searched thoroughly, and an American civilian was thought of as an American spy first and a tourist—my official cover—second.

I had a few days before my final briefing and spent them looking for Maggie. She was well known in Berlin and easy to find. When I learned she was hospitalized I was shaken and thought the worst, but the guys at her bureau assured me she was fine.

On a whim, I stopped at a street cart and picked up roses on the way to the hospital. Walking into the room, I saw her sitting by the window, her cheeks rosy and her eyes radiating, and I knew the trip was worth it. I stared at her for a moment, taking in her features so that I could take every bit of her with me, to pull her into myself whenever I needed her.

I had clearly surprised her, but the shock passed over her face quickly, replaced by a smile that showed off her adorable dimples. She was my baby; there could be no other. I loved her. I knew it as soon as I saw her—my heart filled with warmth and I wanted nothing but to hold her in my arms, to embrace her and shower her with kisses now and forever. She must have felt the same way because it was only a matter of seconds before my wish became reality. We went into the timelessness of our love in our kiss, and once again, my Maggie made life joyous.

I left, satisfied we would be together when I got back, and that we'd be spending a lot of time together from now on. Maybe I would arrange a position in Berlin after I got back—I was sure I could after the successful completion of my mission. We kissed goodbye again, and I treasured that kiss more than any of our past embraces—I felt a new passion in this kiss that wove into the fabric of my soul and told me clearly that she loved me.

From the hospital I headed directly to my briefing, anxious to get the assignment going. The sooner it was started, the sooner it would be finished and I would be rushing back to Maggie.

The briefing occurred in the former Gestapo headquarters on the Niederkircherstrauss, taken over by the Defense Department. I had thought the army was overseeing the operation, but I soon found out differently. Several new organizations had sprouted from the Department, and this one evolved into an organization named the Central Intelligence Agency. I thought I was working for the Office of Special Operations under the Army, but learned it had changed to the Office of Policy Coordination and now this CIA. I didn't like it. It was confusing but then I thought, maybe that was good. I figured the more names, the more layers to get through, the more difficult to determine anything that would bust my cover. What I didn't realize was that the constant changing meant more than impenetrability for the enemy—it also signaled a power struggle within our own agencies. It was downright crazy and, like usual, I was dead center in the lunacy.

When I found my way to the briefing office it had yet another name: the Office of Reports and Estimates. It sounded like an accounting agency, but it was nowhere near that tame or lifeless. First of all, Crowley was there and, although he was a welcome sight, I began to think of his omnipresence. Everywhere I went, there he was. It was a little eerie. But, there was comfort in seeing someone you know when you're half way around the world.

But the other guy who was there rubbed me the wrong way right off. Crowley introduced him as Richard Helmster, and he reminded me of a guy who would give up his mother for a pair of alligator shoes. When he talked his lips barely moved, and he never blinked. He was tall and wiry, and I could see he had a sidearm from the bulge in his suit jacket. It was big, I figured a .45. No one in the building was in uniform except the guards, and it made me think.

"Crowley recommends you highly," he said monotonically, pointing to a vacant chair.

I didn't answer, and I could tell he didn't like it. I guess our senses and thoughts melded.

Crowley interrupted the silent stares. "Do you have any questions about the assignment?"

I had a few, but I asked the first thing that came to mind. "Who am I working for?"

The question took them both by surprise. Helmster squared his shoulders and cleared his throat. Crowley looked to Helmster.

"You're an officer of the United States Army and will be paid as such. You will, however, get premium pay as discussed prior to your acceptance of your assignment. This payment will be dispersed with CIA monies."

That was it. This guy was beginning to make me nervous. "Yeah, so who's my boss?"

"I am."

"And you work for who?"

Helmster leaned back in his chair and steeped his fingers over his chest. Then he leaned forward, placing his folded hands on the desk, and turned his beady black eyes to my face. "The CIA. And for this assignment, so do you."

"Why wasn't I told?"

"Johnny, things are changing quickly and dramatically here in Berlin. It's tough for anyone to keep up," Crowley answered smoothly. It sounded reasonable to me.

"And when I've completed my assignment, then what?"

Helmster smiled and it reminded me of a sewer grate—cold and dirty. "I like that...a positive thinker. You'll have a choice to stay with us or go back to the Army. I hope—we hope—you'll stay on with us."

This guy was a real jewel. "I'll decide when I get back."

"Good. Now for the matter on hand. You have no questions?"

"I meet my contact in front of the post office in Alglienicke District. He will be wearing a black overcoat and brown deerskin cap. He has an identifiable facial scar. He will recognize me by my clothes, and I will tell him Paxter sent me."

"Good. Yes, you have it down. There's a slight change, however."

I looked at Crowley and he shuffled his feet, gluing his eyes to his shoes. Something wasn't right.

"After recognition, instead of handing you the microfilm canister on the street, he will lead you to an alleyway just north of the post office. There he will hand you the film." Helmster stopped and gestured to make sure I followed.

"Okay."

"After it is in your possession, you are to pull this flask from your jacket and offer him a drink." He pulled a pewter flask from the middle drawer of the desk. "Him first. Do not drink it yourself. It will be a liqueur laced with cyanide. It will kill him instantly."

"What? No one said—"

"We can't take chances; the film is too valuable for our nation's interests. That is why you will leave in the casket."

"How do you know the film is real?"

"He's on our side now. We know that. But to insure nothing happens from transfer until you get to the west, we cannot take the chance. He must be neutralized to insure the success of the operation." That word sounded like pure evil in Helmster's mouth.

"He's our guy, and you want me to kill him?"

Helmster sat back stretched his legs under his desk. "Listen, the information is just as important for our protection as for our strength. It will be a matter of days before this scientist gives up everything, either willingly or by torture. These Russians are good at getting information from people. We want exclusive rights on this information. Is that clear, Johnny?"

"I'm really not into killing an ally to quiet him."

"Oh come on, Johnny, you mean to tell me you haven't carried out orders on your own men?"

He knew about Dachau. I didn't know how, but he knew. And I couldn't help wondering what else he knew. It scared me. I remained silent.

"You'll have the flask before you leave. When you open it, be careful: even the fumes can kill you. It has a bitter almond odor, but the booze will overpower the smell. You will also be given the location of the truck with the caskets. It won't be far from the post office. Any questions now?"

My one question was why he was such an asshole, but I didn't ask it. I wanted to get the hell out of there and think a bit, so I shook hands around and left.

This was not the direction I hoped the briefing would take. I'd accepted the assignment, and I didn't think I could have backed out, but I wasn't committed to killing the informant. Not yet anyway.

My walk back to the hotel wasn't pleasant. The briefing brought back all my old ghosts and had me questioning my purpose in everything. And of course, Maggie became the main focus. I didn't know how I would look her in the eye if she ever asked about my work again. And if she never asked, which I knew was unlikely, I didn't know how long it would be before I volunteered the information. Then I thought about changing the assignment, not killing the contact. It would only jeopardize my life, so I wouldn't be compromising anybody else. I figured I'd keep that in mind.

That night I ate a big dinner at a restaurant near my hotel, and the couple of beers I had with it made me tired. I slept soundly that night, holding on to the image of Maggie.

I showered and dressed in my tweed sport jacket and light pants. My gun stayed in my suitcase, but I strapped my knife to the inside calf of my left leg. I never liked going anywhere, much less somewhere dangerous, without some kind of weapon.

Crowley waited for me outside CIA headquarters, which was less than two hundred yards east from Checkpoint Charlie—my entry point into East Berlin. We shook hands in the crisp air, and he handed me the flask. He couldn't meet my eyes when he did it, and I knew it wasn't his kind of killing. Crowley was a battlefield warrior, not a street killer. This smacked of mob tactics.

"The truck will be in the rear of Kirche Church; you'll see it near the post office. The driver will recognize you. Do not talk. He will direct you. Questions?" He was matter-of-fact, all business.

I just shook my head.

"Good luck, Johnny." We exchanged a salute, then he spun quickly and raced up to the door. I was on my own, with my flask of cyanide and my knife.

I walked directly to the checkpoint where two German guards eyed me with suspicion for a few seconds before letting me pass. Their Russian counterparts were on the other side of the small guardhouse and never even glanced at me, so I continued to the street corner and hailed a cab.

It was a short drive to Alglienicke District, and I had the driver drop me a block from the post office. I hesitated a few minutes, drinking in the air. The morning's fog had lifted, and the sun's rays penetrated the white particles, brightening the street. I felt the flask near my chest in the inside pocket of my jacket and wondered if I would use it. I probably should have decided already but I wanted to let the situation develop. If he gave me cause to use it, then it would be that much easier.

Then I saw him. He was older than I'd expected, and his movements telegraphed nervousness. That was no good for him or me. I began walking slowly to him, and I saw him give a slight nod when he noticed me. Then he turned his back on me.

I stopped just before him, making sure the hat and the jacket were a match before speaking. "Excuse me sir." He turned to me and I saw the identifying scar. "Paxter sent me."

He voice was soft and his words leaked slowly from his lips. "Paxter is dead."

"No, he's risen."

He nodded his head, then furtively looked up and down the street. He seemed satisfied and motioned toward the alley with his head. I let him lead. Everything ran smoothly. He stopped midway into the alley then turned to me and took out a small canister, holding it tightly in his clenched hand. "This is all of it. Propulsions formulas, both solid and liquid, and plans for the structures as well."

He waited for me, I didn't know why, and it made him jittery. Finally he asked, "Well?"

"Well, what?" I held out my hand and his recoiled.

"My payment."

There was no mention of payment to me, and then I understood. It would make it easier this way. I had no out but to kill him. "There was no mention of a payment," I said weighing my options, hoping he would capitulate even as I knew he wouldn't.

"Then no film." He backed away.

I reacted quickly, throwing the palm of my hand into the bridge of his nose with enough force to break bone but not shove it into his brain. He dropped quickly. I snatched the canister and walked at a fast pace to the street, his moans beginning to grow louder. I stopped and turned. He was already on his knees. I knew I should go back and finish him—he posed a real danger to me, to the

216

mission now—but I didn't. Following my instincts, I turned up the street and hoped I was right.

Kirche Church was as close as promised and its red-orange masonry walls and spire showed prominently against the gray sky. I rounded the north side of the church found a flatbed truck in its back courtyard. The bed of the truck was covered with a heavy canvas, and I walked quickly to it.

The driver immediately opened the door and jumped to the ground. I jerked back, alarmed at first when I saw who it was, and almost called his name. He silenced me with a fast movement of his hand to his mouth, and I noticed that Thomas's face hadn't changed. He gave me a small wry smile, and I wanted to grab him and give him a hug. We been in it all together. I mean we killed together, we saved each other's lives, we had that bond of just knowing each other's feelings and doing what the other needed done. I remembered his bravery and cunning on the mountainside in Italy as well as his work during the Market garden mission. A guy like Thomas made you feel safe and I felt reassured about the whole assignment after seeing him.

He motioned me to the rear of the truck, then slid off the canvas, revealing fourteen wooden caskets. He looked around to make sure no one was watching, then pulled a knife from the inside of his shirt and pried open the lid of the coffin nearest me.

He smiled and waggled his eyebrows. "Hop in Johnny boy. You gotta take a ride in the box." That was all he said before he helped me into the coffin and nailed it shut.

Through the box I heard him ask, "Did you complete the assignment?" His voice was muffled through the wood.

I knew what he meant by complete. "Almost but the last." He didn't answer, and I began to wonder if he had heard me through the box. I lay in the box staring at the wood. It was fresh and I smelled the pine.

The engine started and I felt the truck vibrate under me when it went into gear. It rolled along the street for a few minutes, then stopped, but the engine remained running. I heard voices but couldn't discern who they belonged to or what they said. Then the truck moved and traveled several more minutes before stopping again with the engine running. A knock rapped against the side of the casket.

"Hey, rap once for yes and twice for no. Understand?"

It was Thomas again. I rapped once.

"Your mission is complete now. I completed it. Understand?"

I let out a long breath. Thomas had killed the contact. That's what the stop was all about. I rapped once.

"Good. Now listen, this is important. These guys, our bosses, they're brutal. This is a new war and these guys are the generals. If they knew you didn't carry out the assignment, I don't know what would happen. Understand?"

I didn't like it but I rapped once, harder.

"You tell them mission complete. That's all they need to know. I did it for old time's Johnny. No more. Okay?"

Again I rapped.

"Next stop is the checkpoint. Don't move. Don't breathe. Okay? No rap needed."

I closed my eyes, checked the film was secure, and began thinking of Maggie to pass the time. As the truck moved again and I rattled along in my casket, thoughts of death and burial began to overtake the prettier thoughts. Was this it? Life ends and the rest is nothing but a pine box buried in some dirt. It all seemed so meaningless. I felt the truck slow and the movement pulled my mind back to the present. Death was far off, or so I hoped as the truck sped up again. I closed my eyes. I didn't want to think about anything, I welcomed the blackness.

I lost track of the time in the vibrating darkness, but it couldn't have been more than ten minutes before we stopped again and Thomas cut the engine. I heard a loud voice that sounded Russian. Thomas responded and I recognized the sharp consonants of German. The other voice turned to German, then there were a few seconds of silence until a swish across the top of the casket alerted me that someone had thrown off the canvas.

I held my breath and felt more out of control than I ever had in my life. Something banged across the side of the box but I remained motionless, listening as Thomas and the unidentified person—I assumed it was a checkpoint guard—continued to speak in rapid German. Then the swish of canvas came again, the engine started, and we were moving again. I knew then we had made it.

The truck took several sharp turns before parking. Someone began prying at the top of my casket, and I helped by pushing against the lid with my hands and knees. It popped off quickly, and the rush of clean air felt wonderful as it splashed against my face.

Thomas stared down at me, then offered his hand and yanked me up. Crowley and Helmster stood at the rear of the flatbed just below me. Thomas shot me a glance, reminding me of his earlier advice. It was the same look he'd given me at the card table on the way to war. We still shared a silent understanding.

"Well?" Helmster stepped back to give me space to jump down.

I pulled the small canister from my jacket and gave it to him. "That's what he gave me."

Helmster looked it over then placed it in his jacket pocket. "We'll take a look. You have any problems?"

"No." I matched Helmster's lifeless tone.

"You completed your mission?"

"Yes, sir." I didn't hesitate when I gave him the beautiful, solid lie.

"Good."

Two soldiers appeared from nowhere, and Crowley barked orders for them to take the truck to the airport. I had forgotten there were actually real dead soldiers in the other caskets.

"I want both of you in my office while we look at the film," Helmster ordered. I would have argued, but I wanted to get the assignment over so I could find Maggie.

219

Helmster and Crowley walked a few yards ahead of Thomas and me. Thomas remained quiet. But me, I had questions.

I elbowed him and asked out of the corner of my mouth, "How did you find him? I left him down on his knees."

Thomas moved his head from side to side, scanning to see if anyone could overhear. He didn't want to tell me. "Listen, it's done. Forget it. No one knows, nor will they ever."

"You know." I said, and Thomas understood my concern.

"My secret."

"Our secret. Tell me so I'll know in case I get quizzed."

Thomas stared straight ahead. "We had a second rendezvous, in case you didn't give him the money."

"There was no money," I said, but I already knew the scenario.

"He was there. You did a job on his nose. You should have gone a few more inches."

"I didn't see the need."

Thomas stopped at that, so I did too, noticing as I did that Helmster had instinctively hesitated. The guy had eyes in the back of his head.

"Johnny, this is war just like before. A different battlefield is all. And one important thing you have to get through your head. We mean nothing to these people, our people, other than to get them information."

"That's reassuring."

"Ah, come on. You're from the streets, what's the difference from your wars there and the ones here? Same kind of people playing the same game."

He was right. I didn't want to believe it or even think about it, but I knew he spoke truly. It didn't leave much room for sanguinity in our fellow man. I knew it all along but didn't want to bring myself to believe it. "How did you kill him?"

"I used my knife. Tell them that when they ask, that you broke his nose, then knifed him."

"How they going to know?"

"They'll know."

"But he was killed elsewhere."

"I brought him back to the alley."

"No, you didn't stop." I knew the stops; there weren't enough.

"I didn't stop. I rolled him out the door when we were moving. He's dead right there in the alley where you made the pickup."

I didn't know whether to believe him or not. This was a new level of trust for us, and we both knew it. I shook my head and we continued.

There was an officer waiting in Helmster's office and I immediately saw his stars. This guy was big time.

"This is Major General William Hales," Helmster said to me. Everyone else seemed to know him already. I immediately went to attention and saluted.

"At ease, Lieutenant," he offered his hand. "We're here informally."

I didn't get it—we were meeting informally, but that didn't explain a major general in our midst.

Helmster butted in, "A quick look shows great work, Pero. The film seems more than perfect, the propulsion systems and fuels better than imagined."

I barely noticed when Helmster handed me my envelope. Inside were several sets of numbers that would give me access to an account set up in my name. My money would be there, tied into an annuity that could be turned to cash whenever I chose. I still didn't get why the major general was there, but it didn't take long to find out.

"Listen, the major general was part of today's operation, albeit in a more behind the scenes role. However, he's here now to help us out on a matter that may seem not so important to you at this time, but could give us all a lot of trouble. Even the smallest things can sometimes mushroom into huge embarrassments. Understand?"

I had no idea where he was going with his little lecture. I shook my head.

"Let me be a bit more blunt. Marguerite Hogan. You know her, yes?

My mouth went dry—I felt completely blindsided, there was no other word for it. I couldn't figure out how they knew, or how much they knew. With my eyebrows drawn tightly together I looked from Crowley to Thomas, but their expressions didn't give up anything. Hales rocked back on his heels.

"Yeah and...?"

"Well, the major general here and Miss Hogan are, shall we say, sweethearts," Helmster's beady eyes were alight—he was taking real pleasure in this.

I was already confused, but now I was getting pissed, too. "What's that got to do with me? No, wait, so what? Because he outranks me, I have to back off?"

"No, no, no," Hales chimed in. "That's not it at all."

I turned to him, ignoring Helmster. "Then what is it?"

Helmster jumped back in, a smile spreading across his face—the first genuine smile I'd seen on him. "Easy, easy. This has nothing to do with whose girl she is. I didn't mean that. It's her drive for truth that we feel might compromise our nation. Compromise you. Get it?"

"No, I don't get."

"Dachau, Johnny," Crowley finally spoke. "She keeps digging. We're afraid that and other things might get exposed."

"I won't, I haven't said anything." I couldn't believe they'd think I'd squeal.

"She's spoken of it to me. Many times," Hales said.

I whirled on him. "Whattaya you know about it?"

He put up his hands. "I know, we know because our lives have just crossed. Maggie is our common interest."

I needed this little chat to come to some kind of resolution. "Okay, so what's this about? Let's get down to it. You want me to kill her, you—"

"Johnny, come on," Crowley said, almost pleading.

"We only want you to stay away from her. End your relationship. Curb your love," Helmster was trying to look sympathetic, but his black eyes were flat.

"Or what?" I looked directly at Thomas for some reason, maybe for support. There was none there.

"It's some good advice. Take it for your safety as well as hers. Hales here will tell her you've disappeared and that will be that. You understand?" Helmster's smile was gone now and menace filled his voice.

The son of a bitch thought I wouldn't recognize a straight threat, and now her sweetheart was sitting there like a king. They had me locked. "I'll take it under consideration," was all I could muster. I would not give them the satisfaction of obeying. If they killed me, so be it. I looked at the envelope. "Anything else?"

"No, we'll be in touch."

I felt the cyanide flask in my inside pocket, reached for it and placed it carefully on the desk. "I didn't need it. I used my knife." No one budged. I stood at attention, then saluted. I don't know why, none of these guys deserved it. Helmster, Hales, and Thomas stayed behind while Crowley walked me out of the building.

"Be careful, Johnny." He put a hand on my shoulder, trying to connect with me. "Listen, think about this conversation. I'll be in touch and when I am, think good and hard about the assignment. We are in terrible times. The Russians want world dominance and we have to stop them. You've accomplished a tremendous setback against them today. You are to be commended and you will receive appropriate recognition when it clears the right people. You're in it now Johnny, so be careful, especially with Maggie. Be smart about it."

I didn't know what I was into. That was my life, and though it took me from place to place, I didn't want to think about it then. I just wanted to see Maggie, to bury this day under her kisses. "We'll see."

Crowley patted my shoulder and winked. "Be well, Johnny." He saluted like the battlefield officer I knew and loved, and I saluted back. He was the only one that really deserved it, and I felt good when I did it.

Crowley, in his trademark pivot, turned abruptly and walked briskly into the building. I shook my head at his retreating form, then cautiously, instinctively, headed for the Tribune's bureau headquarters.

Helmster's words rang through my brain "....your safety as well as hers." I was worried that they would harm Maggie. I looked over my shoulder, my street paranoia kicking in, and thought I caught a glimpse of Thomas ducking around a corner. If Thomas was following me, then things were getting really crazy. I backed off, concerned for Maggie's safety and laid low for two days to let things calm down.

I only left my room to get some bread, cheese, and wine. I searched within myself, coming to the hard realization that if I truly loved Maggie I would leave her to her work and not allow her to risk her own safety in digging the truth from Dachau. But as the callous formed over my feelings of the incident, I had a hard time dealing with why they would actually harm her if the story broke. Then the more I thought about these men, these CIA guys, the answer was clear. They had agendas I knew nothing about and that made them dangerous. Finally, I got it and I didn't like the picture. I knew what I had to do. I put on my uniform and ran to find Maggie to warn her. Then I would fade away.

The office was smaller than I expected, crammed with papers and typewriters, books strewn on the floor with newspapers that could have served as rugs for all I knew. I remembered her old apartment in New York—the space was distinctly Maggie. But Maggie herself was nowhere to be seen. A tall man came from a room off the main office. I didn't recognize him and he was so engrossed in reading some document, he didn't realize I was there.

"Excuse me," I said loud enough for him to look up at me.

"Oh, yes?"

"Maggie Hogan. I'm looking for Maggie Hogan."

He smiled thinly and folded the papers in half, smacking the packet against his palm. His eyes drifted from my face like he was choosing his words, then his gaze returned to me. "Too late sir, Maggie's gone."

"Can you tell me where she is? You know how to get to her house? I'm a dear friend."

He shook his head. "I'm sorry sir. I mean, gone out of Berlin."

The guy's words didn't click, and I kept getting dumber. "On assignment? When is she scheduled to return?"

The man took a few steps toward me, across the hall, and gave me a pitying look. Then I knew. "Sir, Maggie Hogan has been assigned to the Tokyo bureau. There's a war brewing in Korea and they want her near enough to get some stories when it breaks. She left early this morning on a flight out with her officer friend." I must have looked awful, because the man closed the distance between us. "I'm sorry sir, can I get you a drink? I have some scotch."

"No, no thanks. I didn't know."

"Well if it matters, she didn't either. She got word a day or so ago and tried her darnedest to stay for a few more. Maybe she was waiting for you. I don't know, but the home office yanked her outta here."

"Okay, yeah, thanks." I was still numb. I pushed past him and left the office, still stunned. I walked aimlessly a few blocks before heading to my favorite bar in Berlin.

I walked slowly at first, then picked up the pace. My internal alarms were ringing when I heard a puff and got smacked in the shoulder. Lying on the ground, I knew immediately I was shot. I heard screaming and felt weird—wet and paralyzed. Maggie's face flashed before me as I felt my mother's hand touch mine and heard her say, "It's time to come home, Johnny."

## MAGGIE

We flew west avoiding Russia airspace, so we had a layover in London before heading to New York. From there it would be on to Los Angeles, Hawaii, and finally Tokyo. I found out later Bill actually had briefings in each of the cities so the extra thousands of miles were more than just precaution. I decided to stay on the plane as Bill went to the terminal to contact his office. The suddenness of everything had left me a mess, and I felt completely out of control. I felt like a puppet, helpless in the hands of forces I couldn't see much less understand.

Nevertheless, I wasn't completely disappointed. I knew the area was hot for breaking news, especially with Korea's continued belligerence. I really wasn't finished with Europe—the war lingered there, squeezing at the people—but there would be plenty to see and write in Japan.

But, there was still Johnny. I was so confused, so contradictory in my thoughts and feelings toward him. When I was with him, I felt the peace of knowing I was with the man I loved, but there was an undercurrent of fear. Loving him was hard, and sometimes I wished I could stop.

He knew me better than anyone, and he knew eventually I would get the truth out of him about Dachau. Dachau and whatever else was waiting under his polished exterior. I knew there was more—he was into something with this new war—my instincts just burned with it.

Waiting for Bill to return, I couldn't help but wonder if he would find me on the other side of the world. I couldn't believe that my abrupt departure would be the end for us. He loved me and wouldn't leave me. I smiled at my reflection in the small window—he'd joined the army to find me in Europe once, and I believed in my very center that he could do it again. I settled back and, just as sleep overcame me, Bill sat back into his seat next to me. My eyes popped open, and I saw him staring ahead with a blank expression on his face.

"You okay?" I touched his sleeve and broke his reverie.

He turned to me. "Yeah, I'm okay. I just had some disturbing news."

"What, what is it? Not Korea, already?"

"No, no, no. It's… it's one of our guys. You know I wouldn't even tell you this—it's sort of classified—but, well, one of my guys said you should know."

My body went limp. "Why, Bill? Why should I know?" I could feel my throat constricting with fear.

"My guy said that you knew him."

He said "knew." Past tense. I didn't want to hear what he had to say. Somehow, some instinct, warned me that I didn't want to hear what came next. I knew before he spoke, I knew.

"Johnny Pero, people say you knew him. He was killed in action. On assignment."

"I don't believe it." I didn't know what else to say. It couldn't be the truth. I felt a hollowness that was beyond tears—all of my ambition, my motivation, my love was sucked from me like marrow from a bone. I whispered, "Let me off this plane."

Bill blocked my way to the aisle by turning sideways, "There's nothing you can do, Maggie."

I felt all the blood rush to my face as I screamed, "I want off this plane, now."

Bill grabbed my shoulders. "He's gone, Maggie."

"You don't know that. I want to see him."

Bill squeezed hard. "I don't have to tell you this but I will, because, well, because I know you and I want you to realize the situation. This is classified, Maggie, you understand?"

I nodded yes, but I didn't understand. I felt numb, sick, scared even and thoroughly confused.

"He took a bullet, only one, but it killed him. Like I said, he was on assignment and I know you well enough to know you understand what that means. He was a good soldier, trustworthy and brave but his work, people don't know the danger. There are no fronts, there are only bullets that can come from anywhere."

I snapped back at that, even though Bill's voice seemed miles away.

"Where?"

"I don't know where the bullet hit."

"No, I mean where did it happen?"

Bill released his grip and sat back as he squeezed the bridge of his nose with his thumb and index finger then lightly shook his head. "In Berlin."

"East or West?"

This time he winced and leaned back into his seat. "West."

I shook my head in disbelief as I choked out, "One of our men, one of our good men was killed in our own territory. This is what you want me to believe, to accept? How, how does a man like Johnny, after all he's been through get killed on ally soil? Where was his protection? Where —"

"I told you, Maggie, there are no fronts. It's all the same in that kind of business. It's a very, very dangerous war. There are enemies everywhere, even some of our own."

My despair evaporated for a brief second, and my reporter ears kicked in. "What do you mean by that?"

He looked to the aft of the plane then back to me. "I've told you enough."

This was all too fast. "Why can't I see him?"

"You can't," Bill responded curtly. "You know the procedure, an inquiry, these deaths are different."

I didn't know what he meant by that, and I didn't hear anything else. The plane's propellers revved and we began to taxi down the runway. My eyes dried but I wished for the tears to return as I looked out the window at the trees slipping past—I wondered if this new emptiness would remain.

As we lifted off, I watched the ground grow smaller. Japan, Korea, the Orient, it all seemed so unreal. There was no excitement, no grandiose plan fueled by my ambition, my engine for success sputtered to a halt. All I knew was that I was leaving Europe with all my battles, my stories, and my memories sorrowfully wrapped in the cradle of my despair.

# ACKNOWLEDGMENTS

A sincere thank you to George P., a truly perfect soldier who re-lived scarred memories and wondrous feats while steering me into writing this book. My respect and admiration to all female war correspondents who brave death the same as their male counterparts and still get their stories out. My appreciation also goes to Binghamton University for the use of their voluminous library to research the events in this book. A special thank you and appreciation to my editor, Wesley Fairman, for her tremendously amazing work, her truthfulness, good humor and patience with me for a few of my rants.

# ABOUT THE AUTHOR

This is Phil Pisani's debut novel. He is currently working on three more novels and a novella as well as a collection of short stories and screenplays. He lives in upstate New York with his wife Joanne and their three cats. When he is not writing, Phil enjoys fly-fishing in the Adirondack and Catskill streams and deep sea fishing in the Caribbean.

CPSIA information can be obtained
at www.ICGtesting.com
Printed in the USA
BVHW04s2137030418
512422BV00008B/132/P